PRAISE FOR MICHELLE MAGORIAN

Goodnight Mister Tom

'A brilliant story of how love defeats fear' –
Independent
'An assured first novel. Powerful enough to cause the
odd gulp in readers of any generation' – *Guardian*
'The brilliant story of an evacuee with the worst
mother in the whole of children's literature' –
Sunday Telegraph
'This splendid first novel is unashamedly and
gloriously sentimental and it cannot fail to be loved by
readers of all ages' – *The Times Literary Supplement*

Cuckoo in the Nest

'A fascinating story and a vivid picture of Britain in
the 1940s' – *The Times*.
'This is a book for the holidays: big, packed with detail
and gratifyingly emotional in its energy' – *Independent*.
'Teenagers accustomed to the thin gruel of
contemporary fiction aimed at them will enjoy this
meaty story of Ralph's struggle to win over his father'
– *Sunday Telegraph*.

A Little Love Song

'Michelle Magorian has done it again: another
unputdownable read . . . strikes an excellent balance
in portraying the joy of first love' – *School Librarian*.
'Packs everything opera style. Once I started reading
it, I couldn't put it down' – *Times Educational
Supplement*.

A Spoonful of Jam

MICHELLE MAGORIAN

EGMONT

EGMONT

We bring stories to life

For my brothers Jeremy and Simon
And in memory of Nancy

Acknowledgments
Mo and Barry Jehan (under whose roof I wrote this book), and Charlotte
Sutton and Anna Robins (my first 'readers') for their comments.

The author and publisher would like to thank the following for
permission to use copyright material:
Pink String and Sealing Wax by Roland Pertwee and *Arsenic and Old Lace*
by Joseph Kesseiring by permission of Warner/Chappell Plays Limited.
The extract from *Madame Louise* by Vernon Sylvaine is included by
permission of the publishers, Samuel French Limited.
Every effort has been made by the author and publisher to trace the
owners of the copyright of the material in this book. If we have
inadvertently wrongly attributed a quote, we shall be happy to
correct in the event of a reprint.

First published in Great Britain 1998
This edition published 2008
by Egmont UK Limited
239 Kensington High Street
London W8 6SA

Text copyright © 1998 Michelle Magorian

The moral rights of the author and cover illustrator have been asserted

ISBN 978 1 4052 3956 1

3 5 7 9 10 8 6 4 2

www.egmont.co.uk
www.michellemagorian.com

A CIP catalogue record for this title is available from the British Library

Printed and bound in Great Britain by the CPI Group

Contents

Part One *Breaking up*

One

'When did you find out?' asked Elsie.

'Last night. Mum told me when Dad was out. That's why she's so enormous. She said it's coming in August.'

'But that's only a month away!' exclaimed Elsie, amazed.

There was a loud clapping from the front of the classroom. A tall, gawky woman in her thirties was scrabbling around in her desk, her long, ungainly legs splayed out from her chair like a resting spider. She peered at them through tortoiseshell spectacles.

'Not so much talking please.'

They raised their desk lids.

'Everyone seems to be having babies now,' Elsie whispered. 'Your mum. My mum. My cousin, Kitty. Joan's friend, Kay. Everywhere I look I see babies or women about to have babies. There's no escapin' from them. They seek us here, they seek us there. Them babies seek us everywhere. It's an invasion.'

1

Geraldine giggled.

'They'll be taking over the world,' said Elsie, eyeing her friend's reaction. 'They'll be marching to Downing Street. There'll be baby riots.'

'Come on, you two!'

Peering over Elsie's desk lid was a tall, distinguished-looking girl. It was Imelda Francis, the Book Monitress for the last week of term. She was glaring down at them.

They handed their Latin textbooks up to her. She glanced at the brown paper they had taken off, now lying neatly in a pile of other removed brown-paper covers. 'You're not going to use them again next term, are you?'

'Haven't you heard of paper rationing?' Geraldine commented.

'I wouldn't think that would concern you,' snapped Imelda, staring pointedly at Elsie. 'With your father working at the paper-mill.' She spat out 'paper-mill' with as much distaste as if she had mentioned a sewer.

'It's because he does work there that I know how little paper there is,' said Elsie, flushing.

'Ignore her,' Geraldine said when Imelda was out of earshot. 'She's not worth it.'

But remarks like that did hurt Elsie. Not that she would ever let on.

'Are you pleased?'

'About what?' said Geraldine.

'The baby.'

'I don't know. My mother thinks it'll make things better at home.'

'With your dad?'

Geraldine nodded. Elsie noticed the familiar glazed look in her friend's eyes.

'Has he thumped you again?'

Geraldine looked away. 'Yes. I wish he'd never come back. My mum said it's the war that's changed him.' She glanced quickly at Elsie. 'At least he said sorry afterwards. Sometimes when I'm in bed he comes into my room and cries and promises he'll never do it again.'

'If only you could come and stay with me,' said Elsie. 'Are you sure your mum won't let you stay even a couple of days?'

'She wants me to help her. She's always so tired. And she thinks it would be too much for your mother, what with her having been ill and everything.'

'Perhaps we could meet up for a picture.'

'Yeah. That'd be nice!'

They returned to clearing their desks, neither of them saying what was really on their minds, that Elsie wouldn't be going to Geraldine's place. Elsie had been to her flat a few times but the last time, Geraldine's father had locked Geraldine in her bedroom in a rage, leaving Elsie alone with him. He hadn't hurt Elsie. In fact, he had been friendly. But so friendly it made Elsie squirm.

Just then, Alice Brogan's voice could be heard reading a chapter from *Anne of Green Gables*. Elsie peered over her desk lid at her. She was standing at the front of the class.

Alice and Geraldine were Elsie's closest school friends. They were total opposites. Alice had blonde hair, which hung down in two straight plaits, and was nearly always smiling about something, whereas Geraldine had wavy brown hair and, although lively, had a sad expression on her face when off guard. Alice had two sisters, whereas Geraldine was an only child. Alice's father worked in a bank. Geraldine's father was still out of work because of a war injury. Alice was well organised, always near the top of the class and popular. Geraldine was a daydreamer, hovered

4

near the bottom of the class and Elsie was her only friend.

The two things they did have in common were that their uniforms fitted (unlike Elsie's) and Elsie could make them laugh. The problem was that Geraldine was hardly ever allowed out and Alice lived miles away on the other side of the school and she was often away at gymkhanas.

Elsie picked up a clump of ink-stained jotters and crammed them into the well-worn satchel her mother had found in a junk shop. She glanced guiltily aside at Geraldine. What had brought them together was their fathers, who had both been away in the Army for four or five years. Both girls had been disappointed when what appeared to be a stranger began living with them. They had had to endure the rows, the tense silences, the moods, the sudden bursts of rage, their dreams of a wonderful reunion smashed. But life had improved for Elsie in the last few months and she didn't know quite how to tell Geraldine. Her bouts of happiness felt like a betrayal.

'What's your dad like now?' asked Geraldine.

Elsie was startled. It was as though her friend had read her mind. 'He hardly yells at me at all now.

He just ignores me. Like old wallpaper.'

'Lucky you.'

Sometimes Elsie was exhausted with walking round the playground with Geraldine, listening or talking about how bad things were at home. At least Alice was cheerful when they were together, but Geraldine implied that Alice had an easy life and that she was shallow. Elsie suspected it was because Alice was too happy for Geraldine's comfort.

'And you've got Harry to muck around with,' Geraldine added enviously.

'Not for long. He starts at the paper-mill on Monday.'

'But he's only just had his fourteenth birthday! Mum says everyone's got to stay at school till they're fifteen now.'

'Dad found a way round it. Harry would have gone mad if he'd had to stay at school another year.'

'So there'll be no one to protect you next term.'

'Don't remind me!' Elsie laughed, attempting to make light of it.

As she crammed more jotters into her satchel she noticed her hands were shaking. The old familiar nausea had risen into her mouth.

She was aware of a clearing of throats. When each girl had emptied her desk she had to sit quietly with hands clasped on her desk lid and wait for the slow-coaches to catch up. Elsie could feel her face growing hot, which made her even more flustered. She grabbed a handful of loose paper and pencils and stuffed them into the satchel, but then found she couldn't do up the buckles. She shoved some paintings and her remaining exercise books into her shoe bag, and her gym kit into a string bag. As she propped the string bag against the leg of her desk, her chair began to capsize from the weight of her satchel hanging on the back of it. But eventually her hands were clasped on her desk too, and she listened until Alice finished the last chapter of *Anne of Green Gables*.

Miss Pinkerton stood in front of the blackboard and surveyed them all. 'Hands up those who are going to see *Nine Till Six* this evening?'

Elsie and Geraldine raised their hands.

'Usual drill, girls. Come looking your best. The other parents like to see that their daughters are mixing with other well-turned-out girls. A tidy appearance reflects a tidy mind.'

My mind must have exploded then, thought Elsie.

'Freshly pressed dresses, polished sandals, brushed-back hair, but, don't forget, enjoy the play! It will be the last chance for you to see the upper sixth before they go up to university or college or training hospitals, so I do hope you will come and be a good audience for them. One day that will be you up there.'

'Not me,' murmured Elsie under her breath.

'Well now,' Miss Pinkerton said, beaming, 'I doubt any of you will forget your first year at this establishment. The year 1946–1947 will, I am sure, be etched in your memories. Some of you have done exceptionally well in your studies and deserve a well-earned holiday. You have wolfed down some bread and butter for the mind. Now it is time to enjoy some jam. Remember, there is always room for improvement. So I shall expect you to return next year for some–'

'Scones?' suggested a voice at the back of the class.

Elsie swung round. It was Rebecca Stein. A black-haired girl with olive skin, she only spoke occasionally but when she did she nearly always surprised Elsie with her wit. It was strange to think that in three terms they had hardly exchanged two words.

'Quite,' said Miss Pinkerton, smiling. 'Some of you, however, have failed to live up to the exceptional

8

potential I know you possess. You wouldn't have been accepted here otherwise. I hope that when you return, reinvigorated, you will start with a new determination. Now! Has anyone any exciting plans for the summer vacation?'

Elsie watched the hands shoot up.

'Yes, Felicity?'

Elsie gazed out of the window, beyond the lawn and the flower-beds to the sunken tennis court surrounded by high rhododendron bushes. She was vaguely aware of voices mentioning Cornwall, Scotland, Norfolk, and the Lake District. She was half sorry to be breaking up. She was going to miss the fields and the school's large, sprawling buildings with their wide echoing corridors and polished floors. School was a luxury compared to home.

She would miss Miss Pinkerton too. Miss Pinkerton had nicknamed Elsie her 'little dormouse', partly because she was small but also because her work had improved that term. 'It's as though you have been asleep in the winter and have suddenly come out of hibernation.'

'Elsie!'

Elsie looked up. 'Yes, Miss Pinkerton?'

'You haven't said what you'll be doing. Now I know we can't all go away for our holidays and, after all, the government has urged people to take their vacations at home. Less burden on our rather depleted transport. Will you be one of those taking holidays at home?'

'That's right,' said Elsie, relieved. She could hardly say she and her family would be going 'down 'oppin' '. Hop-picking just wasn't 'done'. Even her cousin, Joan, told everyone they were going down to their 'chalet', which sounded like Switzerland, but was really just a posh name for a windowless, tin hopper's hut. She crossed her fingers tightly under the desk. 'And I'll be helping out at the Palace.'

Miss Pinkerton frowned. 'I think you are a little old for fairytale inventions, Elsie.'

'She means the Palace Theatre,' said Imelda Francis. 'One of her brothers is an *actor*,' she added with an air of scandal in her voice.

'As was Shakespeare, of course, before he wrote his wonderful plays,' pointed out Miss Pinkerton. 'Not all members of the acting professions are rogues and vagabonds, Imelda Francis.'

The Book Monitress gave a snigger and nudged

her neighbour, a beanpole of a girl with a long, aquiline nose and the air of a thoroughbred horse.

'And the Palace Theatre is not variety. It puts on some quite good plays between the comedies and the thrillers.' She beamed at Elsie. 'So you'll be sweeping the stage and making tea? That sort of thing?'

'Yes,' lied Elsie.

What Miss Pinkerton didn't know was that Elsie had never been backstage in her life. Her seventeen year old brother, Ralph, had often arranged to show her round but each time the day grew closer she had made an excuse not to go. Whether it was out of shyness or an unwillingness to have her dream of what it was like ruined, she didn't know.

Elsie hated telling lies. Now she would have to undo it by making it come true, and she cursed her big mouth.

'That's marvellous. Very enterprising. I expect you'll have lots of interesting stories to tell the form when you come back. Mind you get out in the sun too, young lady. It will help you grow a bit. We don't want you coming back next term as the smallest girl in the school again, do we?'

'No, Miss Pinkerton.'

Before they were released, Miss Pinkerton gave them a lecture on the dangers of swimming-baths and certain rivers, because of the risks of catching infantile paralysis, which attacked the nervous system, making it impossible to walk without leg-irons or to breathe unaided.

'If you get it you have to live in a big box called an iron lung,' whispered Geraldine. 'I'm going to try and go to the swimming-baths as much as possible so I can catch it.'

'Why?' asked Elsie, staggered at the idea.

'Then Dad can't hurt me any more. I'd be protected by the box.'

'But you wouldn't be able to go to school.'

'Perhaps I could be a boarder here.'

'There aren't any boarders. Geraldine, you don't mean it, do you? About the iron lung. I'd hate not being able to breathe properly.'

Geraldine shrugged. Elsie controlled her exasperation. If only Geraldine would stop feeling so sorry for herself. And then Elsie felt ashamed.

Outside, mothers collected their daughters while hordes of the other girls climbed shrieking on to school buses.

Alice had joined them on the steps, looking like an advertisement for uniforms, her briefcase and sandals polished, her Panama neatly on her head, her brilliant blue eyes radiant.

Elsie, in contrast, felt that she was drowning in a navy blue sack surrounded by other smaller sacks. Even with a giant hem on her dress it still dangled somewhere between her knees and ankles, and the stitching on the sleeves on her voluminous blazer kept coming undone so that the cuffs crept over the tips of her fingers. A piece of old elastic prevented the straw hat from falling off, but not from perching lopsided on her head, while her mousy hair escaped wildly from two tiny pathetic plaits.

'When are you going to the Isle of Wight?' Elsie asked Alice.

'Tomorrow. Mummy says you're very welcome to come and stay. Why don't you? Please say yes.'

'Thanks, but I'm needed at home.'

'Me too,' said Geraldine who, Elsie noted, hadn't been asked.

Elsie was too embarrassed to admit her father couldn't afford the fare. 'Maybe next year. Will you send me a postcard?'

Elsie knew she wouldn't see Alice until the following term and she had doubts about seeing Geraldine. Some 'jam' this was going to be.

She hung back, postponing the inevitable, but before she could dodge the onslaught of girls, she felt herself being dragged, albeit resisting, towards the bus. A cold, sick terror overwhelmed her so that all the strength seemed to be sapped from her body. She wanted to jump off the bus but there was nowhere she could go. She had to carry on with her journey and begin the process of making herself invisible. It was the time of day she dreaded the most.

Two

Crushed against the bus window, Elsie balanced her string bag, shoe bag and tennis racquet on her feet with her arms round her bulging satchel. Her glasses kept sliding down the sweat on her nose. Numb and in pain at the same time, she sat hunched in a daze, surrounded by the shouts and laughter of girls all larger than her. The two third-formers who shared her seat, squeezed her closer to the glass, oblivious of her in their excitement.

As the bus shuddered to a halt at each stop, a rising panic began to fill her chest until Elsie thought her heart would burst. She told herself that since they had finished school early it wouldn't matter that Harry would still be at school and wouldn't be there to meet her. But what if some of the other schools had broken up early too? And what if Harry wasn't there to protect her?

The sun was burning the window. She felt as though

she was being slowly cooked. Perspiration was streaming down the sides of her face. She longed to pull off her damp blazer and hat but it would be just her luck if a prefect spotted her and she was given a conduct mark on her last day. She shoved her fingers up inside her hat and scratched her sodden scalp. She still couldn't get used to having hair long enough to plait. She wanted it cut but her mother said it looked prettier long.

By the time Winford was in sight she decided to kill time in town before catching the next bus so that Harry was sure to be waiting for her by their street. But where could she wait until then?

Elsie caught a glimpse of the little dress shop where her cousin, Joan, worked. She couldn't pop in there for a chat. Her fashion-conscious cousin would be too horrified by Elsie's appearance. She called her Miss Ragbag.

They crawled past the clock tower in the square. Ahead of them, past more shops, Elsie spotted a large shabby Edwardian building with huge doors and windows fronting it, the Palace Theatre. Grabbing her belongings, she pushed her way through the girls and stumbled on to the pavement.

'*Comedy and Thrills*!' she said, reading the placard from a kneeling position. She staggered back to her feet and, resuming her pack-horse stance, Elsie hauled herself towards the road which led to the stage door.

'Can I help?'

The voice belonged to an elderly man who was sitting in a cubby-hole in front of rows of letter racks and a wooden board with numbers on it and keys hanging underneath. His head was surrounded by clouds of steam.

'I think you're on fire,' said Elsie, alarmed.

'Kettle's just boiled,' he said, flapping at the steam with an old tea towel. He peered inquisitively at her, 'Now then, what was it you wanted?'

Elsie suddenly felt tongue-tied.

'You 'aven't come for the audition, 'ave you? Only I got no names down for today.'

'No, sir,' Elsie stammered.

'Autograph hunter?'

Elsie shook her head. 'I just wondered if me brother were around so that I could pass him on a message.'

'Your brother? 'Ere?'

'He's assistant stage manager and small parts.'

17

'Oh, Ralph Hollis.' He glanced at her bags. 'Where you off to then? Somewhere nice?'

'Home. We've just broken up.'

'Ah,' he said. Then he beamed, 'You're Elsie. You're the one Mr Duke and your dad rescued from that flood.'

Elsie felt herself redden. 'Yeah. I got trapped on the bombsite on the other side of the river.'

'From what I 'eard, they only found you just in time. It was your other brother what give the alarm, weren't it?'

'Yeah. Harry saved me life.' She could feel her heart thumping. Thinking of Harry reminded her of why she was here.

'Well, Elsie, I'm afraid Ralph went out looking for a tent for *Desert Highway*. He might not be back for some time. Why don't you drop all 'em bags and stay for a cuppa. You might see him when he comes back. If not, I can pass on your message myself. You look done in. Dump 'em over there. Then they won't be in anyone's way.'

Elsie did so and gazed up at a cast list for *Madame Louise*. She spotted Ralph's name.

'He's got a part next week!'

'Oh yeah? You'll know before he does. Leave your blazer and straw hat on the skip too. You look roastin'.'

The old man pointed to a stool and handed her a mug of tea. It tasted sweet, and to Elsie's surprise it started to make her feel better. With her knees perched up on the stool, her capacious summer dress now covered her feet entirely.

'That the Winford Grammar uniform?'

Elsie nodded.

'You must be bright to get in there.'

'So they say, but I'm only a few places from the bottom. My report says if I listened more and day-dreamed less my work would improve.'

'Oh dear. They never used to let us read our school reports.'

'Oh, I looked at mine. I like to be prepared for the worst.'

'But won't your parents notice the envelope's been opened?'

'I'll take it out and make out that it wasn't in one. I've got away with it before.' Her mother would be so disappointed. It had taken her months to persuade her dad to let her stay on.

There was a sudden silence and Elsie felt awkward.

'Could you tell me about the next play?'

'Plays. This week they'll be rehearsing two. Are you up for the part of Eva?'

She stared blankly at him.

'You don't look more than nine to me, but if you're at the grammar you must be eleven at least.'

'Twelve,' said Elsie.

'So? Are you auditioning? The girl. In *Pink String and Sealing Wax*.'

Elsie nearly choked on her tea. 'Me? I don't have elocution lessons. Only girls who have elocution lessons get to be in plays.'

'But with a bit of coachin'.'

'No. I'm not posh enough.'

'You could copy your brother's accent.'

'He learned it when he was evacuated. It took him years! Anyway I'm not brave enough. This is the first time I've ever been backstage.'

'So how come you decided to stay for a cuppa?'

' 'Cause you're not as fierce as I thought you'd be.'

'Oh no. You're thinking of Mr Neville.'

'You must be Wilfred!'

'That's right. Ralph told you about me, did he?'

Elsie nodded. 'Nice things,' she added hurriedly.

'Mr Neville's the one who's producing *Pink String and Sealing Wax*. He's the one you'd have to see.'

From what Elsie had heard, Mr Neville had a temper which would make a lion whimper.

'He's going to London to see some girls from stage schools this Sunday to audition them.'

'There you are then, Mr . . .' she stopped. 'I'm sorry, I don't know what your surname is.'

'Everyone calls me Wilfred.'

'I wouldn't stand a chance. Thanks for the tea, Wilfred,' she added awkwardly. She caught sight of a clock, and a rush of nausea so intense and so sudden nearly caught her off balance.

'You all right? You've gone an awful colour.'

Elsie nodded and forced herself to smile.

It was when she reached the pavement that he called after her. 'You forgot to leave your message.'

'I'll tell him at teatime.'

She dragged herself to the bus stop, where she caught the bus to the end of their street. She willed Harry to be waiting for her there. She pulled off her hat and carefully placed her spectacles in the inside pocket of her blazer. She glanced round quickly to make sure there wasn't a prefect. Satisfied, she tried to find a bag for her hat to go into. And then it was her stop. Clumsily she stepped out, looking round frantically for Harry, but there was no sign of him. It was while she was attempting to stuff her hat into her shoe bag that she heard the voice.

'No one to guard you today, Elsie?'

Elsie swung round. She shaded her eyes from the glare of the sun behind the girl's back. She could see Marjorie was flanked by the usual half-dozen assorted boys and girls. She was huge compared to Elsie, but then most people were. Stocky with legs and arms like a docker's, Marjorie Bush stood, legs apart, her hands on her hips, a sneer on her face.

'What a lot of bags you've got,' she commented in a sickly singsong voice. 'Shall we help you carry them?'

Elsie by now had managed to hang her satchel and shoe bag crossways across her chest. Her tennis racquet jammed under one arm, she picked up the string bag and headed for the road.

'Get her!' screamed Marjorie.

Elsie felt herself sinking under the weight of flailing fists and scratching fingernails, conscious of trying to

22

protect her spectacles from being smashed. As her blazer was dragged down and hands groped into the pockets, she suddenly remembered she had to look smart that evening, and then there was an awful sound. A tearing seam. And she was aware of the skin of her shoulder being exposed to the air.

Three

'Leave her be!'

Elsie heard the sound of feet running away, but before she could gather breath Marjorie Bush yanked at her hair and pushed her face towards the ground. This was followed by a great roar which she knew was Harry. As he dragged Marjorie Bush off her, Elsie sat sprawled across the pavement.

'I'll get you!' Marjorie shrieked. 'I've got all the holidays to get you. You won't have *him* around next week, will you?'

Elsie stared up at her demented, distorted face.

'Thought I didn't know, eh? Well, your precious brother'll be at the paper-mill and there'll be just you and me and this,' she said, presenting her fist. 'Sprat!' she added with venom. And she ran off.

'My dress is torn,' Elsie said lamely.

'I'm sorry, Elsie. They kept the ones that were leaving longer 'cause it was our last day. They gave us

biscuits and stuff and there was a speech and everything. And then the other kids wanted to give us all
bumps in the playground. I got here as soon as I could.'

'It's all right. She's gone now.' She gazed up at
Harry. Seeing his face always comforted her. Compared to other fourteen year olds he was short, but he
was quick on his feet and extraordinarily strong. With
his thick crop of black hair he was almost a miniature
version of their father to look at. Unlike their father, he
spoke with a Hertfordshire accent like their mum.

'Come on,' said Harry, and he grabbed her hands
and hauled her to her feet.

Elsie thrust her hand into the inside pocket of her
blazer and drew out the spectacles. They were un-
damaged but her relief was short-lived when she spotted
her hat. 'Oh no!' Someone had put their foot through
it. She felt the tears welling up.

'You'll have to tell 'em now,' said Harry.

'No! It will make it worse.'

'But how are you going to explain the mess you're
in?'

'I'll think of something.'

It was only when they had traipsed through the
rubble of their badly bombed street, and had stepped

over loose bricks and planks of wood to the lane which led to their back yard, that Harry asked the question that had been whirling round Elsie's head all day.

'What are you going to do this holiday without me? You can't stay in all the time.'

'I'll be going down 'oppin' so I'll be away then, won't I?'

'But that's not for a month. What are you goin' to do till then?'

'I dunno.'

There was no one else on her street to play with now. There were only five houses left standing. The house at the far end of the street was lived in by an elderly couple, their son and his wife and baby, and their two grown-up daughters. The house at the other end was empty and had become a playground for the gang in the next street when Harry and Elsie weren't hiding in it. Their house stood between two others and faced nothing but rubble and the back walls of the next street's yards.

Harry was really Elsie's best friend. Out of school they had been inseparable until her dad had started taking Harry with him to the allotment on Sundays. She hated Sundays now. And it looked as if the holiday would be one long Sunday. Nowhere to go. No one to play with.

They sneaked into the yard, past the coal shed and lavatory, and quickly opened the scullery door and dropped her bags on the floor. Elsie grabbed the dishcloth, rubbed her face vigorously with it, and put the Panama hat back on her head. She had just finished when the kitchen door opened. It was her mother.

'Elsie!' she wailed. 'Oh, how could you? You know you've got to look nice tonight.'

'I fell off the bus, Mum. It moved off before I was ready.'

'That hat's ruined. And look at the state of your blazer. You'd best take it off so I can brush it down. Oh, Elsie, your dress is filthy. I'll never get it washed and ironed in time.'

Elsie stared numbly at her.

'I said take it off!'

Slowly Elsie did.

'Oh my Lord! It's torn right across the seam. How could that happen falling off a bus? Have you been climbing trees again? Harry, have you two been larking around in that empty house?'

They shook their heads. Elsie was too hot and tired

even to cry. There was a long silence.

'You'll have to wear your winter uniform tonight.'

'In this heat wave? I'll roast.'

'What else can you wear, love? Your uniform is the smartest thing you have.'

Elsie knew she was right.

'You'd best put your old togs on for tea and give me your gymslip, blouse and tie in case they need ironing.'

Her winter uniform was in a box under the bed and weighed down by mothballs. People would be able to smell her from the school drive.

Her cousin Joan's clothes hung on a hook at the back of the door. They shared what used to be a small parlour. The mantelpiece was scattered with Joan's curlers and Kirbigrips and had a mirror propped up on it. There was one bed on a wooden floor which Elsie shared with Joan. The curtains on the windows were made of dyed sacking.

In each alcove, makeshift shelves had been made using orange boxes on top of one another. Joan had the left-hand alcove for her belongings and Elsie had the right-hand one. Elsie kept her battered schoolgirl annuals and comics there. Her thin, floppy rabbit, which was six years old, called Bugs, sat in the empty fireplace. Joan said Bugs was a very good name for it. It was so old and grubby it looked as though it might be breeding them.

Elsie dumped all her bags on the bed. She knew Joan would complain if she didn't put them away but she felt too exhausted to do it. The weather had been so hot at night that Joan had insisted on sleeping with the window open, but Elsie had protested. She begged her mother to intervene but her mother had said, 'Who would want to rob this house?' Elsie couldn't say Marjorie Bush might climb in to finish her off in her sleep.

She peeled off her dress and stood barefoot in her knickers in front of the small mirror. Already she could see a bruise forming across her shoulder and chest, and her head smarted. She touched it lightly with her fingers and, to her amazement, a clump of hair fell out. Suddenly she felt sick and began to sweat even more. She ran out of the room, into the hall, and past her mother in the kitchen, but before she could get to the sink she vomited over the scullery floor.

She felt her mother's hand, cool and gentle on her forehead.

'Sorry, Mum,' she blurted out.

29

Her mother put her arm round her but she yelped with pain. 'Elsie, what are all these marks?'

'It's where I hit the pavement,' she murmured.

It was only half a lie.

'I've a good mind to ring up the bus depot and speak to one of them inspectors.'

'Please don't make a fuss.'

'It's not right. Now you go and wash your face and have a lie down.'

'But, Mum . . .'

'You want to be all right for tonight, don't you? Do you still want to go?'

'Yes, Mum.'

'Oh good. I'm looking forward to it. We'll have a nice time. You'll see.'

Elsie dragged herself back to her room and flopped down on the bed. She must have slept deeply because, when she awoke, the bags from the bed had been removed and unpacked and all her exercise books were in one of the boxes in the alcove. Elsie sat up sharply. She had just remembered her school report. She hadn't taken it out of the envelope.

She heard voices from next door. It sounded like everyone was at home. The door opened and an eighteen year old girl with long brown crimped hair stuck her head round the door.

'Oh, you're awake,' Joan said, surprised. 'Auntie Ellen sent me in to wake you. She's got some toast for you and a cuppa.'

Elsie saw her glance at her chest and arms.

'You're so clumsy, Elsie.'

'I was carrying a lot.'

'Auntie Ellen says to put on a skirt,' and Joan disappeared.

Elsie put on the dress she wore at weekends. She didn't want everyone staring at her bruises and asking awkward questions.

In the kitchen her father and Ralph were having an argument. A few months ago Elsie hated them arguing so much she would fly out of the room. But since her father had, to everyone's amazement, allowed Ralph to work at the Palace Theatre, they now argued in a different way.

'If you're not in it,' her father was saying, 'there's no point in us coming to see it. That's the only reason we go, ain't it, Ellen?'

'Oh, I quite like going to the theatre,' said Mrs Hollis.

31

'That's because you're a woman,' Harry quipped. He was sitting close to the wireless, his ear almost attached to the dial.

'It's about soldiers in the desert,' Ralph added.

'I do know rather a lot about that,' his father said wryly.

'Exactly!'

'If I know about it already, why go and see it?'

Elsie sat at the table and stared at them. It always puzzled her how unalike they were. Her father was stocky and square, while Ralph, although just as strong, was small and wiry with springy brown hair. Ralph talked posh, her father spoke with a London accent. The only things they had in common were their tempers and stubbornness.

'But they'd be saying some of the things you perhaps can't find the right words for, and if Mum saw it too, she might understand better.'

'I don't think we need you to tell us how to talk to one another.'

'But it's more than that, Dad. It's about life. And history. And morality.'

'I'm 'ungry,' said Harry.

'It's just bread and drippin' tonight,' said Mrs

Hollis. 'We'll have a nice bit of fish paste on Sunday.'

Elsie noticed her father was staring at her.

'I hear you had an accident on the way from school today.'

Elsie could feel herself reddening. 'Yeah. Daft, eh? Ralph?' she said, turning to her brother hurriedly. 'What was that all about? The soldiers in the desert?'

'*Desert Highway*. It's by J B Priestley. It opens on Monday. I want Dad and Mum to see it.'

'We'll see you in the next play you've got a part in,' said Elsie's father.

'*Madame Louise*,' said Elsie.

Everyone stared at her.

'I saw the cast list.'

'Oh yes, Wilfred told me you popped in to see me.'

'Oh?' said her mother curiously.

'He said you had a message for me. What was it?'

'Um,' said Elsie, pretending to rack her brain. 'Blow it! I've forgotten. It wasn't important though.'

'I hope you weren't making a nuisance of yourself,' said her mother.

'He said you should put yourself up for the girl's part in *Pink String and Sealing Wax*. Why don't you?'

'I've never been on the stage.'

'Yes you have,' said her mother. 'At your elementary school.'

'Don't encourage her,' said her father. 'One in the family's bad enough.'

'Anyway, Mr Neville's seeing some girls on Sunday and they go to a stage school.'

'You've got as much chance as them,' said Ralph.

'No she ain't,' said her father. 'She don't talk lah-di-dah. I admit she's beginning to get lah-di-dah. But she ain't fully lah-di-dah yet.'

'But she reads lovely,' said Elsie's mother. 'And she can mimic people when she's telling a story.'

'Dad,' said Elsie, suddenly, 'you know you go to see Ralph when he's in a play?'

'Yeah.'

'If I ever did get into a play, ever, would you come and see me too?'

'Course I would. Though there's as much chance of that happening as an elephant dancing *Swan Lake*.'

Elsie forced herself to smile, but she was aware of a sudden ache at the back of her throat.

'When are we going to eat?' Harry pleaded.

34

'Put some plates on the table, Joan.'

Joan looked up from the film magazine she was reading. 'That's Elsie's job.'

'I know, but she's not been well.'

'It's all right,' said Elsie.

'Sit down, love. You'll be helping me enough in the holiday.' She gave a sudden yelp.

Elsie glanced at her mother's large abdomen.

'Ooh, the little blighter. It kicked again.' She laughed.

'Geraldine's mother's going to have a baby,' said Elsie. 'Any minute too.'

Her mother frowned. 'That must be a worry to her. Geraldine's father's still got no job I take it?'

'No.'

'Have you finished with that yet, Ralph?' asked Joan impatiently.

'You can have the rest of the paper.'

'I'm only interested in the bit you're reading. I want to know what's on at the flicks.'

'It's *Tarzan and the Huntress*. Johnny Weissmuller and chimpanzees. Not many fashion tips in that I should think, unless you like the hirsute look.'

'Do they wear suits in the jungle?' asked Joan.

'Hirsute. It means hairy,' said Ralph.

'Why didn't you say so?' said Joan, crossly. She grabbed the paper. '*Frieda*.'

'That's good,' said Ralph. 'I saw it at the Palace as a play.'

'It's an Ealing film. I want to see an American film. They're more glamorous.'

'There's plenty of those.'

'Good. Oh, Auntie Ellen. There's a Sweet and Swing Ball at the Town Hall tomorrow. Max Rogers will be playing. Can I go?'

'If you go with someone. How much is it?'

'Four and six if you get it at Ellis Brown's, or five shillings at the door.'

'What? Give me that!' She took the paper from Joan.

Joan looked awkward.

'Joan, there's loads of other dances here at two and sixpence. *And* you get a buffet.'

'But that's during the week.'

Elsie switched off the sounds of their voices and bit hungrily into her bread.

'This'll please Win,' her mother exclaimed. 'The *Sunday Despatch* is going to publish the latest James

Hadley Chase adventure story. Oh dear. There's another suicide.'

'Now that'll really please Auntie Win,' chipped in Harry.

'No it won't,' said Mrs Hollis. 'It's just she notices these things.'

'It'd please her even better if it was a man,' said Mr Hollis.

Elsie smiled. There was no love lost between her father and Auntie Win.

'That's an awful thing to say,' said Mrs Hollis.

'But true,' added Elsie, giggling.

'Eat up,' said her mother.

'Auntie Ellen,' said Joan. 'I was reading that.'

But Elsie's mother had pulled out her massive men's glasses.

'John, there's another case of infantile paralysis.'

'Oh yeah?'

'It's another child.'

'In this area?'

'No. It's in Heaton Rural District. They had the same trouble last summer.'

Elsie was about to tell her mother what Geraldine had said, but decided against it.

'Oh, John. We're going to be on the housing queue for years. It says here that people are already asking for priority to be given to nurses, midwives, teachers and police. And the farmers are worried sick when their prisoners of war go back to Germany. They'll be desperate for farm workers but they 'aven't got anywhere for them to live. So they reckon they won't have enough farm-hands to do the work.'

'Why can't they build their own?'

'They want to, love. They say they'll willingly give some of their land for building new houses on. They want special consideration given to them since they need to produce food.'

'Everyone wants special consideration,' commented Mr Hollis.

Elsie pricked up her ears at this. Her parents had put themselves on a list for a new council house on a new estate. It would mean moving away from Winford and her going to a different school.

'So there's not much chance of us moving?' said Joan casually.

'Not for years. What are we goin' to do? I don't want the baby suffering from the damp.'

'If that ceiling leaks again,' said Mr Hollis,

38

'we'll swap rooms with the girls.'

'But we get the warmth from the range up there.'

'Don't worry. We'll sort something out. Anyway, it's summer now. I've collected quite a few slates and there's the empty house down the road. I'll get some slates off there too. If the landlord don't mend the holes in the roof I'll get some mates round to do it with me. You'd best get a move on if you want to get to Elsie's school.'

'Oh, Lord. Joan, are you sure you don't want to come with us? The play is all about a dress shop. I know you saw it at the Palace but . . .'

'Molly's coming round.'

'What colour's her hair now?' asked Ralph.

Elsie and Harry glanced at each other and grinned. Molly had dyed her hair blonde to be like Jean Harlow, only it had come out green.

'Purple?' Harry suggested.

'You shut your mouth,' said Joan.

'Funniest thing I ever seen,' Mr Hollis said, chuckling.

'Yes, more like Green Harlow,' said Ralph.

Joan pouted.

'Come on, Elsie,' said her mother. 'You'd best get your uniform on.'

Elsie stared at the navy gymslip now hanging above the range. The very thought of it made her skin prickle.

'Cheer up, love,' said her mother. 'It'll all be over in a few hours' time.'

Four

After the play, Elsie and her mother hovered near the doors surrounded by hordes of girls in checked summer dresses, their parents and relatives all decked out in frocks, hats and gloves. Geraldine was there with her mother, who was looking enormous. How Geraldine hadn't guessed that her mother was pregnant staggered Elsie. To Elsie's dismay, Miss Castleford, the head-mistress, a tall, well-built woman with a surprisingly soft voice for someone with such a robust frame, joined them. She eyed Elsie's winter uniform.

'We had just got Elsie all spruced up in her summer dress, looking really lovely, when I come over all faint and I'm afraid I spilled steak and kidney pie all over her. There was gravy everywhere, and her two other frocks was in the wash.'

'Oh dear,' said the headmistress. 'Were you burned? I must say, you do look a little flushed.'

'No, Miss Castleford,' Elsie replied politely,

41

thinking that if anyone was going to faint it would be her if she didn't get out into the fresh air.

Miss Castleford and her mother rabbited on about opportunities for girls, and the heat wave, and the fifth- and sixth-formers in the all-female play. Suddenly she heard the headmistress say, 'And will you be going anywhere special in the holidays, Mrs Hollis?'

Elsie stepped quickly behind the headmistress and shook her head wildly, making attempts at a pantomime of hop-picking.

'We thought,' said her mother slowly, trying not to catch Elsie's eye. 'We thought we'd stay at home and enjoy the garden.'

'Oh, very wise, Mrs Hollis. All this dashing around in the vacation can be so very exhausting and at least at home one has one's own creature comforts.'

'Exactly,' said Elsie's mother.

It was only when they were well clear of the school on a bus that they clutched each other and burst into laughter.

'Oh, Elsie,' Mrs Hollis choked. 'Creature comforts!' And they just howled. Elsie was glad Joan hadn't come with them. Joan would have found something to complain about. Elsie had her mother all to herself for the first time in ages.

'What does it feel like walking around all 'em big polished halls?'

'I felt a bit lost at first. But now it's like there's lots more space to run free. Which is daft really, since we have to be so ladylike when we walk down the corridor.'

There was a silence.

'Elsie.'

Elsie knew what was coming from the softness in her mother's voice.

'About your report.'

'I'm sorry, Mum. I really am. I know I'm not concentrating enough but I drift off. I can't help it. I really try.'

Often she used to go through an entire class hardly taking in a word, her energy taken up with a fight not to let her upper eyelids meet her lower ones.

'The thing is,' her mother said slowly, 'I know you're bright. Any fool can see it in your eyes. And you're quick too. Your mind is sharp as a knife, so I can't understand it really.'

'Maybe I've got the kind of brain that don't come

out in essay writing. If they'd let us write stories I'm sure I'd do better.'

'Those glasses are helping you? They don't need changing?'

'No.'

'You'd tell us if they did?'

'They're fine.'

'There's something else.'

'Oh?' said Elsie, dreading what was coming next even though she was sure she hadn't done anything bad.

'It's about Harry.'

'Oh, Mum, I know you don't like me getting into his and Ralph's bed at night, but I get desperate with Joan's snoring. I nudge her but she only stops for a few seconds and then starts all over again. I've really tried to sleep in our bed, but I need the sleep.'

'That's not what I want to talk about.'

'There's nothing wrong, is there?'

'No. But with Harry starting at the mill he'll be making new friends.'

'And he won't want his little sister hanging round so much.'

'Nothing of the kind. That's not what I meant. Harry

would fight a dragon for you, you know he would. It's just that he's growing into a young man. He'll be bringing in a pay-packet this time next week. What I'm trying to say is that when he first starts he'll be tired out at nights so don't expect . . .'

'Him to be interested in me when he comes home.'

'Something like that. I know you're both close, but some of his school mates will be at the mill too. They might not want you around, that's all. Especially if they're all boys.'

Elsie didn't need her mother to tell her. Many times she had been looked on as a hanger-on. Not by Harry. He liked her being there with him. It was because she was so small. Everyone thought she was just a little kid.

'I expect you'd like to see your own friends this holiday. I'm glad you've made some. Alice and Geraldine are nice girls.'

Elsie remained quiet and stared out of the window.

'Come on, love. It's Winford.'

'Where's my satchel?'

'At home, you chump. You're on holiday now. Remember?'

Elsie gazed up at her mother. She loved her so

much. She was always surprised at how suddenly she would appear pretty without warning. Even with the baby growing in her, the rest of her was slender and she still darted around with quicksilver movements and then would laugh at herself for not being able to tie her shoelaces because of her 'bump', as she called it. Sometimes she had to go through the strangest contortions. She had to ask Elsie to cut her toenails now.

Elsie always felt safe with her mother. She had heard her mother have nightmares at night after the war, when Dad came back, but when they had hidden under the stairs during the bombing-raids she had never let on that she was frightened. She had just put her arms round Harry and Elsie, and held them tight. It wasn't that Elsie believed her mother could protect her from everything. It was just that she knew her mother was fiercely proud of them all.

She wished her father could feel the same too. Sometimes after supper she would stare awkwardly at him while he whittled away at a piece of wood by the range, racking her brains for something interesting to say about herself in the hope that he would glance up at her and smile. But she could never find the right words.

And then it was time to get on the next bus. Immediately fear overwhelmed her like a familiar reflex. Her mother's voice chatted gaily over her head. She felt a hand on hers.

'Elsie. What's up?'

'Nothing.'

'You look like something's botherin' you? Is there?'

'No,' said Elsie, glancing nervously out of the window. 'It's our stop, Mum.'

They stood on the pavement by the bus stop.

'Have those kids been teasing you again?'

'What kids? I'm just a bit tired, that's all.'

'That's all right then.' Her mother gave her a squeeze. 'My lovely girl,' she said, beaming down at her. And Elsie felt comforted.

The full impact of Marjorie's latest assault didn't hit Elsie until late into the night. From the kitchen next door, she listened to the reassuring voices of her parents chatting and laughing about something while the wireless blared out music. And then it was quiet and she heard a stumbling from the hallway. Ralph was returning from the theatre. Then it was silent again. Elsie found herself whispering, 'Why?' She buried her head under the sheets and began to sob uncontrollably, because she didn't

47

know the answer and so felt helpless to do anything about it. What was it about her that caused such hostility, such premeditated attacks? Harry said it might be because she wore glasses or because she was so small. But what could she do about that? Perhaps it was something she had said or done and, without realising it, she had deeply offended Marjorie. If only Marjorie would tell her why she hated her so much.

When she was drained of tears, Joan's snoring seemed even more jarring than usual. Elsie sneaked out of bed and made the familiar route up to her brothers' bedroom. She was just tucking herself up next to Harry when Ralph raised his head at the other end of the bed.

'Elsie!' he grunted.

'It's Joan's snoring,' she yawned.

'I know, but can't you get used to it?'

Elsie gave him what she hoped was a withering can-pigs-go-to-the-moon? sort of look.

'I give up,' he moaned, and Elsie watched his head flop back on to his pillow.

She pushed her head into the nape of Harry's neck. Life wasn't so bad, she thought, and promptly fell asleep.

The sheikh climbed over the wall and leaped on to a passing horse. A great cheer went up in the crowded cinema. The villains were chasing him across the desert. Elsie and Harry jumped up and down in their seats, booing loudly. The chase continued, the villains getting closer, the sheikh finally breaking free of them. Elsie watched him galloping up a hill, the fine sand rising up behind him, his robe billowing round him. He was over the hill! But waiting for him on the other side was a band of mean-looking tribesmen.

'To be continued' splashed across the screen and the lights went up. Elsie sat back in her seat, her sandalled feet dangling over the edge. Two boys in the seats in front of them leaned over eagerly to talk to Harry, ignoring her.

'Coming round to the park for some footer?' asked one.

'Without old four-eyes,' his friend added.

'She's no problem,' said Harry brightly. 'She can watch and keep score. You always forget.'

Elsie was used to pretending to be invisible at the sideline. It didn't upset her usually. It was enough that

Harry wanted her there to see him play. No one else in the family bothered.

'When we start at the mill,' said one boy excitedly, 'we can use their field. It's really good.'

'I can't wait,' said the other.

'Are you nervous?' asked his friend.

'Nervous?' said Harry. 'Nah. What's there to be nervous of?'

'What they'll do to you.'

'What does he mean?' Elsie asked.

'They do something to all the new apprentices,' Harry explained. 'It's a sort of initiation ceremony.'

'Why?'

'To be one of them.'

'But it's going to be worse for you,' said one of the boys. 'Because of your brother being an actor.'

The other boy made his wrist go limp. 'Nancy, nancy, nancy boy!' he chanted.

Harry grinned. 'They'd better not go too far or they won't get me in their football team.'

'They might not want you.'

'Anyway, I don't go anywhere near the theatre. Well, only to see him sometimes.'

'You go in!'

'You'd better shut up about that.'

Harry shrugged.

'And about hanging around with girls,' the boy added, staring meaningfully at Elsie as if she was an inferior sort of insect.

'Harry,' said Elsie, 'I won't be coming this afternoon.'

'Don't take no notice of them. They're all talk.'

'I said I'd go somewhere else, see.'

'With one of your schoolfriends?'

'Hoity-toity grammar snob,' said one of the boys.

'You want me to play with you this afternoon?'

'Yeah, of course,' said the boy.

'Then you'd better stop calling my sister names.'

'Ain't she got a tongue?'

Elsie was relieved when the lights went down for the main film.

When they left the cinema they stood outside adjusting their eyes in the brilliant sunlight.

'Do you mean it about doing something else?' said Harry.

'Yeah. You don't mind, do you?'

'No. Not really.' He grinned. 'I'm glad you've made friends. It's goin' to be odd not havin' you around though.'

Elsie was tempted to tell him she had made it up, but she remembered what her mother had said. She gave him a playful punch and headed quickly down Winford High Street in a miserable daze.

She stopped outside Joan's dress shop and peered inside. Joan was being spoken to by a tall, smartly dressed man. Elsie was about to push the door open when she caught sight of her reflection in the window. Her hair had been fought into plaits again. She wasn't even wearing socks, and her sandals looked as though a dog had chewed them. Seeing Joan's crisp appearance she knew she couldn't get away with pretending to be a customer, not in her faded blue frock. And then, to her horror, she saw five children reflected in the glass behind her, and one of them was Marjorie Bush.

Elsie ducked quickly as Marjorie reached out for her head. She shoved her way through the group and sprinted down the road, the yells of the gang in her ears. She bolted across the road while drivers beeped their horns furiously at her. All she could think of was her spectacles. Her father told her that if she didn't look after them he wouldn't be able to afford to buy her another pair. Without glasses she wouldn't be able to read and it was reading which kept her sane.

Ahead of her she could see the Palace Theatre. She dived down the street on the left and there was the river where she had so very nearly drowned because of Marjorie. This time there would be no Harry to rescue her. Behind her, she could hear the gang drawing closer. She leaped across the road. The stage door was closed! She threw herself against it and, to her utter relief, it gave way and she tumbled headlong on to the floor. Sprawled out in front of the cubby-hole, she found Wilfred gazing down in astonishment.

'Hello, Elsie. What brings you back? Changed yer mind?'

'Yes! Tell me, what do I have to do?'

Five

Mr Neville lived in an upstairs flat a few doors away from the theatre. Elsie pressed the button. She stroked her hair back and attempted to polish her sandals on her calves. She could hear footsteps and then the door was flung open.

Towering above her was a tall, distinguished man in his fifties. Greying hair Brilliantined back, a cigarette in his hand, a cream linen jacket over an open-necked shirt and cravat. 'Yes?' he enquired, gazing down at Elsie.

She took a deep breath. 'I'm Elsie Hollis and I'm putting myself up for the part of Eva.'

There was a long silence as Mr Neville drew for what seemed like an eternity on his cigarette. 'I see. Perhaps you had better come in.'

No roaring yet, thought Elsie. A good sign.

It was blissfully cool in the tiled hallway. Elsie followed Mr Neville up some narrow stairs.

'Who is it, Adrian?' shouted a deep female voice.

'Someone come to audition.'

'Here? From Italia Conti?'

'No. From Winford, or is it Braxley?' he enquired of Elsie.

'Braxley.'

The door at the top of the stairs opened into a small hallway with walls covered in playbills and theatre posters, and Elsie was led into a sitting-room. The windows were open to the sounds of the trams and hooting cars in Winford High Street. Mr Neville removed a pile of slim books and newspapers from a wicker chair.

'Take a seat,' he mumbled, the ash from his cigarette dangling over the pile in his arms.

A striking, handsome woman in her fifties peered into the room.

'Where . . . ?' she began, and then she caught sight of Elsie and stared at her, amazed. Elsie suddenly became conscious of the dirt on her knees and tried to cover them with her dress.

'Eloise, may I introduce another member of the Hollis family. Elsie Hollis.'

Elsie slid to her feet. 'Good afternoon.'

The woman gave a huge smile and started waving wildly towards the door, as if milk was boiling over in a saucepan somewhere.

'I will leave you to attend to your business.'

Elsie sat down again and watched Mr Neville, cigarette still in his mouth, flicking through one of the slim books.

'The play is called *Pink String and Sealing Wax.*' He glanced at Elsie from under his eyebrows. 'Or do you know that already?'

'Yes.'

'Do you know anything about Eva?'

'She's twelve.'

'And you are . . . ?'

'Twelve.'

'Of course. Though one needs to be more than just the same age of a character in a play. In rep, that is repertory theatre, an actor or actress has to play people of all ages every week.'

'Oh?' said Elsie, puzzled. 'Ralph says he plays nothing but old men. He says he's getting to be a real expert at wrinkles and white hair even though he's seventeen.'

'Yes, well, we all have to begin somewhere.'

56

'And he says the actors that are really old, about forty or fifty, play the young parts.'

'Does he now?'

'Yes. Does that mean you'd prefer someone much older to play Eva?'

'Not quite.'

'So I'm still in with a chance?'

'That remains to be seen. Now tell me, what plays have you been in at school? You're at Winford Grammar School for Girls, I know.'

Elsie was amazed. 'Did Wilfred tell you?'

'Wilfred? No, your brother did. He appears quite proud of you.'

'Really?'

'So tell me about your school plays.'

Elsie now realised she had not a hope in hell. 'Um. I'm afraid the girls in the plays are the ones that have elocution lessons.'

'Ah,' said Mr Neville. He stubbed out his cigarette and proceeded to light up another. 'Yes, I noticed the Hertfordshire accent.'

'I can do other accents. And I know what you *require*,' she added politely, hoping to impress him, 'is more Dick Barton than Snowy.'

'More Dick Barton?' he repeated slowly.

'Posh. Oh, I don't suppose you have much time to listen to the wireless. You see, Snowy is Dick Barton's sidekick. He speaks like my dad.'

'Cockney,' said Mr Neville.

'And Dick Barton–'

'Special Agent.'

'Yes,' said Elsie excitedly. 'So you know?'

'I know. I think, however, if you read Eva's lines at the speed of Dick Barton, the audience might get the wrong impression.'

'So you'd need unhurried posh?'

There was a strange muffled explosion from behind the door. Elsie looked over at it anxiously.

'Are you telling me you haven't had any acting experience at all?'

'Well no, except . . .' She paused and then shook her head. 'No. You couldn't really call it acting.'

'Any information is valuable and, to be honest, Elsie, at this moment you need all the help you can get.'

'I used to read to my mother. And I did all the different voices too, of course.'

'That's something, I suppose.' He sighed. He

walked up and down the room, a copy of the script of *Pink String and Sealing Wax* in his hand.

'Eva is one of a family of six children, though we never see the two youngest on stage. Her father is a pharmacist who has to do post mortems.' He hesitated. 'I don't suppose you know what a post mortem is.'

'Oh, yes I do,' said Elsie enthusiastically. 'You see, my Auntie Win used to bring home all these green paperbacks.'

'I know them. Detective stories. That sort of thing?'

'Yes! So I know that a post mortem is essential if a person has died in suspicious circumstances. The dead body has to be opened up to see if there is any sign of arsenic or other poisons.'

'Exactly. Sometimes Eva's father is asked to do this, but as a pharmacist he has to give drugs to people. He also has to experiment with the poisons on guinea-pigs.'

'Guinea-pigs,' said Elsie horrified. 'You don't mean he kills them?'

Mr Neville seemed to be suppressing a smile. Elsie thought him very callous.

'I am afraid so.'

'Well, I think that's terrible!'

'So does Eva when she finds out.'

'Does she rescue them? Is that what the play is about?'

'Not quite.'

'What does she do then?'

'She comes down at night and feeds them and talks to them. And one night when she does this she sees and overhears something which upsets and angers her very much.'

'To do with the guinea-pigs?'

'No. It concerns her brother, Albert, whom she is very fond of. But you don't need to know that yet.' He opened a page. 'Let's hear you read then.'

He held the open book out for Elsie to take. Elsie pushed her glasses back up to the bridge of her nose and looked down at the page. Luckily she had seen plays in books before, with Ralph.

'It's a conversation between Eva and her mother, about Eva's father. Take your time to read it through quietly and when you're ready you can start.'

Elsie noticed to her surprise that her hands were shaking. Just pretend Mr Neville is Mum, she thought. As she read through the scene, she learned more about Eva's father. She looked up when she had finished.

'Now?'

He nodded.

'*But Albert doesn't want to be a chemist, and I was only looking. But there's nothing to look at – is there? Is there? Albert puts a finger on his lips warningly.*'

'Stop.'

Elsie stood up. 'Thank you for seeing me, Mr Neville.'

'No, no. I only wanted you to read Eva's parts, not her mother's words and the stage directions.'

Elsie blushed. Of course, how could she be such an idiot.

'I'm so sorry,' she spluttered.

'Don't worry. We all do strange things when we're nervous. I'll read Mrs Strachan's part. Let's start again.'

'*Public analysts do murders, don't they?*' said Elsie.

'*Eva!*' said Mr Neville.

'*I don't mean themselves, but to bits of people who've been murdered.*'

'*Albert, you haven't been talking to the children?*' said Mr Neville.

'*Of course not,*' he replied as Albert.

'*They boil up their tummies to find out who did it,*' read Elsie.

'*Eva!*'

'*I 'spect Pa's boiling one up now.*'

'That'll do, Elsie.'

Elsie closed the book and gazed hopefully at Mr Neville.

'That was a very intelligent reading, Elsie. Tell me, why do you want to be in this play?'

Elsie hadn't expected this question. Should she say it was because she wanted to be a great actress one day? Because she didn't. She stared up at him. 'Do you want the truth?' she asked falteringly.

'I think I can take it.'

'I wanted to avoid being beaten up.'

Mr Neville looked surprised. 'By Ralph?'

'Oh no. By Marjorie Bush.'

'Marjorie Bush? Am I supposed to know this Marjorie Bush?'

'Oh no. And you wouldn't want to either. She's the leader of a gang in the next street and her favourite pastime is to sit on my head. I don't know why.'

'So being in *Pink String and Sealing Wax* would be a way of keeping you off the street, so to speak?'

62

'More than that, Mr Neville. It might just save my life.'

Mr Neville took the play from her hands. 'Tomorrow I'm meeting some young girls who have been trained at stage schools where they have acting classes and dance class.'

'And elocution,' added Elsie dismally.

'Yes. And, of course, some of them have already acted with professional actors.'

'Well, thank you for hearing me,' Elsie said, suddenly conscious of her eyes stinging.

'I haven't finished yet. I'll be honest with you, Elsie. I'm not sure that you're experienced enough to play the part and, to be fair, I must give the other girls a hearing too.'

'Yes, of course.'

'But I think you have talent.'

'You do!' Elsie was astounded.

'And I would like to see how you cope on stage now and how well you take direction. You may not get a part this time, young lady, but, who knows, maybe next year.'

Elsie found it difficult to smile for, although this was good news, next year would be too late. By next year she would probably be dead. She might even be having *her* tummy boiled up at a post mortem.

He opened the door and the woman called Eloise almost fell into the room. 'Oh, I was just going to see how you were getting on.'

'We'll take the same scene again,' said Mr Neville from the auditorium. Eloise, who Elsie discovered was Mr Neville's wife, was on stage with Elsie to read the part of Mrs Strachan.

'Now, during this scene you are sewing a sampler,' Mr Neville explained. 'Can you sew, by the way?'

'Badly,' said Elsie.

'So does Eva,' said Mr Neville.

What happened next was a great whirl of things. Mr Neville wasn't fierce at all. He was very insistent with his directions, but that made Elsie feel safe. When it was all over, she felt disappointed.

'I'll let you know on Sunday night,' said Mr Neville. 'I presume your father knows about this.'

'Not exactly.'

Mr Neville raised an eyebrow. 'Nothing changes much in your family, does it?'

As Elsie was led to the door to the front of the

theatre, she realised that her reasons for wanting to be in *Pink String and Sealing Wax* had changed. She suddenly understood why Ralph was so drawn to the theatre. It was the sheer exhilaration of stepping into someone else's skin and entering an entirely different world. It was the excitement of being stretched, of being asked to do something she would never have believed possible, and enjoying it at the same time. And it didn't matter whether she was any good at acting or not. She had experienced a moment of magic and she knew, as she stepped out into the heat and hubbub of the busy High Street, that she wanted to return to it. The magic had ensnared her.

Six

'Elsie!' But she couldn't find her key. Scrabbling around on the pavement amongst her belongings there was no sign of it anywhere.

'Elsie.' She began to sweat. Without the key there was no way of getting back to safety. She had to find it. Then she spotted it glinting in the sunlight through a grid in the pavement. She slid her fingers through the grid but she couldn't reach it.

'Elsie.'

It was too late. A hand touched her shoulder and it began to shake her.

'Elsie.'

She opened her eyes. She was in church sitting between Harry and her mother.

'You fell asleep,' Harry whispered. 'It's over. It's time to go home.'

'You're always falling asleep,' said her mother quietly. 'If you didn't read so late and then go wandering around in the night . . .'

'I don't go wandering.'

'Up to the boys' room,' continued her mother.

'That's so I *can* get to sleep.'

'Joan don't snore that badly.'

Elsie sighed. It was useless trying to convince anyone. At school, it was all she could do not to fall asleep in class sometimes. How was she supposed to do well when she couldn't stay awake to hear what was being said?

At least falling asleep in church made the service go quicker. She often wondered what all the strange singing, the words that made no sense to her, and the hush and the pomp had to do with a man who preached out in the open on hills, and by the sea in Galilee. She was convinced that if ever Christ came back he wouldn't spend five minutes in a church. He would probably be too bored or be asked to leave for wearing unpolished sandals. She looked up quickly in case a thunderbolt came down for having irreverent thoughts in a church.

'Was the sermon any good?'

'The vicar just went on and on again about the people who didn't go to church.'

That was another thing that perplexed Elsie. Why rant and rave about the people who hadn't come to church to the ones who had come? Sometimes it made Elsie want to walk out there and then and yell, 'Add me to your collection, since you'd take more notice of me if I wasn't here.'

'I suppose you'll be going to the allotment with Dad again?' she asked Harry matter-of-factly.

'Yeah. Can't wait to get out of this,' he said, tugging at his collar. 'I wish I could take it off now.'

'The vicar would have a fit,' Elsie smiled.

'I don't know how Ralph could've lived with a vicar for five years!' exclaimed Harry.

'Ralph said he wasn't as stuffy as this one. That he liked reading other books besides the *Bible*. That he even took him and his son out in an old dinghy sometimes.'

Harry humphed in disbelief. Round them, the congregation were drifting towards the door.

'Why don't they get a move on?' whispered Harry, impatiently.

'Shall we shout "fire"?' Elsie suggested.

'They wouldn't hear,' said Ralph, glancing at a group of elderly women.

'Don't be rude, Harry,' said their mother, leaning towards them. 'You'll be old one day.'

'No I won't. I'll live a life of adventure and then pop me clogs just before me fortieth birthday.'

'Oh, life ends at forty, does it? Don't give me many more years, do it?'

Elsie and Harry glanced at one another. Elsie never thought of her mother being any particular age. She was just her mum.

'Dad's gone already!' Harry said urgently. 'And Ralph.' He began to jig around impatiently.

At last they stepped out into a blast of hot air. Elsie swiftly removed her straw hat with the artificial flowers on it, and gave her scalp a vigorous scratch.

'Don't do that, Elsie,' exclaimed her mother. 'People will think you've got nits.'

But Elsie's attention was riveted on Harry, who was racing along the pavement trying to catch up with his father.

'They'll have a lot to talk about today,' her mother commented. She sighed. 'His last day as a schoolboy.'

'That was Friday.'

'You know what I mean.'

Elsie swallowed back her tears. She longed to spend

69

the day on the allotment with her father, but he had no interest in her whatsoever.

She remembered when she had nearly drowned, trapped under fallen rubble, waiting for Harry to return with help. Terrified, she had felt the water slowly rising and had sung like mad to stop her teeth chattering so violently. And then there were voices and she had recognised one of them as her dad's. He had freed her and lifted her angrily in his arms. And she knew he wasn't angry with her, but angry because he might have lost her. It was the first sign since coming back from the war that had shown he loved her.

He had carried her back to the house where Ralph worked, and after she had been given dry clothes and had been wrapped up in a blanket, he had held her on his lap and she had flopped exhausted against him, feeling his warm chest moving up and down as he breathed and she had drifted off to sleep.

A week later he had said that she could stay on at the grammar school until she was sixteen so that she could take the school certificate examination. And everything began to change. Life at home stopped being filled with rows and unexpected explosions. But now it was as though she didn't exist. Elsie realised it was because she was a girl and so there was nothing she could do about it.

Her mother put her arm round her. 'Do you want to take a bus out to Geraldine's?'

Elsie shook her head. 'They wouldn't like me just dropping in. They're a bit more formal than us, Mum.'

Joan was now walking on ahead.

'I expect she wants to get home before Molly arrives.'

'They'll bag the room all day,' groaned Elsie. 'What can they find so interesting to say about hair?'

'And fashion,' her mother reminded her.

They looked at one another and smiled.

'When we get back, we'll sit out in the yard and you can help me shell peas.'

'Oh, lovely,' said Elsie, wryly.

'Cheeky! And we'll have a nice chat. A nice cuppa. Just the two of us, eh?' At that moment she gave a sudden laugh and she touched her abdomen. The baby had kicked again. 'The three of us, I mean.'

The day drifted by in a soporific haze. In the afternoon Elsie wandered down the street, picking her way through the bombed buildings, lifting up broken rubble, looking for bits of wood they could use for kindling in the range. Sometimes Elsie would come across some torn curtain material that her mother used for cleaning rags. Her father was always pleased when anyone found some bricks intact. If she had a good collection, perhaps he would take a bit of notice of her.

The street was almost silent but for the sound of a wireless coming through the windows of the end house. Elsie felt shy of going near it. The people who lived there called Elsie 'little titch' after the music hall comedian and, every time they did, they rolled around laughing as if they had only just thought of it. Elsie had lost the ability to smile politely. She didn't like looking younger than her age. It meant people talked *down* to her. Ha. Ha. Ha.

When her father and Harry returned in the evening, more red-nosed and brown than ever, they were talking rapidly, or rather Harry was talking and her father was nodding and adding the odd word. Elsie pointed at her collection of 'new' bricks, but her dad just nodded and said, 'Good. Good,' and went back to listening to Harry.

It was late at night when their visitor arrived. Elsie had already gone to bed. She was woken by a loud knocking at the front door. There were murmurs from the kitchen and footsteps in the hallway and the sound of the door being opened.

'Mr Neville,' she heard Ralph cry out.

'I've come to see your father. Don't worry, it's not about you. I'm quite satisfied with your work.'

Elsie slid out of bed and pressed herself against the door. She could hear her father in the hall.

'Ah, Mr Hollis, I've come to talk to you about Elsie.'

Part Two *Eva*

One

Elsie crouched down outside the kitchen door and peered through the keyhole. She tried listening through it but could only make out, '. . . had no idea. Talked about it but never thought . . .' And then her mother opened the door. 'I'm sure you'll be more comfortable listening in here.'

Mr Neville and her father were sitting at the table. Her mother was standing looking hot and flushed by the range where a kettle was beginning to steam. She had removed her apron and was looking quite overcome. Elsie sat down next to Ralph, opposite Mr Neville, who smiled at her. He seemed even more elegant in their kitchen. But, she noted, he also seemed at ease and treated her parents with enormous respect.

'But she ain't done nothin' like this before,' her father was saying.

'I think she can pick it up. She's quick.'

'Oh, she's that all right,' said Mr Hollis.

'Because of her lack of experience she'll have to work very hard. She would have a chaperone, who would attend rehearsals and escort her home,' he added meaningfully, looking directly at Elsie. 'Right to her door.'

'There's no need for that,' said her father. 'She's a big girl now.'

'It's the accepted manner of doing things at the theatre, Mr Hollis.'

'I see.'

'She would have to be available in the mornings, when we set the scenes. And she would need to study the lines in the afternoons. I believe you know my secretary, Mrs Egerton-Smythe?'

'Yes, sir.'

'The first week we shall be rehearsing at her home, while the other cast rehearse *Madame Louise* on stage. The following week we rehearse in the theatre. Mrs Egerton-Smythe has kindly suggested that Elsie has help with learning her lines at her place in the afternoons.' He paused. 'Mr Hollis, I know you have had a few misgivings about the theatre, but your daughter is on holiday and it would be an educational experience for her.'

'And she's local and free,' added Mr Hollis.

Mr Neville smiled and passed him a cigarette.

'Not at all. She will receive a little pocket money for her troubles. Not much but . . .'

Out of the corner of her eye, she noticed Ralph looking horrified that their father was so blunt with Mr Neville.

'She ain't going to be helpin' in a series of emergencies like what he was,' he said, waving his hand at Ralph, 'is she?'

'No, Mr Hollis. I auditioned other more experienced girls in London and I would like Elsie to play the part.'

'The others asked too much, did they?'

Elsie wished the floor would open up and swallow her. Didn't her father think she was good at anything?

'Mr Hollis, this is our first exchange with the Redmond Theatre and we want to make a good impression with our opening play. I would like Elsie for the part of Eva because I think she's the best candidate I've seen.'

Elsie was flabbergasted. She reached for Ralph's hand under the table. He gave it a squeeze.

'Don't get me wrong, Mr Neville. But I don't see how she could be.'

Elsie reddened.

'Your daughter has a freshness that the other girls lacked. She's also more intelligent. More natural. Her lack of sophistication is a positive bonus. Naturally, I understand if you are doubtful. I know that Mrs Hollis has been ill and perhaps needs Elsie to help around the house.'

'I've got bags of energy!' Mrs Hollis protested. 'The only thing I want to know is would she be finished by August the 29th?'

'Yes. It'll be two weeks' rehearsal, two weeks' performance. Last performance August the 23rd.'

'Only we're goin' on holiday, see.'

'How lovely. Where?'

'Kent.'

'Beautiful county.'

Elsie stared intently at her father. She watched him glance at her and her mother, and then at Ralph. He shrugged helplessly and gave a nod, at which point Elsie leaped up with a cry, and Ralph flung his arms round her and began jigging her round the kitchen.

Her father glanced in despair at his wife. 'Don't you go auditioning next, will you?'

She was smiling broadly. 'Oh, John. It's so exciting. Our Elsie!'

Mr Neville handed Elsie a copy of the play. As he rose to leave, he suddenly asked, 'Will you be coming to see *Desert Highway* this week?'

Her father looked awkward. 'Well, Ralph ain't in it you see.'

'No, but Basil Duke is. And he's first class. And I know you were in the same unit together in the war and are drinking chums.'

Her dad gave an embarrassed cough. He didn't like people to know he went to a pub with an actor. 'I'll think about it,' he said evasively.

They followed Mr Neville quietly to the hall door. Suddenly a loud trumpeting came from the front room.

'Good Lord!' whispered Mr Neville. 'What on earth?'

'Joan, snoring,' chorused Elsie and Ralph.

'Extraordinary.' And with that he left.

'I don't know,' Ralph commented. 'Is it fair? I spend months and months hanging around the theatre, working my fingers to the bone, and I get elderly bishops to play, and you walk in and get a huge part.'

'You don't mind, do you?' Elsie asked anxiously.

'You bet I do. I'm as jealous as hell.' But he was grinning. 'If we play our cards right, we'll get the whole family working there.' He winked.

'Over my dead body,' said Mr Hollis vehemently.

'Oh, John,' said Mrs Hollis, smiling. 'They're only pullin' your leg.'

'Yeah, well.'

'Dad,' said Elsie, touching his arm. 'You said you'd come and see me if I was in it. Will you?'

'Course he will,' said her mother. 'We wouldn't miss it for the world, would we, love?'

'No,' said her father, looking resigned.

Elsie grinned. Now I'll show you, she thought.

Breakfast was special. Elsie kept looking at Harry, who was jigging around on his chair, his hair slicked back with some of her father's Brilliantine. His bread and dripping was only nibbled at the corners. In the end, Elsie's mother cut it in half and turned it into a sandwich. 'Eat it later, when you've calmed down.'

Elsie's father was frowning. 'It'll be hard work, you know. Repetitive. Lots to learn.'

'Yeah,' responded Harry eagerly.

'You'll probably be on envelopes.'

But nothing could squash Harry's exuberance at going off to work.

Elsie spotted her parents give each other an anxious look.

'Newcomers come in for a bit of raggin'.'

'I know, Dad.' Harry gave a dismissive wave.

Ralph said nothing.

It was when they were outside watching their father wheeling his bike out into the street that Mrs Hollis gave Harry a hug. Harry looked at her, amazed. 'What's that for?'

His mother gave a watery smile. 'I dunno.'

'I'm not going off to war,' Harry laughed.

'That's what he thinks,' Elsie heard Ralph mutter.

Harry sat on the bar of his father's bike and they were off.

Minutes after they were out of sight the atmosphere was back to normal. Joan was looking for a particular belt which matched her dress. Ralph was swallowing down tea and hopping on to his creaky old bike. 'I've underlined your part for you,' he yelled to Elsie.

And then Joan was running for her bus and it was suddenly quiet and her mother was clearing the table. Monday was wash day. 'You read out in the yard. It'll be steamin' in the scullery. I'll 'ave the copper goin'.'

When Elsie opened *Pink String and Sealing Wax* she found that every time it said EVA on a page, Ralph had underlined it as well as Eva's dialogue and her moves, so that Elsie could spot them easily. She had pages of lines to learn and her heart fell. But Mr Neville had told her not to start learning them yet. Over the next week she was to concentrate on Eva's story within the story of the play. To find out everything she could about Eva from what Eva and her family said. The playwright, Roland Pertwee, had left all the clues there for her to find.

The play was set in 1880 in one room, the parlour of the Strachans' house. Mr Neville asked her to imagine what he called the story off-stage, so that when she entered the parlour she would be coming, not just from the wings, but from another part of the house where she had been involved with other people and their gossiping, pleasures or dramas. Elsie didn't understand what he meant, but he must have guessed because he said it would all make sense if she took it step by step. First of all, she must read the play.

She opened it and began.

'*Mama,*' she whispered.

'*Yes, dear,*' Mrs Strachan answered.

'*Lucy caught a mouse this morning.*'

'*Poor thing!*' exclaimed Mrs Strachan.

'*But she didn't drown it. Pa said to give any mice she caught to him.*'

Elsie carried on reading.

'How you gettin' on?'

Elsie blinked up at her mother, feeling dazed. 'I've nearly finished Act I.'

'Dinner's on the table.'

'Dinner!' Elsie cried. She suddenly felt panicky. 'Oh, no! I've got two more acts to read. I wanted to finish it before everyone gets home. I won't have any time once they do.'

'Come on. Your eyes need a rest.'

Her mother was right. While she read Act II in the yard, refreshed after the break, her mother came out and Elsie helped to hang the washing on the line, chatting some more about the play.

'Now don't you go telling me the end,' Mrs Hollis said, and suddenly Elsie realised with apprehension that her mother would be coming to see the play.

Joan was the first to arrive home. She and Elsie put a clean sheet over the mattress of the three beds in the house and put the bottom one as a top sheet. The top sheets would be done the following week. After Elsie had laid the table for supper, she returned to the yard, but hardly had she opened the play again when she heard the sound of a bicycle chain. She leaped off the stone step and ran out into the little lane. But it wasn't Harry. It was Ralph.

'You've caused quite a stir.'

'Have I? Why?'

'Anyway,' he said suddenly, ignoring her question, 'I thought you might be interested to see the cast list. Your name has been added this morning. It's in order of appearance, which is why your name is at the top.'

Elsie pushed up her glasses and stared at what appeared to be a sea of names.

'Mr Neville has a part,' she exclaimed.

He pointed to 'Mrs Strachan'. 'Annie Duncan will be playing your mother. She's a really good actress. She's been working at the Palace for ages. She lives near Winford too. Most of the others travel backwards and forwards from their digs in London, except of course for the ones at Mrs Egerton-Smythe's.'

Mrs Egerton-Smythe was an exuberant middle-aged widow, who lived in a vast old house with a massive lawn and trees which sloped down to the river. Since the terrible winter earlier that year, she had started taking in actors, and sometimes actresses in an emergency. Ralph still earned money as her gardener.

'You'd best go looking your best, Elsie. An actress has to put in a good appearance for her public.'

Elsie laughed and gave him a playful punch.

'Seriously, though. Some of them go to rehearsal looking really glamorous. I'll go in and have a word with Mum.'

'Glamorous!' Elsie repeated. She had about as much glamour as an old mattress. And then she heard another bicycle chain and she sprang excitedly to her feet. The door of the yard opened and her father wheeled the bike in. 'Where's Harry?' she asked excitedly.

He was behind him. Elsie was shocked. Harry was one of those people who was always grinning. Nothing worried him much. But now his face looked ashen and tired.

'Harry!' she said, running up to him.

'He's had a hard day,' her father muttered. 'Leave 'im be.'

Her brother managed a small grin. They looked at

84

one another, realising that neither of them could speak freely.

As soon as they entered the kitchen Elsie's mother was all over him. 'You look done in. Sit down. I'll get you both a cuppa. A bite to eat and you'll be fine.'

And then the evening's ritual took on its usual pattern. Supper was eaten and cleared. Elsie did the washing-up, the wireless was switched on, and while their mother ironed her way through the week's washing, Joan moaned about how she couldn't afford a new-look skirt, which was flared and down to the calves. And how she was looking out of date in the dress shop and how humiliating it was. Mr Hollis whittled away at a piece of wood and Harry and Elsie listened to *Dick Barton, Special Agent*.

Usually her mother frowned at her during *Dick Barton*, which was her signal for 'Don't forget your homework'. But Elsie had no homework that night. And then she remembered she needed to read Act III.

She was so lost in the play she was surprised to be told to go to bed, and was aware that everyone else was going too. Once in bed she carried on reading. When she had finished she went upstairs and found that Harry was still awake. He looked pleased to see her.

'Finish it?'

'Yeah.' She slipped in beside him.

The window on the other side of the room was opened so that a cool breeze drifted across the bed to their faces. There was silence for a moment.

'They gave you a hard time, didn't they?' she whispered.

'Yeah,' he said, and she noticed his voice was shaking.

'Because of Ralph working in the theatre?'

'Yeah. I'm not cross with 'im. It's not his fault. It's just,' he faltered, 'I think my initiation's going to last a bit longer than the others.'

'Oh, Harry. And you've been so lookin' forward to work. Have you told Dad?'

'No. But I think he guessed.'

'Did he say anythin'?'

'Sort of. He just looked at me and asked me if I was all right. And when I said I was, he said, "Well done, lad".'

Elsie put her arms round him. Harry was looking so sad. He gazed down at her and then he gave an enormous grin. 'Don't you worry, Elsie. I can take it.'

'But I can't bear the thought of them hurtin' you.'

'I'll find a way round it. They 'aven't got the better of me yet.'

Two

Miss Benson, who was to be Elsie's chaperone, was waiting for her at the stage door. She was tall, broad, and looked ageless, dressed in a navy blue dress, large navy blue cloak, navy blue hat, navy blue gloves and navy blue shoes. She was carrying a large tapestry bag. She peered down at Elsie without moving her head. A no-nonsense sort of person, thought Elsie, as she stood there conscious of her straw hat itching her head, her hands folded one over the other so that the woman wouldn't see the mess of darning on the fingers of her pale blue cotton gloves. They had been worn by her cousin, Kitty, who passed them down to Joan, and then down to her. They were miles too big but they were all her mother could find.

Miss Benson was to escort Elsie to the rehearsals at Mrs Egerton-Smythe's house. Elsie had a horrible feeling that any magic in rehearsals would be snuffed out by Miss Benson with a glance, and wondered why

Mr Neville had chosen someone so grim. And then the penny dropped. Of course. Marjorie Bush! Miss Benson would frighten off a dozen Marjorie Bushes. Walking down the street with her would be like travelling with your own Sherman tank.

Elsie was overwhelmed with such relief that her shyness evaporated and she found herself smiling up at her. Miss Benson emitted an 'harrumph!' and swept out of the stage door, the implication being that Elsie should follow.

Elsie caught sight of Wilfred. 'Well done, girl.' He was grinning.

Outside, the heat of another scorching summer's day was beginning to fry the pavements. It wasn't till they were in sight of Mrs Egerton-Smythe's house that Miss Benson acknowledged Elsie's existence.

'There are a few things that ought to be explained to you, young lady. First of all, I am used to chaperoning professionals.' She enunciated the word with grandeur. 'Young ladies who are self-disciplined, who speak well, who present themselves impeccably, who have, in fact, been trained in the art of the theatre. I hear from Mr Neville that,' and here she stopped as if to gain strength from some invisible source, 'that you are a local girl who has had no experience.' She swallowed. 'And no training whatsoever.'

Elsie watched mesmerised as Miss Benson's jowls began to wobble like an earth tremor before a volcano. She watched her purse her lips and force them into a controlled smile, but even more fascinating was the ever changing range of colours of Miss Benson's skin until her entire face went white except for her nose, which seemed to blush at the tip. It was as though all her anger was harnessed and was now residing in the area above her nostrils.

'So,' Miss Benson said breathlessly. 'As I am not accustomed to accompanying such inexperienced ladies, and you are not accustomed to being looked after by a chaperone, I will have to teach you what is required.'

'But isn't Mr Neville going to be doin' that?' Elsie asked.

Miss Benson winced. 'Not on stage, Miss Hollis. Off stage. Off-stage behaviour. The rudiments of etiquette. And, if I were you, I shouldn't talk too often while you still have that execrable accent.'

She swung her tapestry bag back with as much force as if she were about to throw a discus and strode up the road, Elsie running beside her.

Elsie stood awkwardly by the French windows which led on to the veranda and stared towards the summer house and river. It was the room her father had brought her back to after she was nearly drowned, and she had not been in it since that night. Looking out now, everything was green except for the flowers Ralph had planted. And the river looked invitingly cool. A row of chairs had been placed with their backs to the French windows, and smaller furniture had been set on chalk marks on the floor. The thought of reading her part in front of all these strangers, who were now casually browsing through their newspapers or mail, seemed terrifying. After Miss Benson's outburst, she wondered what the other members of the cast would think of her voice. Miss Benson had found herself a chair and was knitting what appeared to be a navy blue blanket, but Elsie thought it was probably a sock for Miss Benson.

There was a gentle touch on her shoulder. Looking up she found a woman of her mother's age smiling down at her. 'I'm Annie Duncan. You must be Elsie Hollis.'

'You're playing my mother!'

'Which is why I thought it would be a good idea for us to get to know one another. I expect you're feeling very nervous.'

Elsie nodded.

'Don't worry. All newcomers to a production feel like that. It's just that some hide it better.' She bent over and leaned closer to Elsie to whisper. 'Who's the giant navy blue bat?'

'My chaperone,' Elsie giggled. 'Miss Benson.'

Elsie noticed Annie Duncan was dressed in the latest fashion: a black new-look skirt which flared to mid-calf, a blouse, a small red jacket, a black rounded hat and heels. In fact, glancing round, Elsie was relieved that Ralph had warned her. They did look glamorous. One of the women looked like a film star. She wore a hat with a black net clouding over her face.

'That's Fabia Delmar. She's playing Pearl Bond.'

'The one who steals the strychnine from my father's laboratory and poisons her husband with it?'

'That's right,' said Annie, surprised. 'I see you've been doing your homework.'

'Which one is my brother Albert?'

'There,' said Annie, pointing to a distinguished-looking man in a cream linen suit and tie and straw hat.

Elsie guessed he could be anywhere in his twenties or thirties. Albert, was supposed to be nineteen. 'He doesn't look a bit like I imagined him.'

'Oh, he will. His name is Felix Venning. And that man over there is playing your father.' The actor was tall with black hair and an intent look. 'He's called Arnold Swann.'

'He produces plays at the Palace as well, doesn't he?' Elsie asked.

There was a loud clapping of hands. It was Mr Neville. He was standing in the centre of the room.

'Good morning, everyone. As you know, this is our first exchange venture with the Redmond Theatre and we hope it will be an experiment which will flourish. By swapping every other week, the audiences in both Winford and Redmond will continue to have a new play every week. The difficulty of course will be the travelling, but we think we can cope. We seem to be able to cope with most things.' He smiled. 'Most of you know one another and have worked together often, but we have two members from the Redmond Theatre here. Sheila Darbisher who will play Emily Strachan.' My older sister with the voice of an angel, thought Elsie. 'And Roger Douglas.' Who plays Ernest O'Shea.

93

He loves Emily and wants to marry her, and helps Albert and Emily out of a fix. He is Doctor O'Shea's son, she added internally.

It was while she was attempting to take all of this in that she heard her name being called out. 'And Elsie Hollis. Sister of Ralph, who some of you know. She will play Eva.'

Elsie saw Felix Venning grinning at her and, in spite of her face growing hot, she couldn't help smiling back.

'As we don't have an auditorium for those who are not in a scene, Mrs Egerton-Smythe has said you may use the library or sit out here on the veranda. Just don't go out of hearing. I don't want Geoffrey, my stage manager, or Rosemary, one of the assistant stage managers, to have to chase you when we need you. It is delightful here but we need to make the best out of our two-week rehearsal period.'

As some of the cast went to sit on the veranda with their play scripts, Elsie, Annie and Felix were asked to remain and, to Elsie's relief, Miss Benson was despatched to the kitchen. As Elsie opened the play, she noticed her hands were shaking.

'Geoffrey,' said Mr Neville to the young man who

was sitting next to him with a large book, 'give Elsie a pencil, will you.'

'Yes, sir. Of course, sir.'

The young man leaped eagerly towards her. Elsie was mystified. Did Mr Neville want her to draw a picture?

'This week we will be setting the play, which means I will be telling you where to move. Geoffrey will be writing down everyone's moves so that if you forget he can remind you. But before I do that, I had better tell you about the different parts of the stage. Do you know what I mean when I say stage right or stage left?'

'Yes,' said Elsie. 'Stage right is from where I'm standing on stage, not your right or left.'

'Correct. Now stand in the middle for me. That's that round chalk mark there.' He indicated a chalk mark in the middle of the room.

Elsie did so.

'Has Ralph told you about downstage and upstage?'

'Yes, sir.'

'Sir,' said Geoffrey tentatively. 'May I make a suggestion? It is relevant, sir.'

'Go on then.'

'Simon says, sir.'

Mr Neville glared at Geoffrey as if he had just lost his senses.

'Simon says do this. Simon says do that,' Geoffrey elaborated.

'Oh yes,' enthused Felix. 'Five minutes. I'm sure it would save a lot of time in the long run.'

Mr Neville gave a sigh. 'Geoffrey!'

Geoffrey sprang to his feet. 'Simon says upstage right.'

To Elsie's amazement, the elegant Felix Venning and Annie Duncan sprinted up to the back of the room on the right-hand side, Elsie ran after them.

'Simon says centre stage.'

And so it went on. At the end of the five minutes the entire room had collapsed into hysteria, watched by other members of the cast through the windows. And the joy of it was that Elsie discovered her way round the set immediately, and felt much more at ease with Annie and Felix.

Once they had calmed down, Mr Neville pointed out where the doors would be on the set.

At the opening of the play, Elsie as Eva had to sit

on a stool by the fireplace next to the armchair where Annie as her mother was mending socks. Felix as Albert was drawing on a piece of paper at the centre table.

'Now, you'll be sewing a sampler, Elsie,' said Mr Neville. He turned to Rosemary and gave her a nod. She wrote something down. 'Let's begin.'

Elsie took off her hat and gloves.

It was when everyone had left the room to go their separate ways for lunch that Elsie suddenly realised how much she had to learn. This time tomorrow they would have done a run of Act I without books and have been set another act to learn for the next day!

'Come along, young lady,' boomed a voice behind her. 'You're wanted in the kitchen.'

'But I have to learn my lines, Miss Benson!'

'Food!' she ordered. 'You are to have an hour's break. Then you can look at your lines.'

In the kitchen sat Queenie, a local woman who 'did' for Mrs Egerton-Smythe. Waiting for Elsie on the table was bread with a scraping of butter and a bowl of soup. As soon as she began eating, she could feel her head clearing and energy returning.

'I will teach you how to eat soup correctly,'

announced Miss Benson. 'You eat soup from the *side* of the spoon. And you tip the bowl *away* from yourself as you reach the last dregs. Useful to know, especially if you have to eat on stage.'

'Oh. Thank you, Miss Benson,' said Elsie quickly.

'Not at all. Now, when you have finished lunch you will go out and play.'

'But I have to learn my lines.'

'You will *play*. Mrs Woods here has kindly allowed me to borrow her bell. At two p.m. I will ring it. You will learn your lines between then and four p.m. One of the ASMs, will return to hear you. And in case you don't know what an ASM is, it's an assistant stage manager. Elsie knew already. An ASM was general dogsbody and prop hunter, Ralph had said. 'Now go along with you.'

'Where?' Elsie asked.

'The garden!' Miss Benson said, a slight note of exasperation creeping into her voice.

'Yes, Miss Benson.'

She noticed Queenie giving her a wink. She suppressed a smile and left the kitchen.

The lawn had massive high hedges on either side, but facing her on the other side of the sprawling house was a coach house. Elsie walked past two sheds and headed towards the little summer house and jetty at the bottom of the garden. She sat on the old wooden planks, her legs dangling above the water, and watched the river drift by, her thoughts floating down into the fronds and weeds below.

She woke up to the sound of a bell ringing. She scrambled to her feet and ran up the lawn. She could see Miss Benson standing on the veranda. One of the doors to the rehearsal room was open. 'I shall collect you at five p.m,' she said. And she swept round the corner.

Elsie climbed up the steps and into the rehearsal room, and picked up her copy of *Pink String and Sealing Wax*. Mr Neville had said to learn the lines with the moves at the same time. But every time Elsie opened her mouth to speak, she felt curiously exposed. She was conscious of how different she sounded to all the other actors. Her voice sounded tinny and horrible, and she began to panic.

The minutes raced ahead and Elsie realised with mounting horror that she was going to be tested on her lines and she didn't know them. Within hours Mr Neville would be informed of the terrible mistake he had made. Her mother would be disappointed. There would be no play for her father to come and see her in. And, worst of all, she would have to spend four weeks alone, avoiding being beaten up.

'Downstage right,' she muttered. And then she realised she was attempting to put on a posh accent, even to say her moves. By the time it was four o'clock she had not learned a single line. She listened miserably to the footsteps crossing the polished wooden floor in the hallway towards the door. It was too late. The ASM had come to hear her.

The door opened. When Elsie saw who was standing there, it was the final straw.

'Oh, Ralph!' she cried, and she burst into tears.

Three

'I'm Eva. I'm twelve years old and have chickenpox. Had chickenpox. I'm over it now, but father still won't let me go out.

'I have two brothers and three sisters. We live in a big house in Brighton near the sea, with my parents and Lucy, the maid.

'My eldest brother is Albert. He's my favourite. He's nineteen. He wants to be an engineer and invent things. He's always drawing some idea in his head. But father won't hear of it. He wants him to be a chemist and druggist, like him. In fact, father doesn't want anyone to do what they want to do, especially if they enjoy it.

'Then there's my sister, Jessie. She's sixteen and wants to be an actress. She's always 'doing' characters in front of mirrors, and exaggerating everything as if she's on stage. She's very pretty. Not at all like me.

'Emily's my older sister. She's eighteen, but looks older. She has a beautiful singing voice. Of course,

father doesn't think so. If she could be discovered, I'm sure she would be famous overnight. But she says it doesn't happen like that. You have to work hard and have dedication. She wants to take lessons and get better and better. Instead, she has to give lessons to two horrid little girls. And when she's there, they stuff their faces with food and never offer Emily so much as a crust.

'My other sister is little Vickie, 'cos she's the littlest. She's seven. And my other brother is Malcolm who's nine. Malcolm gets pocket money from my father, a penny a week, which he has to put straight into a box. That's when he hasn't done anything to annoy father.

'Then there's Mother. She's very kind and means well. It's just that she doesn't really seem to understand what we're talking about, so we don't tell her everything. Especially important things. She'd only tell father. She reads to us at night, which would be a lovely experience if it weren't so dull. She's reading us Pilgrim's Progress at the moment, which seems to go on for ever. Jessie has been trying to persuade her to read us Hans Anderson, but I'm afraid it hasn't had any effect. Pilgrim's Progress is supposed to be good for us. Like sewing samplers. Although what good sewing a sampler is doing for me, I don't know, except *teaching me to endure boredom and pain.*

'But best of all is Albert. He's handsome, and the most wonderful person in the world.

'Oh no, my "N" is upside down. I hope no one notices. It took me ages to sew and I don't want to have to unpick it and do it all over again.'

Elsie stopped. She felt a hundred times better. Her brother was smiling.

'Now, tell me what you do in Act I.'

'I sew and chat about my father. I admire Albert's drawing, but I keep it a secret from Mother in case she spills the beans to Father and Albert gets into trouble for not studying. I go upstairs with her and Jessie to listen to her read from Pilgrim's Progress *to me and my brothers and sisters.*

'My second scene.

'I return. As I sew and everyone else is chatting, I am thinking of the guinea-pigs my father has brought home, and how I can feed them. I go downstairs to give Lucy a message from mother.

'My third scene.

'I'm very excited. I rush in to tell everyone the news that not only is Lucy not feeling well, but she has a spot on her bottom. What a place to start chickenpox!

'*Jessie is asked to recite a poem. The poem is about someone called Lucy. This is too funny for words, and we rush out giggling uncontrollably.*

'My fourth scene.

'*It's night-time. I'm in my night-dress. I sneak downstairs to give the guinea-pigs some lettuce. I hear my father coming and I hide behind the curtains. After he has left, I come out of hiding and head for the kitchen. I return with some lettuce for the guinea-pigs, and I'm just about to enter the laboratory when I hear strange noises coming from the jars and I run out. Then I realise that what I had heard were the cats outside. I laugh at myself. I hear Albert's voice and I hide in the shop.*

'My fifth scene.

'*My beloved Albert is not alone. There is a woman with him. She persuades him to go out into the garden for a bit of a kiss and a cuddle. I've overheard it all. I step out. I'm frightened, and I don't know why. I'm jealous and hurt. The smell of the woman's scent revolts me. I throw myself on to the settee. My heart is breaking and I sob angrily.*

'That's my story in Act I.'

Elsie laughed with relief. It was all beginning to make sense.

Before they could finish the act, Miss Benson walked in. She frowned at Ralph.

'I presume you are one of the ASMs?'

'Yes, Miss Benson,' said Ralph. And he beamed. 'I hope we haven't kept you waiting.'

In spite of herself, Miss Benson smiled.

I do love you, thought Elsie, as she gazed up at her brother.

'And how did Miss Hollis do?'

'Oh, she's coming along famously, Miss Benson.'

'Have you been with the company long?'

'Off and on since November, but I'm on a proper contract now. ASM and small parts.'

'Oh, a good start to your career.'

'Yes. I feel very lucky. And privileged. This company has a high standard.'

'Indeed,' she gazed pointedly at Elsie. 'Let's hope it will continue.'

Outside, Miss Benson insisted that Elsie put on her hat and gloves before she began striding along the pavement again. A glowing monologue came from Miss Benson about the nicely spoken ASM.

'A real gentleman if ever there was. Good breeding. That's what you need to aim for, Miss Hollis. He's young but I can see he will go far. He has that air about him. I've worked with the best, you know. The best. Oh, yes. He may be on the bottom rung of the ladder, but he'll rise. You mark my words. He'll rise. I shall keep my eye out for him. You're fortunate that he's the one hearing your lines. Well educated too. I can tell. I should have asked him his name.'

Elsie waited until they had turned the corner into the High Street for her *coup de grâce.*

'It's Ralph, Miss Benson. Ralph Hollis. He's my brother.'

'The new look!' Joan gasped. 'All the actresses?'

'Yes,' said Elsie.

'But how could they afford it? Ralph said rep actors and actresses are always broke.'

Joan stood up and looked at her skirt, which barely covered her knees. 'How can I go out lookin' like this? With all this leg showin'. I feel vulgar. And old-fashioned, too.'

'Can't you buy them with coupons?' Elsie asked.

'Nah. It's all this bloomin' utility stuff. The government still says clothes in shops can only be made of so much material. Look at this skirt. I've let it down as far as I can, but it still don't look anything like the new look. How come the women in France can wear long flared dresses and skirts and not us? It's not fair! So tell me what they looked like. Every detail.'

Elsie sighed. 'Will you let me learn my lines afterwards if I do?'

'I'm not stoppin' you.'

'Fabia Delmar is the most glamorous. She was wearing this red dress with a belt in the middle. There was so much of it. And it swished. Her waist looked very small. The sleeves were short, but the neckline was all sculptured and bits stuck up.'

'Bits?'

'And she wore gloves. And she wore a hat with a net veil thing.'

'And?' said Joan, impatiently.

'Annie Duncan wore a little jacket and a wide, Chinese looking hat. The jacket went in at the waist.'

'That's what I'd really love. I'm so fed up with these square-shouldered jackets in the shops. I want to feel pretty. Elegant.'

'You look pretty already.'

'You're just sayin' that to get me out of the room.'

'No, I'm not.'

When she was happy, Joan did look pretty.

'I have to learn my lines for Act I by tomorrow,' Elsie pleaded.

'I thought you were supposed to learn them this afternoon.'

'I started learning them, but I have to learn where to go as well.'

'Molly's comin' round.'

That'll be the two of them moaning together, Elsie thought. She picked up the play and went next door to the kitchen.

Her mother smiled. 'You're a mind-reader. Time to lay the table.'

Elsie was about to protest when she noticed Harry leaning near the wireless as if wishing himself down the tubes.

'You look like you could do with an early night, Harry,' Mrs Hollis commented.

'Yeah,' he yawned. 'After *Dick Barton.*' He caught Elsie's eye and they smiled at each other.

'First few weeks are always toughest,' Mr Hollis said. 'But you're doin' all right.'

'Course he is,' said Mrs Hollis. 'I'm just not used to him bein' so quiet!'

After supper Elsie tried to learn her lines in her parents' room, but it was difficult to concentrate because of the wireless blaring from downstairs. She stuck both thumbs in her ears, but then kept losing her place.

Her mother appeared. 'Want some help, love?'

'Oh, Mum. Yes please. Would you hear me?'

It was all she could do not to laugh. Her mother looked so comical in her men's spectacles, and she read everything out laboriously slowly in her Hertford-shire accent. But it was helpful. 'You know it very well,' she said.

'Ralph helped.'

'That's nice.'

'It's easier when you know what you're talkin' about and what's goin' on.'

'Well, yes. It would be.'

'Oh, Mum,' Elsie giggled. 'You are funny.'

'Am I?' said Mrs Hollis, surprised.

Elsie sat on the bed next to her. Her mother put her arms round her and let her rest against her. 'My lovely girl,' she murmured.

'Will you really come and see me in the play?'

'Course I will. And more than once. I'll stick a bivouac up in the gods and come and park there.'

'And you'll bring Dad?'

'Yeah. Don't you worry.' She ruffled her hair. 'It's still like draggin' in an unwillin' donkey, but I usually succeed.' She sighed. 'If only he'd stop scratchin'.'

'Scratchin'?'

'Haven't you noticed him doin' that once we get into our seats upstairs.'

Elsie had never thought about it before, but her mother was right.

'Sometimes I almost expect him to come out in hives or a rash.'

'Why does Ralph want him to see *Desert Highway*?'

'He wants us both to see it.'

'Will you?'

'I doubt it, love. He only goes when Ralph is in somethin'.' She lowered her voice. 'He don't say so, but he's proud as mustard seeing 'im on stage, but don't let on I told you.'

'Cross my heart and hope to die.'

'And I'm proud of you,' she said, beaming.

Elsie knew that already. She even took it for granted. So why wasn't it enough? Why did she need her dad to be proud of her too?

Four

'Go to where Mr Neville set you for the beginning of your first scene.'

Elsie sat on one of the dining-room chairs. She was wearing a long practice skirt that Rosemary had brought in for her at Mr Neville's request, so that she would get used to wearing a long dress before the opening night.

'Ralph, what happens in the afternoons?'

'What do you mean?'

'Why are there only rehearsals in the mornings?'

'It's so that the actors can learn their lines, get any make-up they might need, sometimes do a matinée, sometimes even get a film job. But most of them go to a pub in the middle of the day, sleep all afternoon, perform in the evening and learn their lines into the early hours.'

That morning Act I had passed by in a haze. Elsie had managed to get through it without the book, but through the run all she could see were the pages turning over in her head. She hadn't dared look up at the cast because she knew it would make her forget her lines. It was a mess. An embarassing humiliating mess.

There was a knock at the door. 'Oh, no!' said Elsie, alarmed. 'It can't be Miss Benson yet.'

'She wouldn't knock.'

'Come in.'

A freckle-faced fifteen year old girl with crossed front teeth and long, wiry, red hair, poked her head round the door. Ralph leaped to his feet and gave an enormous grin. 'Jessica!'

'Am I interrupting?' she asked, smiling.

'A bit,' said Ralph. 'I have to finish at five. What time is it now?'

'About four-thirty. I'll see you later then. Mother says you can stay for tea.'

'Good-o.'

The door closed. Elsie watched her brother leaping round the room like a cat on hot bricks who has got the cream at the same time. Mum referred to Jessica Egerton-Smythe as Ralph's sweetheart, which made Ralph blush. Elsie felt uncomfortable.

'Shall I start?' she said.

'Yes. Fire away.'

Elsie began sniffing, as though she had a foul cold. Slowly and steadily she went through her first scene in Act II while Ralph read the other characters' lines. It seemed to take for ever.

'Right,' said Ralph, eagerly, when she had finished. 'What happens next?'

'You are a bully.'

'I'm not, am I?' said her brother anxiously.

'No,' she laughed. Her brother had a temper but there wasn't an ounce of malice in him.

'That's it. That's my last appearance in Act II.' She gave a sigh of relief.

'Well done.'

'Really? Mr Neville said I had to imagine what goes on in the other rooms in the house when I'm not in the parlour. Because I have to keep walking on and off.'

'You're doing that already,' Ralph said reassuringly.

'Yeah, I suppose I am. But it don't seem to come out when I speak the lines.'

'It will.'

Elsie gazed at her brother's eager face. She wanted

more than anything not to let him down. Or Mr Neville. Or her mother. She knew what a low opinion her father had of her. If she failed to prove him wrong, if she humiliated him in public he might never speak to her again. She had found out that some members of the cast thought that Mr Neville had made a mistake in giving her the role, but had to keep their opinions to themselves because he was the boss. 'Lines now,' said Ralph. 'Before Dracula reappears.'

Elsie giggled.

'*Go on*,' said Ralph, reading Jessie. '*Didn't you think she was pretty?*'

Ralph entwined an arm with Elsie and they walked over to where the fireplace would be.

'*No*,' said Elsie as Eva. '*Awful looking. She had paint on her face!*'

Outside it was hot and airless. Elsie stumbled silently alongside Miss Benson trying to keep up with her as she swept boldly down the High Street. Aside from the occasional harrumph, Miss Benson didn't speak a word. They stopped at the stage door and Miss Benson picked up a letter. Elsie saw Miss Benson in a new light. She hadn't imagined anyone wanting to write to her. Later, getting off the bus Elsie spotted Marjorie and three of the gang sitting on a wall, looking bored.

'Come on, Miss Hollis,' ordered Miss Benson. 'Chin up.'

Looking out of the corner of her eye, Elsie spotted the girls leaping off the wall. I bet they can't believe their luck, she thought. Acutely aware of her spectacles and her Sunday-best hat, she readjusted them firmly.

'Oooh. Look at little Miss High-and-Mighty,' sneered Marjorie.

Miss Benson swung round and glared at the four girls. 'Are you referring to me?' she boomed.

'You're not exactly little,' sniggered Marjorie. She and her friends collapsed into a fit of giggles.

Elsie stayed close to Miss Benson's side. Nobody moved. By now Elsie was sweating so profusely, she was sure the gang could smell her terror. And then, to Elsie's utter astonishment, Miss Benson raised her arms inside her voluminous cloak and gave a deafening roar. The gang was so surprised they ran off. Once they were out of sight, she resumed her normal brisk manner and began walking again. Elsie trotted along beside her, gazing up at her in awe.

'Paper tiger,' Miss Benson explained.

Elsie didn't care what kind of tiger it was, as long as it got rid of Marjorie Bush and her pals.

As on the previous day, Miss Benson insisted on taking Elsie right up to her front door. This afternoon, her mother was ready. She had removed her apron. And, as on the previous day, Miss Benson politely declined the cup of tea Mrs Hollis offered and turned on her heel, sallying back, past the ruins and rubble in the street, with a strange kind of dignity.

There were two letters in the kitchen. The letter for the family was from Kitty, Joan's older sister, and was filled with chatter about her baby and her husband, Frank, and how hot the hut that they were squatting in was, but how grateful they were to have a home for the baby. And how kind people had been. And that she was looking forward to seeing them in Kent when they all went down 'oppin'.

The other letter was in Geraldine's handwriting. Elsie looked at the envelope and immediately felt depressed.

'Ent you goin' to open it?' said her mother, surprised when she put it back on the table.'

'In a minute.'

'Gets you down, does she?'

Elsie nodded.

'Some people are like that, love. Some people tire you out. Some people buck you up. Don't let it get to you.'

'It's just that things aren't so good at home for her.'

'Yeah, I picked that up on the night at your school. It's hard for a man to be out of work. Hurts his pride. Do you want me to read it out to you and leave out all the horrible bits?'

Elsie smiled. 'No.' She went to tear the envelope open.

' 'Ere,' said her mother, handing her a knife. 'We could use that envelope again.'

Elsie sliced it open neatly.

Dear Elsie,

I can't believe we only broke up three days ago. It seems like three years. How I'm goin' to get through the rest of this holiday I don't know. Mum's had to go into hospital. They say she's got blood pressure problems. Something called toxaemia. So I'm left here with Dad. I try not to make him cross, so I make myself invisible.

Elsie sighed. Her eyes drifted down the page.

I can't even run away, because I've nowhere to go, and Mum would be upset. And she says she's looking forward to me helping with the baby and the housework and that.
I wish they were rich and could send me off to boarding-school. I'd love that. No I wouldn't. I'd miss Mum. Maybe she's right. Maybe the baby will make everything better. Sometimes I count the years I've got left before I can leave home. When they have rows, I pray that I'll die in my sleep. Is it still bad when your parents row? Six weeks to go! It's like a prison sentence, isn't it? I wish I could see you soon. Write to me, won't you?
Your special friend,
Geraldine

'That bad, eh?' said her mother, who had been watching her from the range.

Elsie held it out for her to read.

'I'aven't got me specs. You'll have to read it to me yourself.'

When Elsie had finished, her mother stared at her for a moment. 'Did you tell her that things was bad 'ere?'

Elsie blushed. 'Ages ago,' she mumbled.

'When me an' your dad rowed a lot? We've still got a way to go, love. The war's messed things up a bit. Everything's a bit topsy-turvy. At least Dad and I aren't strangers like . . .'

She stopped.

'Like Geraldine's parents,' Elsie finished for her.

'Don't take the rows personal, that's all I'm sayin'. No man's good at sayin' what he feels, so sometimes they get angry instead.'

'So when they're not cross, how do people know?'

'By what they do.' She paused. 'And a bit of guesswork, I suppose.' She smiled. 'Now get that dress off so as I can wash it all over again for tomorrow morning. And then, if I'm quick about it, I can hear your lines.'

But at that moment there were footsteps in the yard. Elsie kneeled up on the little truckle-bed which was

119

used as a settee under the window, and peered out. It was her dad and Harry. Harry waved at her. But Elsie could see he was almost reeling with exhaustion. She watched her father put his arm round Harry's shoulders. Harry beamed up at him. Elsie was aware of a lump hurting at the back of her throat.

Five

Elsie stared intently down at her words. If only they were all near one another they would be easier to learn. There was so much to read between each of her bits. She had fallen asleep while trying to learn them in bed, and had woken up with her face buried in Act III when Joan had joined her.

She couldn't even learn much at breakfast because it was her job to lay and clear the table.

Sitting on the back of Ralph's bicycle as it sprang like a bucking bronco over strewn bricks, she clung on, feeling shattered with exhaustion.

Miss Benson, as usual, said nothing. She gave her usual nod followed by her usual harrumph, and strode out of the stage door with brisk and gargantuan strides.

When they reached Mrs Egerton-Smythe's garden room, Elsie glanced at the cast. Felix Venning was doing a crossword in a newspaper. Annie Duncan was pacing up and down by the French windows, glancing periodically at her script and then quickly looking upwards and mouthing silently. Arnold Swann, who played her father, was standing puffing a cigarette and staring thoughtfully at a page.

'Do you want me to hear you?'

It was Isla Leighton, the girl playing Jessie. She had a round sort of beauty, thought Elsie. Round face, round eyes, and a broad mouth which fell into a dazzling smile. Mum said that Ralph had had a soft spot for her once, and she could see why.

'Yes, please,' said Elsie, relieved. 'I fell asleep last night in the middle of reading them.'

'It happens to us all. One of the advantages of having freezing digs in the winter.'

Elsie tried to make sense of this remark.

Isla laughed. 'If you're learning lines in bed, it keeps your mind going. If it's too snug and warm you drop off to sleep.'

'Oh yeah. I get it,' said Elsie.

'Here,' said Isla, holding out a safety pin. 'I thought this might help.' Elsie stood up in her practice skirt. 'I don't think they realised quite how small you were,' she said, clumping the material of Elsie's long skirt together at the waist. 'There. How does that feel?'

Elsie walked around in it. 'Much better. Thanks.'

'I'll read the other lines,' said Isla. And she began.

The next morning during the run, all Elsie could see was the print floating around in front of her eyes. It was as though she was a tightrope walker with vertigo, and if she dared take in her surroundings she would fall. Or in her case, 'dry'.

She had overheard Fabia Delmar comment to someone after the run of Act II, 'Poor little scrap. She's just not up to it.'

Felix Venning had said, 'Darling, it's her first week.'

'But she shouldn't be doing her first week with us. She should be doing it in her school play.'

Several times, Elsie was tempted to go to Mr Neville and admit defeat. In fact, she couldn't understand why he hadn't ditched her already. And then it dawned on her why she wasn't ever chosen for the school plays. It wasn't because of her Hertfordshire accent at all. It was because she was no good. But as soon as she began to lose courage, she reminded herself of Marjorie Bush who loathed the very sight of her, and that gave her the strength to keep going.

*

'*Now here's the hell of a thing!*' cried Mr Neville, as Dr O'Shea, his accent thickly Irish. '*Adelina Patti herself in a carriage outside, and she's in a divil of a rage.*'

Mr Neville turned to the others and said, 'Now just give me a look. And you, Emily.'

'I give a cry and thrust you aside and run from the room,' Sheila added as Emily.

'Yes,' said Mr Neville.

Elsie watched enviously. The cast were so quick to pick up on things.

'Curtain,' said Geoffrey as they finished the act.

'Thank you, everyone,' said Mr Neville. 'Run of Act III and Act I tomorrow. We'll have a stagger through the whole play on Saturday. Elsie.'

Elsie was pencilling in her rush to the window. She felt her heart sink. She closed her book and went over to him. He took her aside. 'Miss Benson tells me that she has found you asleep these last two days after lunch. Are you having problems sleeping at home? I mean, is there anything worrying you?'

Elsie didn't know which question to answer first.

'You're learning your lines. That's good.'

124

'But I can't look at anyone,' she burst out, then wished she had kept her mouth shut.

'You give a wonderful performance away from the cast but when you're in rehearsal it all falls by the wayside?'

'Yes!' said Elsie, amazed that he knew.

'I don't know if this helps, but imagine a piece of elastic. Every time you work by yourself, you stretch it, then when you rejoin the cast it springs back.'

Elsie didn't think this was going to help her in the slightest.

'But the elastic doesn't quite go back to where you left it, because it has been stretched, so although it seems as though you've gone backwards . . .'

'I get it!' interrupted Elsie, excitedly. 'You're still making progress?'

He nodded.

'But I heard someone say no one will hear me.'

'Did you? Well, it's true that you can only just be heard. But,' he said, holding up his hands before she could protest, 'what I can hear makes sense, which is what is most important. Later, I'll tell you when I want you to speak up. Understood?'

'Yes, sir.'

'Will this help you sleep better?'

'Not really. Unless I pop upstairs first.'

'I'm afraid I've lost you.'

'I sleep with Joan. Or rather, I don't.'

He frowned at her for a moment and then his eyebrows suddenly shot up. 'The trumpeter?'

Elsie giggled and nodded.

'Good Lord.'

'But Auntie Win is coming to stay next week and she usually tells her to sleep in the bed in the kitchen. The only snag is, Auntie Win kicks. But I should know me lines by then, so it won't matter.'

'It matters if you're tired for rehearsal, young lady. Now, let me get this absolutely straight. Next week there will be three of you in the bed. After Joan is thrown out, your aunt will begin kicking you until eventually you flee to your brother's room.'

'Yes, sir.'

'Which brother?'

'They share. They sleep top "n" tail.' Elsie suddenly felt herself redden. 'I'm ever so sorry. Ralph wouldn't want you to know that. I think he likes everyone to think we're more—'

'Suburban?'

126

'Is that swanky?'

Mr Neville hesitated and then nodded. 'I think Ralph has given up on that. But that is not our problem. Our problem is how do we ensure you get an un-interrupted night's sleep while we rehearse?'

'Search me, sir.' Suddenly Elsie felt very sorry for Mr Neville. She touched him gently on the arm. 'Don't worry, sir. I'll manage. I'm used to it.'

'Wake up!'

It was Jessica.

'Was I asleep?' Elsie asked.

'Like a log,' Jessica said, amazed. 'Miss Benson's been ringing the bell and I've been yelling like mad. I was beginning to think you'd fallen in the river and drowned.'

Elsie sat up and yawned. 'You are lucky living here.'

'I know,' sighed Jessica.

'Do you miss it when you're at boarding-school?'

'Yes. But then I can get away from my brother, Charles. So it's worth it.'

'I can't imagine not liking my brother. I like both of mine.'

127

'I liked Laurie. I loved him actually.' She suddenly looked sad. Elsie knew Laurie had been killed in the war. 'I hope we don't have to leave here.'

'Why should you?'

'It's a long story. But Mother's getting married, you see. And she might have to move out because of it. It's to do with my father's will.'

'So why get married?'

'Romance!' said Jessica, smiting her chest with her hand, and making gooey eyes. 'No, really,' she said, smiling, 'she wants to marry him.'

'Is it someone you know?'

'Yes. And he's nice. Thank goodness. But it's going to cause the most awful scandal. At least, that's what Charles thinks. He's dead against it.'

'Why?'

'Because the man my mother is going to marry is not only one of her lodgers here, but he's also an actor!'

'What's wrong with that?'

'Well, my father was a very well known K.C.'

'What's a K.C?'

'King's Counsel.'

Elsie was still no wiser.

'It's like a grand barrister. Defends or prosecutes people in court.'

'Like in murder trials?'

'Yes. So, you see, an actor is not top drawer enough for Charles. And, of course, as an actor he doesn't have a penny. And he's eleven years *younger* than her!'

'But who is he?' Elsie asked.

Jessica gazed at her in silence for a moment. 'Basil Duke.'

'Basil Duke!' Elsie yelled. 'My dad was in the war with him. Course, he didn't know he was an actor then. By the time he found out it was too late. He already liked him. He goes to the pub with him sometimes, only it's supposed to be a secret. He don't want any of his mates to find out. Gosh! Basil Duke!'

'Shush,' said Jessica, looking round nervously.

They were interrupted by the sound of the bell being rung.

'You won't mention this to anyone, will you?' said Jessica.

'No. Of course not.'

The bell was now even louder. Elsie sprang to her feet. 'Act III.'

They ran up the lawn.

'Tell Ralph that Mother's invited him to tea again,' panted Jessica.

Elsie nodded, trying hard to take in this information, because her head was already being flooded with Eva's thoughts.

Six

The next day, when the cast had gone their separate ways to have lunch, Miss Benson appeared on the veranda.

'Now that you've learned your lines, your brother's been sent out prop-hunting with one of the other ASMs.'

'Oh, no.'

'So I'll be taking you home early.'

'But I wanted to go through my lines again before the run tomorrow morning.'

'Ah. I take it you weren't DLP this morning then?'

'DLP?'

'Dead letter perfect. You took prompts. Extrapolated. Went off the rails a bit.'

Elsie nodded.

Miss Benson gave a sniff. 'I could hear you, of course.'

Elsie could feel herself reddening. It was difficult enough hanging on to the tiny crumb of confidence

131

she had without Miss Benson removing it.

'I won't tell you what to do, if that's what you're worried about. Never do. Very unprofessional. I leave that to the producer. You have your moves written in, should you forget?'

'Yes, Miss Benson.'

Miss Benson held out her hand for the play script. Elsie swallowed. Execrable. That's what Miss Benson had called her accent. To Elsie's surprise, Miss Benson was very helpful. She prompted in a calm way, correcting her and making her go over each scene until she began to feel so confident that she even started to enjoy it. Although Mr Neville had told her that the Saturday morning run was not a test, it was just to see where the weaker spots were so that he could concentrate on them the following week, Elsie was still very nervous. She felt she could now cope with it. The elastic had been stretched quite a bit.

Miss Benson didn't make any comment about her performance on the way home but, by the time they reached Elsie's front door, Elsie couldn't hold back any longer. 'Miss Benson,' she blurted out. 'Was I all right?'

Miss Benson stopped in mid-harrumph and glanced down at her. 'You'll do.'

So, when her mother answered the door, Elsie was too dazed with happiness to notice the look of anxiety on her mother's face.

'We have a visitor,' she said quietly.

'Is it Auntie Win? Has she come early?'

'No, Elsie. It's Miss Castleford.' Her mother looked up at Miss Benson. 'She's the headmistress of Winford Grammar School for Girls.'

'But why is she here?' Elsie whispered.

'You were mentioned in the *Winford Observer* today.'

'Me?' Elsie said, amazed.

'It said how the Palace Theatre had auditioned girls for the part of Eva, and how they had chosen a local girl. You. And they mentioned what school you attended.'

'Isn't that kind of her?'

'I don't think you understand, Elsie.'

'Coming to congratulate me!' added Elsie, happily.

'She hasn't come to congratulate you. In fact, she's not very pleased. She wants to know why she wasn't informed. Why her permission wasn't asked. And she wants to know what kind of play it is, and if it's suitable for a Winford Grammar School girl to appear in.'

'Oh, Mum. She couldn't stop me, could she?' Yes she could, thought Elsie. And she knew why. 'It's 'cos of me accent, Mum. If I walk on stage in front of everyone like me, a Winford Grammar School girl . . . Oh, Mum.'

'Elsie, I'm so sorry, love. I had no idea.'

It was at this moment that Miss Benson reminded them of her presence. 'Perhaps I could have a word with her?'

'Oh, Miss Benson,' said Elsie's mother. 'Would you?'

Miss Benson swept back her navy cape. 'Where is she? In the parlour?'

Elsie and her mother glanced at one another. 'We don't exactly have a parlour,' they began.

'Well, we do,' said Elsie. 'But it's a bedroom now.'

'So where is she?'

'In the kitchen,' said Elsie's mother, indicating the door.

To Elsie's amazement, Miss Benson flung it open and then they heard her say, 'Good afternoon. Miss Castleford of Winford Grammar School for Girls, I presume? This is an honour.'

Elsie and her mother found they were holding hands

tightly. They followed Miss Benson into the kitchen. Elsie was relieved that her headmistress had seen her in her best dress, gloves and hat. She stood quietly by the range, attempting to be invisible. Miss Benson sat at one side of the table, her mother opposite, while Miss Castleford sat at the head of the table nearest the wireless.

'A murder!' Miss Castleford exclaimed. 'By a woman!'

Elsie felt sick. She knew what happened to young ladies who disgraced the name of the school. Expulsion.

'But the play isn't about that,' said Miss Benson, stoutly.

'It isn't?' said Miss Castleford. 'Then tell me, Miss Benson, what is it about?'

'Family unity!' said Miss Benson triumphantly. 'The strength of family love against terrifying odds. Death itself.'

'I see,' said Miss Castleford.

'Elsie plays the twelve year old daughter of a middle-class family.'

'I'm sorry to interrupt you, Miss Benson,' said Miss Castleford, lowering her voice, 'but I don't think that's possible.'

'Oh, but it is. And the beginnings of a very fine performance, if I may say so. A credit to your school.'

'Really?' said Miss Castleford, looking astounded.

There's no need to look quite so disbelieving, thought Elsie.

'I heard her lines this very afternoon. An exceptionally bright child.'

Elsie caught her mother breaking into a smile. She looked flushed from the heat and the difficulty of sitting in a chair that looked as if it might topple over with the extra weight of the baby.

'Might I suggest that you have a word with Mr Neville?'

'I really think he should have had a word with me first.'

'I'm sure he would have done had it been term-time,' said Miss Benson.

'That might be the case but–'

'And I'm sure he will be very anxious to clear this matter up. I know for a fact that it was because Elsie was a pupil at Winford Grammar School that he knew what calibre gel he was taking on. He has an extremely high regard for the school.'

Elsie had never heard an adult lie with such bare-faced bravado. And for her sake too! Eventually the two women left together. Elsie and her mother hurried into Elsie and Joan's bedroom and peered out at them as they walked down the street. Elsie's mother began to shake with suppressed laughter. 'They look like they're goin' to some garden party,' she gasped.

Elsie sat on the bed and they collapsed backwards, laughing hysterically.

'Oh, she's sharp!' gasped her mother. 'She's very sharp.'

The door opened and Elsie's father peered in. 'What's goin' on? You sound like you're laying eggs.'

'I'll tell you about it later,' wept Elsie's mother.

'Good. Because Harry's in the kitchen waitin' for you.'

'I was goin' to have the table all laid by the time you got back. Never mind.'

Harry was standing by the table, his cap in his hand, looking a little awkward. He held out a small, bulky envelope to Mrs Hollis.

'Your first pay-packet,' his mother breathed. She beamed at him.

Elsie's parents insisted that Harry sat at the head of the table at supper. Mr Hollis put his hand on his

137

shoulder and said he was a man now, but Harry was so overwhelmed he looked about ten.

They had steak and vegetable pie. Elsie realised her mother must have saved coupons and queued for hours to get the ingredients, and it was obvious that Harry appreciated that too, especially when chocolate cake followed. The meal took on a party atmosphere, so much so that Joan didn't moan about the length of her skirts once.

Elsie found Harry was still awake when she went upstairs.

'Too excited to sleep?'

'Sort of. I was just thinkin'.'

'About bein' a man?'

'Yeah.'

'What does it feel like?'

'No different, really. So I don't know how to be, or what I'm supposed to do.' He grinned. 'But don't tell anyone, will you?'

Seven

'I'm sorry, sir,' Elsie had blurted out. 'I didn't hear him. I was feeding the guinea-pigs!' And, in her mind, she *had* been feeding them. She had seen them so vividly in their cage, prisoners between the rows of jars and tubes and foul-smelling liquids. To her relief, the cast had laughed.

'I think they've probably eaten enough for the moment,' Mr Neville had quipped, and he asked Geoffrey to give Elsie her line again.

Sitting collapsed in the chair, Elsie had no idea how she had done. She was just relieved to have made it through the entire play. Also, watching the scenes when she was off stage, she could now see the shape of the story. And it all made sense.

'Well done!' said Annie Duncan, who put her arm round Elsie and gave her a squeeze. By now everyone in the cast was chatting excitedly to each other.

'Thank you, everyone,' said Mr Neville. 'We now

139

have the luxury of another week's rehearsal ahead of us. We will be on stage on Tuesday but we'll start with Act I on Monday here, same time. Have a good weekend.'

'Elsie, are you doing anything tomorrow?' Annie asked.

'Shelling extra peas, I should think. My aunt's coming.'

'So it wouldn't be convenient to come to my place for tea?'

Elsie was stunned. Tea with an actress! 'Yeah,' she blurted out. 'Please.'

'After lunch, perhaps?'

Elsie nodded.

'But don't dress up. I shall have my comfy togs on. And then I thought we could perhaps go through our bits together. Would you mind?'

'No,' said Elsie, shyly. 'I'd like that.'

'With you looking at me instead of that world inside your head?'

Elsie gave an embarrassed laugh.

'Yes, it's difficult making that leap from lines in a play to responding to a real person in the flesh.'

'I'm scared to look,' said Elsie.

'In case you're thrown forward from 1880 to 1947?'

'Something like that.'

'Maybe then if we have some time together with no one watching?'

'Oh yes, please,' began Elsie. Just then she heard her name being called out. It was Mr Neville. He beckoned her over.

'Two-thirty, then,' said Annie Duncan, as she left her.

Elsie looked up at Mr Neville. He peered down at her. 'Miss Benson has informed me of the visit from your headmistress.'

'Yes, sir.'

'I shall be taking her out for lunch today.' He smiled. 'So there's no need to give the matter another thought.'

'Thank you, sir!'

That evening, to everyone's amazement, Elsie's parents went to see *Desert Highway*. Joan was furious to be left alone with Harry and Elsie on a Saturday night, so Elsie and Harry promised to keep quiet if Joan wanted to go to the flicks with Molly. Joan agreed, which meant that as an exception Elsie and Harry could stay up late to listen to the Saturday night thriller.

'Why aren't you downstairs?' Joan had said crossly, when she found Elsie asleep in her brothers' bed. 'I thought somethin' awful had happened to you.'

'I was too frightened to sleep on my own,' said Elsie. But she knew that Joan's crossness was guilt at having left them by themselves. Joan insisted that Elsie come downstairs in case her mum and dad checked up on them when they came in. But when her parents came home, they spent ages in the kitchen talking excitedly. Elsie sat up in bed trying to make out what they were saying. They weren't having a row, but they had lowered their voices so as not to wake her, she guessed. Elsie had never heard her parents talk together so much. Usually they just acknowledged one another's existence, saying the odd word now and again, especially her father, who hardly talked at all.

Elsie must have fallen asleep because the next thing she knew, she had been woken up by Joan's snoring. She stumbled sleepily out into the hall. As she crept gingerly up the creaking stairs, she was surprised to hear her parents still talking in their bedroom. Behind her, through the stained glass at the top of the hall door, the first signs of dawn were filtering through. She made her way quickly into the boys' room. Ralph still wasn't back from the theatre.

The next morning all of them kept drifting off to sleep in the pews at the back of the church. Joan's chin had slumped on to her chest, and within seconds her snores began echoing and bouncing off the stone walls of the church. The elderly ladies in the pew in front turned their outraged faces, yet again, in their direction.

'Can't you stop her?' whispered one, furiously.

'It's an affliction,' Elsie's mother murmured to them.

'An affliction?' remarked the woman's elderly companion. 'It's an unholy racket. That's what it is.'

'Joan!' urged Elsie, and she gave her a nudge.

Joan's head shot up. 'Have you ironed me blue cardigan?' she said loudly. Then she suddenly realised where she was, and blushed crimson. 'Pinch me if I drop off again,' she begged Elsie.

'Can I pinch her too?' Harry asked eagerly.

'No!'

'Some people,' hissed the woman in front of them, 'come here to worship the Lord and pray.'

Once outside, Mr Hollis walked on ahead while Harry trotted to keep up with him, but Elsie noticed that even her father was a bit more sluggish than usual.

'I heard you talkin' last night,' Elsie remarked to her mother casually.

'Oh yeah?'

'And I heard you later on, and in the morning.'

'Did we keep you awake?'

'No! It was only a couple of times when I woke up. I couldn't make out what you were saying, though.'

'We were talking about *Desert Highway*.'

'All night?'

'Yeah. We talked about other things too.'

'What was the play about?'

'All sorts of things really. Life. How history repeats itself. War.'

'Oh,' said Elsie.

Her mother laughed, and then she looked serious for a moment. 'There was a lot in it, you see. I didn't understand it all, but there were some things that made me think.'

'Like what?' Elsie asked.

'Like we're all God's creatures. And that as long as we remember that, we'll be strong inside. But if people behave in an evil way, they're rotten inside, and that makes them weak and eventually they'll be destroyed. But if people care about each other and do what's right, then that gives the person another sort of strength to fight off an attacker. And that's what's worth dyin' for.'

She put her arm round Elsie. 'I dunno if that's what it was supposed to mean. But that's what it meant to me. The thing is, it got Dad talking about his time in the desert. His mates. The ones who had died or got wounded. Yeah,' she said softly. 'A lot of things.' She frowned at Elsie. 'Do you know that his unit were told not to talk about it when they got home?' She gave a wry smile. 'Not that he would have done anyway.'

'So, did Dad like the play?'

'I dunno. I think he was a bit shocked. He thought it was goin' to be all running around and play-acting, not seeing soldiers on stage in the desert.'

'Did he scratch himself?'

'Well, it's funny you should say that. He did at the beginning, but I noticed towards the end he stopped. The bit in the middle of the play, when they went back in time, was a bit strange. He nearly went home after that, but I said, "We paid a shillin' for the seats. We might as well see the last four penn'orth worth." So we stayed for Act III. And that was the one that got to him. We didn't even get a bus afterwards. We walked, and just kept talking the whole way home. Well, your dad mostly. After that, we started talking about everythin' really. Like we used to do when we was courtin'.'

'Shall we start?' said Annie within minutes of Elsie arriving.

Elsie began to feel nervous. Annie insisted that they sat opposite one another and that every conversation they had in the play, they would look into each other's eyes. It was terrifying and Elsie felt totally at sea.

'I can still see you reading the lines on my retina,' commented Annie at one point. 'Remember, I'm your mother.'

Gradually lines began not to feel like lines! When that happened, there was room for other thoughts about what was happening in the play to filter through. She felt more at ease, as if she was having an ordinary conversation with her mother.

'I understand where I fit in now. And I don't feel so lonely. I feel part of the family.'

'And there's something else,' said Annie. 'When you're being Eva your accent disappears.'

'You mean I won't have to learn to talk posh?' she asked in surprise.

146

'Not if you're Eva,' smiled Annie. 'You really have got under her skin.'

Elsie laughed with relief.

'Now,' said Annie, 'time to stop hiding behind your glasses. Off they come.'

Tea was pancakes spread with some molasses sent by an actor friend who was touring in a Shakespeare play in Canada.

'Is he your boyfriend?' Elsie asked, in the middle of licking the stickiness from her fingers.

Annie seemed amused. 'I like him. And he appears to like me.'

'He must do if he sends you molasses. Are you going to marry him?'

'He hasn't asked me.'

'How old are you?'

'Thirty-five.'

Elsie gasped.

'That shocking, is it?'

'You only look twenty-five. Except when you're acting older.' Elsie had always believed that women who weren't married with children were either rather staid, like the teachers at her school, or man-hating, like her Auntie Win. But Annie Duncan was having a wonderful, exciting time *and* she wasn't married. Joan was always moaning about how awful it was to be on the shelf. And she was only eighteen. Once she met Annie it would cheer her up. In fact she was supposed to pick Elsie up at five o'clock, but when six o'clock came round and she still hadn't arrived, Elsie realised with dread that she was going to have to go home alone.

'Are your parents on the phone?'

'No.'

Her Uncle Ted was on the phone. It was a shared phone in a hallway, but Uncle Ted refused to take messages for their family from anyone with a hoity-toity voice.

'I'll be fine,' said Elsie, brightly. She knew her mother would be cross if she was late, with Auntie Win coming. They had already had a row about Elsie wearing her glasses, which Elsie had refused to do until her mother forced her.

At seven o'clock Elsie left Annie Duncan's house. At least it wasn't dark, although that didn't console her much.

'I'm sorry I can't walk you home myself,' said Annie.

'Would you look after my spectacles? I sometimes have accidents when I go home.'

Annie looked at her, puzzled.

'Please. If they get smashed I won't be able to read.'

'Won't you want to read in bed tonight?'

'No. I need to catch up on some sleep.'

Elsie placed the precious spectacles in Annie's outstretched hand.

'Why don't I look after your *Pink String* script too? I can bring it in tomorrow to rehearsal.'

Elsie walked down the steps to the pavement. Already her legs had begun to buckle. She stopped and turned. Annie Duncan gave her a wave. 'You're sure you'll be all right?'

'Of course. I'm a big girl now,' Elsie said jokingly. 'Well, sort of. Inside.'

Annie Duncan laughed and closed the door.

Elsie crossed the road in a daze of mounting nausea and panic.

Eight

They shut her in the coal bunker of the bombed house at the end of her street.

As soon as Elsie had spotted Marjorie sitting on the wall with the others, she knew it was pointless even to try to escape. Resistance would only make Marjorie angrier. She made a half-hearted effort to cross the road, but within seconds she was on the pavement underneath them. A strange feeling came over her, as if she had been chloroformed. She wasn't inside her skin any more. She felt stunned, yet removed, as though looking from a great height down at herself being pummelled. It was only when she realised where they were dragging her, that horror jolted her back into herself again. Remembering how she had been left trapped in rubble in rising flood-water, she began to put up a struggle.

But nothing could match Marjorie's fury. Elsie had no sooner been shoved into the coal bunker when she

150

heard the entrance being blocked with the surrounding rubble. For what seemed like hours, Elsie listened to them talking outside. Every now and then they would call her names or make jokes about her size, throwing heavy objects at the bunker. After a while there was silence, but Elsie suspected it was a trick, that if she attempted to push the lid open, they would pounce again and do something even worse to her. Marjorie said that if she tried to escape, she would drop a live rat in there and shut them in together. Elsie believed her.

Sitting there, crouched in the dark, she tried to think logically. By now, her mum would be angry with her for being late. Dad and Harry would still be at the allotment. Ralph would still be gardening at Mrs Egerton-Smythe's. Joan and Molly might have returned from Molly's place by now. Why hadn't Joan picked her up?

Elsie leaned her head against the brick wall. The dust was choking her, and because of the heat wave the coal bunker felt like an oven. She was sweating so much she could even feel it trickling down her legs. She counted on her fingers the things she had in her favour. 'One, I'm alive. Two, me spectacles ain't smashed.'

She remembered how Marjorie had scrabbled round her dress frantically, looking in vain for pockets, how she had kept shrieking, 'Where are they? Where are they, you little toe-rag?'

'Three, me *Pink String and Sealing Wax* is all in one piece. Four, lots of people will miss me some time, and come looking for me. And they'll find me like they did when I nearly drowned.' Hot tears suddenly spilled down her face. They wouldn't dream of looking for her in a coal bunker. She could be there for weeks.

She had just dropped off to sleep, dreaming about Annie Duncan's room, all colour and words and music, when she heard a scrabbling outside. She froze, not knowing whether to call out or not.

' 'Ello there, little mouse,' sneered a familiar voice. 'Thought I'd bring you a few things to keep you company.'

Elsie pushed herself away from the lid. She heard more heavy objects being dragged and heaved over the top of it. Mustering up all her courage, she yelled out, 'Why are you doing this to me?'

There was a tumbling of falling bricks and she heard the girl throwing herself against the bunker. 'Because you're an ugly little bug,' Marjorie whispered venomously. 'Just lookin' at you makes me feel sick.'

'Why don't you avoid me, then? Why do you wait for me?'

'Because I want you to go. For ever.'

'But I've done nothin' to you.' Elsie's voice was shaking.

'Every day you're 'ere, in this street, you do somethin' to me. And I don't like it.'

Bewildered, Elsie heard Marjorie throwing more bricks at the coal bunker. She listened to her pacing up and down, muttering angrily to herself. And then suddenly it was quiet. Elsie gathered in her knees and rested her face on them. It was the nearest she could get to hugging herself. With shame, she suspected it was not sweat running down her leg, but something else. She made fists with her hands.

She decided to think through all her scenes in *Pink String and Sealing Wax*. Much later, having heard no movement from outside, she began to pray.

'They will find me,' she muttered, 'they will.'

She awoke with a start. The scrabbling outside had begun again. She felt sick. To her horror, she heard several voices. If Marjorie had returned with the gang, it would mean that she would need to show off in front of them. And that's when Elsie remembered the rat. She backed away into a corner and made herself as small as possible. Terrified, she heard the debris being removed from the bunker. She began to whimper and shake uncontrollably. Suddenly the lid was lifted and a flashlight dazzled her eyes.

'No!' she shrieked.

'Elsie?'

Looking down at her with blazing eyes was a very familiar face. A face which seemed to speed into a point. It was wearing a khaki cap.

'Auntie Win!'

'It's wonderful, Joan. More interesting work, hot baths. And you'd meet lots of people. I've made more friends in the last four months than I did in a year and a half of being demobbed. You get all your clothes provided for you.'

'Uniform,' muttered Joan.

'Lots of underwear and stockings.'

'Thick brown ones,' Joan murmured. 'The only pink bit of your clothing is your corset.'

'Warm coat for the winter. And freedom from domestic duties. Now, that should appeal to you. You'd be doing something really useful!' she emphasised.

' 'Ere, love, get that down you.'

Elsie looked down at the plate her mother had passed to her. It was bread and butter with sugar sprinkled over it and a mug of tea. In spite of the heat and the fact that she was wearing her mother's cardigan over her nightdress and a pair of her father's woollen socks, Elsie still felt chilled.

Once they had arrived home, Auntie Win had insisted on wrapping her in a blanket while her mother put pans of water on the range. Then her father and brothers were sent out of the room so that Elsie could have a soak in the tub in privacy. She watched as the brick and coal dust floated to the surface. It was quite obvious from the bruises and grazes on her legs what had happened.

While Auntie Win regaled Joan with the delights of life in the women's army, ignoring the fact that Joan was looking more disgruntled than ever, Elsie's mother said very quietly, 'I s'pose you fell off a bus again?'

Elsie couldn't speak.

'Why didn't you tell us, love?'

How could she say, because I could never find the right moment or the right words, that I was scared things would only get worse, that I thought you and Dad would accuse me of doing something to rile her. And maybe it was all my fault? Then there was the shame. She bowed her head and looked at the filthy water in the tub.

It was Harry who had spilled the beans. When Joan had returned home without Elsie, she had protested that she thought Ralph was picking Elsie up. By this time Auntie Win had arrived in her uniform, Cockahoop having just passed out as an officer.

When Ralph also returned alone, Elsie's mother began to worry. As soon as Mr Hollis and Harry had arrived back from the allotment, Harry blurted out, 'They must have got her.' He was forced to explain and then took them to the place where Marjorie and the gang usually pounced, and together they made their way methodically back towards their street. Harry noticed something odd about the empty house at the end of it, but he couldn't put his finger on what. And then Auntie Win had said, 'It looks as though someone's built a bonfire on the top of that bunker there.' And Harry had begun running, pulling all the wood and bricks off in a frenzy. 'Gently,' Auntie Win had said. 'Let your dad and I deal with this. We don't want it to collapse.'

Harry had been left pacing up and down, slamming a fist into his open palm. Elsie had watched her Auntie being pushed aside. Two muscular arms reached down for her and pulled her out. It was her dad.

'I'm gettin' the police on to this,' he muttered angrily, as he carried Elsie back to the house.

'Please don't, Dad. She'll do something worse to get back at me.'

'Why didn't you tell us?' he stormed.

'I dunno. I just want to forget it, Dad. Please.'

'Who is she? She's in that gang in the next street, ain't she? I'll give her a good tanning. Just because she's a girl.'

Elsie burst into tears.

'Let's leave it till the morning,' her mother had said quietly.

By the time Elsie was tucked up in the truckle-bed in the kitchen, it was already dawn. Her mother wondered if she ought to turn up for the rehearsals, but Elsie begged her to let her go. She needed to escape into 1880 and be someone else.

In the morning, as usual, Ralph perched her on the back of his bike and pedalled her to the theatre. They did not speak. In fact, there had been almost total silence throughout breakfast, and Elsie found she couldn't swallow any bread. At the stage door, instead of leaving her with Miss Benson, Ralph said he would come with them.

'You don't need to,' said Elsie.

'I want to see Mr Neville about some props. I won't have time later with the dress rehearsal of the other play this afternoon.'

So the trio had walked on in even more silence until Miss Benson asked her how she had enjoyed her tea with Miss Duncan.

'It was very nice,' Elsie murmured into the pavement.

For some reason she couldn't look Miss Benson in the face. It was as though her whole body was being pulled by force towards the ground. A tightening in her chest made it difficult to breathe.

Annie Duncan was sitting out on the veranda. Overcome suddenly with shyness, Elsie picked up her practice skirt from the prop table, put it on and sat in a chair in the corner. At least the skirt hid the bruises on her legs. Felix Venning and Arnold Swann were walking up and down as usual, murmuring lines to themselves. As she watched them, she began to soak herself into the set, trying to imagine what it must really look like as a Victorian parlour.

Mr Neville called for everyone's attention. 'Before we begin today's rehearsals,' he said, 'I have something to say to the cast.'

Elsie looked up expectantly.

'Last night, young Elsie here was beaten up by a gang and locked in a coal bunker, where she remained trapped for hours until, very fortunately, her family found her and took her home.'

Oh, no. Elsie whispered inside her head. Not here. Don't do this to me. Please. Stop!

'We are very pleased to have her with us safe and sound, and I appreciate the great act of courage it has taken for her to turn up here this morning when she must have had so little sleep last night.'

It was the worst thing that could possibly have happened to her. Who had told him? And then she realised it must have been Ralph. How could she look anyone in the eye now? Didn't Ralph realise that this was her other world, that he had brought Marjorie Bush and all her hate into the rehearsal room? Now the cast might discover what she had yet to discover herself, the reason for her being beaten up. And even if they didn't, they would ask themselves, 'Why? There's no smoke without fire.' Everything swam around her in a daze of piercing and numbing pain. If she could have died there and then, it would have been a blessed relief.

It was Annie Duncan who broke the silence.

'Oh, my darling.' And she threw her arms round Elsie and held her tight.

A shudder ran through Elsie as she took in a deep gulp of breath. And then the room was filled with a great howl. And Elsie realised that the howl was coming from her, and she was helpless to do anything to stop it.

Nine

That afternoon after the rehearsals, she and Miss Benson were taken to tea. Miss Benson wasn't going to let Elsie out of her sight. Ralph had also told her, and Queenie. In fact, everyone knew. And they wouldn't allow her to feel ashamed. They showed how appalled they were, whereas her family had hardly referred to it at all. It was almost as though she had brought shame to the family.

The cast made her talk about what had happened over and over again, and they held her hand or put their arm round her, or perched her on their knee. At first she was embarrassed at such shows of affection, but it was nothing like when Geraldine's father touched her. There was a naturalness about it. It was the way they all behaved with one another, and she began to relax.

'Wrong place at the wrong time,' some of them said and recounted incidents they had experienced or known. 'Wrong colour eyes, wrong religion, wrong nose.' And Elsie heard herself adding, 'Wrong height.'

Earlier, at the end of Act I, Elsie, as Eva, was left on her own. She had been hiding while her brother, Albert, had been speaking secretly to a strange woman. Once they had left, she came out of hiding and tiptoed towards the chair where Fabia Delmar, as Pearl Bond, had been sitting. Trembling with fear, she had stared at it. There was an odd smell. She sniffed. Suddenly she felt sick and angry. How could Albert love someone else besides her? How could he? Furious and hurt, she yelled out, '*Filthy, beastly scent! Horrible! Horrible! . . . Oh, Albert!*' And, in despair, she threw herself on the settee and wept.

'Curtain,' she heard Geoffrey say quietly.

Elsie opened her eyes. Mr Neville came and sat on the settee and handed her a handkerchief. She took it gratefully. 'It's all right, sir,' she laughed through the blur of tears, 'it's not me crying. It's Eva! I mean . . .' she began, struggling to make sense of it.

He ruffled her hair. 'I know what you mean. You've made great strides today. Do you think it's because you're not wearing your glasses?'

'No, it's because I've come off the tightrope.'

'In plain English, please.'

'I can look into people's eyes without being Elsie.'

Mr Neville nodded.

'But I don't have to all the time. I can talk and sew at the same time. Well, I don't think you can call it sewing exactly.'

Mr Neville smiled. 'If you had a nap now, do you think you could rehearse again this afternoon?'

Miss Benson was called in. She huffed and puffed, pointing out what Elsie had been through, but Mr Neville tried to convince her. Elsie went and joined Annie on the veranda while they hammered it out. Eventually a compromise was reached. Miss Benson would let Elsie rehearse if they finished early.

Elsie was enjoying the rehearsals, but her head was beginning to spin, so she was grateful to have Miss Benson fight her corner for her.

Tea was in a chintzy, olde worlde tea shoppe, on the top floor of the department store where her Auntie Win used to work. Never in Elsie's wildest dreams did she think she would ever be taken there. Elsie was grateful for her gloves and hat, but acutely conscious of the unsightly bruises on her legs. Annie, who seemed to read her thoughts said, 'I have all sorts of scraps of material. You're so small I could probably run you up a new-look skirt. That would hide your knees.'

'Miss Hollis is not going anywhere without me,' interrupted Miss Benson.

'But, Miss Benson, I took it as read that you would be coming too. Will you? Please?'

She made it sound as though Miss Benson would be doing her a huge favour. Elsie could see that Miss Benson, underneath her pudgy hands which were now clasped firmly beneath her ample bosom, was deeply flattered. She opened her mouth for a second, closed it, and gave a nod in the grand manner.

Elsie's other companions round the table were Felix and Isla. Felix, tall and elegant in his cream suit, Panama, silky cravat and cane, attracted a great deal of attention. He smiled and waved at the other tables, lapping up the adulation. Elsie noticed Isla and Annie giving each other a quick smile. Annie leaned closer to Elsie.

'This is why we have to pay attention to what we wear, even when we go out. As performers at the Palace, the public like to see their actors and actresses looking like film stars.'

Elsie pulled at her baggy cotton gloves self-consciously. If only hats didn't itch so much.

After a waitress in black and a lacy white apron and cap had brought them cakes and tea, Isla suddenly leaned conspiratorially towards Annie. 'Is it true Basil Duke is getting married?'

'No idea,' said Annie. 'Why don't you ask him?'

Isla's eyes grew wide. 'Me? Ask Basil Duke?'

'I'll ask him,' said Felix. 'I'll get it out of him.'

'Why would he keep it secret?' Annie remarked.

'Shall I be mother?' said Miss Benson.

Elsie was aware there was only one cake remaining.

'Go on, Elsie,' said Felix. 'Looks like you need it.'

Elsie glanced aside at Miss Benson, who gave the regal nod. It was when Elsie had her mouth full, that Felix began talking to her.

'I was once a scapegoat. I began to think I had some terrible disease or that I was a ghastly person. Yes,' he added dryly. 'Difficult to comprehend, eh?'

'Go on,' Annie interrupted.

'You know that feeling when you're having a nightmare and you wake up with a start, and this tremendous relief floods through you because you realise it's just a bad dream and all's well with the world? When I was the scapegoat it was like being in a nightmare, waking up and finding yourself still in a nightmare. By the time I left that particular set-up, I was so used to being insulted or ignored that I became quite buttoned-up.'

'Now, that I find difficult to believe,' said Annie.

'So when I met a new lot of people,' Felix continued, 'I was a little reticent. Stand-offish, you know? I thought I might receive the same treatment. After all, I was the same person, wasn't I? But I found myself with a group of people whom I made great friends with, who actually liked me.'

'What are you trying to say, Felix?' asked Isla.

'The point is,' he said, arching one eyebrow, and here he looked at Elsie, 'I like you. And I think I can speak for my fellow artistes. They like you too. And anyone who doesn't like you, or treats you badly, has no taste. In fact, I'll say more than that–'

'Oh, dear,' said Annie.

'In fact,' said Felix, undeterred, 'their head needs examining.'

'Here, here,' said Isla.

A crumb had lodged itself at the back of Elsie's throat and she began coughing so violently that the tears ran down her face. Miss Benson thumped her back firmly, which nearly sent Elsie reeling across the room.

'Now look what you've done,' said Annie.

'I think it's dried eggs in the mixture that's done that,' Felix remarked.

Ten

Ralph took Elsie to the theatre for her rehearsal. Surrounded by exotic flowers, Elsie found herself in a cream, turquoise and gold world. Piled upstage was the *Madame Louise* furniture. Downstage was the furniture they had rehearsed with, ready for the breakfast scene at the beginning of Act II.

Elsie spotted her practice skirt on the back of one of the chairs. She slipped it on and fixed it as usual with the safety pin Isla had given her. Her fingers were shaking, but it wasn't from fear any more, it was excitement. She gazed out at the lit auditorium, the rows and rows of crimson-covered chairs, up to the dress circle, the upper circle and to the gods, where she and her family usually sat. Now she was on the other side looking up.

Lying on the table was Eva's handkerchief. She picked it up.

Arnold Swann came on stage deep in thought. Elsie

was rather in awe of him. He didn't approach her much and she was too shy to talk to him. 'Speak when you are spoken to,' Miss Benson had advised. But as soon as he became her father, and she became Eva, they could talk to one another.

Elsie watched Fabia Delmar make her entrance, so glamorous and sophisticated. She was in another new-look outfit, with the most beautiful shoes Elsie had ever seen. There was such a swish of her petticoated skirt that you could hear her coming from the wings.

Felix was with her. He looked as elegant as usual, but he never appeared cool. He always looked as if he had some private joke going on in his head, as if he would explode into laughter unexpectedly at any moment. He and Fabia were having an animated discussion about a new play when suddenly he gave an enormous smile. With a loud, 'Elsie!' he rushed over and swung her into the air, where he held her in his arms. 'We can now talk eye to eye,' he quipped.

To Elsie's surprise, she found herself putting her arms round his neck as if it was the most natural thing in the world to do.

'Have you been measured by Florrie yet?'

'Measured?'

'For your cossie, you poppet.'

Elsie had completely forgotten about the Victorian clothes they would be wearing. Then a vague memory of Miss Benson running round her with a tape measure came back to her. 'Miss Benson has them.'

'I've got them too,' said a voice behind them.

Felix put her down.

It was Annie. 'I've made you a skirt. It just needs hemming. I need you to stand on the table when we break for lunch.'

Elsie caught sight of Miss Benson lumbering into the wings with her bag, and a pale blue and cream skirt over her arms. Before Elsie could thank her, there was a clapping from the auditorium from Mr Neville. Rehearsals for Act II had begun.

And Elsie loved it. Once the initial fear had worn off, she revelled in the exhilaration of being on stage and listening to the others. One minute she was laughing, the next she was furious, then anguished, and when she wasn't on stage she watched the rest of the cast from the wings.

After lunch Miss Benson, Annie and Elsie went off to the café where the actors ate, and Annie treated Elsie to a pie. From there they went back to Annie's flat. Miss Benson squeezed herself into a wicker chair while Elsie took her shoes and socks off and sat barefoot on Annie's bed amongst the cushions. Elsie loved her flat. It was ordered chaos. Hats and gloves, wigs and silky scarves spilled out of the brightly painted boxes turned on their sides and stacked one above the other. Annie put a record on the gramophone which, Elsie could see, pleased Miss Benson enormously.

'What do you think, Miss Benson?' Annie remarked later, when Elsie was standing on a chair, the hem of the skirt pinned into place.

'Stylish,' Miss Benson replied. 'She'll look very stylish. As long as she doesn't droop when she walks.'

'Do I droop?' exclaimed Elsie.

'Well, yes,' said Annie. 'When you first came I was worried you were permanently round-shouldered, but the more confident you've become the less rounded your shoulders are.'

'They look square and military now, do they?'

'Cheeky,' said Annie.

'Annie, can you hear me on stage?'

'Yes.'

'But do you think Mr Neville can hear from the auditorium?'

'He can obviously hear you from the stalls or he would've said something.'

'But do you think I can be heard from the gods?'

'I don't know. But Mr Neville will tell you if you can't be.'

'But if I can't, what shall I do? If I shout, I won't be able to think about what I'm saying.'

'Let Mr Neville tell you,' said Annie. 'I can give you some exercises for diction and for resonance if you like.'

'What's resonance?'

'I'll explain it more fully when I've ironed this skirt and hemmed it on the machine. But the exercises will bring your voice into your face and forward.'

'Humming! Ralph does it till his lips tickle. Is that it?'

'Partly, yes. Now, let's iron this skirt and then I'll tell you.'

Elsie wondered if her father might think the skirt was charity. Joan might be jealous, and it might make Elsie more noticeable when she walked home. The other thing was that Elsie wasn't particularly interested in fashion. But she didn't want to hurt Annie's feelings and she knew her mother would be delighted.

172

Annie insisted she wore her skirt home. When they stepped off the bus at the end of their street and Elsie began looking around wildly, Miss Benson took her hand and clasped it very firmly.

'Oh, Elsie!' were the words her mother greeted her with.

'Miss Duncan made them from scraps which were of no use to her,' Miss Benson stated with authority. 'It hides the bruises and other war wounds.'

'Will you come in for a cuppa?' her mother asked politely.

'Thank you, Mrs Hollis, but no thank you.' She released Elsie's hand and swept back down the street.

Elsie and her mother watched her kick up the dust like tumbleweed rolling through a ghost town.

'Mum, has Dad said anything about Sunday to you yet?'

She shook her head.

'Is he angry?'

Elsie's mother nodded.

'With me?'

'For not being told. But I don't think it's that.'

'With Marjorie Bush?'

'Oh yes, he's angry with her all right.' She looked

at Elsie as if she wasn't quite sure if Elsie was old enough to be told.

'I think he's more angry with himself, love.'

'Himself? Why would he be angry with himself?'

'For not protecting you.'

'But he weren't there.'

'He feels he should've been.'

'If I'd been a boy, I could've fought them all off.'

'You'd have to have been a mighty strong one.'

'Like Harry?'

She smiled sadly. 'Yes. Though there are some battles that even Harry finds difficult.'

'Why don't they go for Ralph instead of Harry? It's him they're angry with.'

'Because,' said her mother with a note of resignation, 'Harry's there.'

Elsie suddenly wondered if that's why she was attacked. Was it possible that Marjorie Bush was angry with someone else? But because Elsie was conveniently there, she was the target? But if so, who? Elsie tossed the thought aside. The truth was that Marjorie Bush hated her, and that was that.

'Mum, why won't Dad speak to me?'

'He finds it a bit awkward, I think. He's so used to being with men, see.'

'Is it because I'm a girl? Is that it?'

'Yeah, love. I'm afraid so.'

Eleven

'Any minute now!' Elsie whispered urgently to her mother.

The family were sitting in the front row of the gods at the last performance of *Madame Louise*. Elsie's father had gone through his usual scratching routine until, Elsie noticed, some pretty young women began dashing round the stage.

'This is a bit saucy,' Elsie heard her mother mutter quietly. 'I don't think you should be 'ere.'

'I notice it's keeping John awake,' said Auntie Win, who was sitting on Elsie's left.

'As long as it keeps Joan awake,' Elsie added.

Suddenly a young actress wearing a dress which could be used for three different occasions stormed on to the set, with a strange man called Mr Trout following. '*I tell you, I can't wear the damn thing!*' she protested.

Elsie laughed. Her aunt gave her a dig in the ribs. 'I can't help it,' she whispered, 'he looks so funny.

Anyway,' Elsie added, 'you're allowed to laugh. It's a farce.'

'*But what's the matter? What's wrong with it?*' yelled Mr Trout.

'*Everything! Just what the hell is it supposed to be?*'

'*It's my new invention. It's called "A Poem in Economy" or "The Charlie Trout Up and Down Treble".*'

Suddenly the door of the shop opened and in walked an elderly bishop and his equally elderly wife. It was Ralph and Rosemary.

Ralph gazed around the shop, shocked.

Mr Trout leaped towards them. '*Ah. Bonjour, Modom. Bonjour, Your Holiness!*'

'Here it comes,' whispered Elsie.

'*Eh, I think we're really looking for a Madame Louise,*' croaked the bishop.

'*Yes, yes, of course!*' said Mr Trout, the smarm in his voice growing ever smarmier. '*But, meanwhile, could I interest you in this completely shattering creation?*'

Elsie watched as Mr Trout tried to demonstrate how the 'Poem in Economy' dress could be used for different functions. Suddenly the dress fell off the model, leaving her standing in her underwear. Throughout the demonstration, Ralph had been looking on aghast, Mr Trout turned to the bishop and said, '*The bishop himself won't wish for anything better!*' At which point the bishop and his wife turned tail and left, and the curtain fell.

'Did you see the expression on his face!' gasped Elsie's mother.

'Is that it?' Auntie Win exclaimed.

'No, there's another scene.'

'No, I meant is that all Ralph does?'

'Yeah,' said Elsie. 'It takes two hours to put that make-up on. Good, eh?' She turned to her mother. 'Will Dad want to leave now?'

Auntie Win gave a snort. 'Not after seeing that pretty young girl in her undies. He's a man, isn't he? He'll want to see if it happens again.'

'And if there'd been a murder, Win, you'd be just the same,' commented Elsie's mother, pointedly.

The curtain rose on scene two. '*But, Eve, darling, how perfectly awful for you,*' said a young female voice.

One of the other young models was lounging on a sofa in the showroom while the other one stood behind her and manicured her nails. They were both wearing lingerie and wraps.

'*Of course, I gave him a jolly good slap in the face – but you can't go around just slapping faces – it makes such an awful noise.*'

'Wouldn't bother me,' Elsie heard her aunt mutter, and she and her mother glanced quickly at each other, trying not to laugh.

Elsie lay awake beside Harry, waiting for Ralph to come home. She was too excited to sleep and desperate to talk to him. In two days, four hundred pairs of eyes would be looking at her, and she began to panic. All week she had been copying Ralph's humming exercises and doing strange diction exercises, which were mostly Gilbert and Sullivan songs, which she would whisper.

She noticed the doorknob turning slowly. The door opened.

'Ralph! Is that you?'

Her brother jumped. 'No,' he whispered crossly. 'It's the Hunchback of Notre Dame. Of course it's me, you idiot. What are you doing here?'

'I wanted to talk to you.'

'We'll wake Harry.'

'Ralph, nothing wakes Harry.'

'So what is it? Are you worried about Monday?'

179

'Sort of. But I wanted to talk to you about tonight. You were ever so funny.'

Her brother grinned. 'Thanks.'

'There's something else.' She didn't know how to say it tactfully.

'You look like you're trying to be polite.'

'I am.'

'Well, forget it. You're hopeless at it.'

Elsie took a deep breath. 'Are you cross about me getting such a big part and you getting—' She hesitated.

'A spit and a cough.'

'What?'

'A tiny part.'

She nodded.

'If you'd been male and my age, and had the same experience, I probably would be. But I couldn't possibly play Eva unless I walked on my knees and spoke in falsetto.'

'Like St Joan,' Elsie giggled, remembering a disastrous audition Ralph did when he first approached the rep.

'Shut up, you beast,' said Ralph, sitting on the bed and pretending to be about to hit her.

Elsie already felt much better. 'It's goin' to be

strange not rehearsin' next week. I'll miss it. Do you miss it when you don't have a part?'

'Yes.'

'Are you in the next play?'

'Not yet. But I plan to be.'

She could see he was bursting with excitement. 'Tell me,' she begged.

He leaned towards her. 'The next play is called *No Medals*. Arnold Swann is producing it. Some of the scenes have been crossed out by Mr Neville so that he can employ fewer people.'

'And that's why you don't have a part?'

'At the moment.'

'I don't understand.'

'You know Wilfred gives everyone who's in the next play their copy on Saturday night?'

'Yes.'

'I persuaded him to let me glance through one of them, and I discovered a certain scene which had been cut. A woman is trying to tell her husband something which she finds difficult to say. She wants to tell him the news at the right moment. In the original play there's this sentry in the background who keeps appearing, and that makes her feel self-conscious. And Mr Neville has cut him out. So I'm going to ask Mr Swann if I can play him. There aren't any lines, but I feel that the presence of the sentry adds a certain tension to the scene.'

'And gets you on stage again,' added Elsie.

'Not at all.'

'But don't you think it'll make the audience laugh?'

'No. I shall do it seriously.'

Elsie stared at her brother's comical face. His hair had conquered the hair-cream and was now sticking up, still white in places from the talcum powder. She smiled. Her brother tweaked her nose.

'I can be serious, you know. Anyway, I shall approach Mr Swann with my argument on Monday night after the performance if he has been received well. If not, I'll do it Tuesday morning, at rehearsals.' He stood up. 'Now, I wish to get undressed. This isn't a peep-show, so close your eyes, or else.'

Twelve

Elsie and Miss Benson were given dressing-room six. It was up several flights of steps, which was fine for Elsie, but Miss Benson was speechless by the time she reached the top. There was a tatty old armchair in the corner of the room. Along the wall, hanging on a rail, were three long Victorian dresses. Below them was a pair of long, tapered ankle boots with a row of buttons at the side. Miss Benson, still panting, opened the window. It was stifling. She drew a tin box from her voluminous bag and placed it on the dressing-table.

'I realise that you won't have had experience in make-up. But I know what you need for a juvenile one.' She switched on the remaining three light bulbs which surrounded the cracked mirror.

'Miss Benson,' said Elsie, suddenly aware of a new kind of terror emerging, 'I feel sick.'

'Quite normal!' said Miss Benson, briskly. 'Now, let's try and sort out which is your Act I dress and which are your Act II and Act III dresses.'

Her Act I dress was powder-blue. A tiny frill of lace emerged from the cuff of the long sleeves and high neck. The cuff, large hem and top of the shoulders which scooped over the chest, were a navy-and-red check. Down the closely fitting bodice of the dress were twenty or more buttons. The dress fell to just below her knees. Miss Benson produced garters to keep her stockings up. 'Always useful,' she commented. 'Take your dress off and I'll begin putting your make-up on in your petticoat.'

'Miss Benson,' began Elsie, falteringly.

'You don't have a petticoat? Of course not. In this weather. Foolish thought. No vest either, I presume?'

Elsie shook her head.

There was a knock at the door. 'Come in,' sang out Miss Benson.

It was Florrie. 'Undies,' she said, poking her head round the door, and she held out a collection of white lacy garments.

'Thank you,' said Miss Benson, taking them. She handed them to Elsie whose face grew hot with embarrassment.

'Change behind the curtain.'

Once Elsie had put her clothes on, she stepped out to look at herself in the full length mirror. Underneath the petticoat, she wore black stockings under long, lacy bloomers. She really looked like a girl in the last century. She took off her glasses and blinked at herself. She had now rehearsed without them in the theatre and had grown to like the exposed feeling of not being hidden behind them.

Miss Benson beckoned her over. 'Buttons.'

'There are so many of them. And on the dress. Will I have time to change between the acts?'

'You'll have help,' said Miss Benson, calmly. She produced a large hairbrush from her bag, unplaited Elsie's hair and brushed it away from her face in long, sweeping strokes. Elsie yelped as Miss Benson untangled the knots. She had never had her hair brushed so vigorously. She glanced up at Miss Benson's face in the mirror.

'A hundred strokes,' Miss Benson announced, catching her eye.

Elsie's heart plummeted. But after a while the brushing began to relax her. And then it was over, and the brush was set aside on the dressing-table.

'Turn,' said Miss Benson, suddenly. She was

holding a pinky-coloured greasepaint stick. She made strokes across Elsie's forehead, several down her cheeks, by her nose, over her chin and above her lip.

'Close your eyes.'

Elsie felt the stick being drawn across her eyelids.

'Foundation,' muttered Miss Benson. 'Gives me a clean sheet to work on.'

Elsie felt Miss Benson's fingers moving in a circular motion into every nook and cranny of her face.

'Overture and beginners,' said Rosemary, peering round the door.

'That means five minutes to curtain-up,' said Miss Benson. 'We go down now.'

'Why?' asked Elsie.

'Time is five minutes ahead when there is a performance in a theatre,' explained Miss Benson. The "quarter" means twenty minutes before curtain up, the "half" means thirty-five minutes. That's why we have to go down now.'

Elsie began to panic. 'What if I dry?'

'Geoffrey will prompt you. You will pick it up and carry on. I expect that will happen a lot this morning.'

'You don't think I'm very good, do you?' Elsie stammered.

'On the contrary. So don't fish. You'll dry because you'll be adjusting to the set, the costumes and the lighting. Mr Neville may even have to stop if something goes seriously wrong. But everyone will try and keep going, whatever happens. And I'll be there to help you.'

'Thank you, Miss Benson.'

'Now get a move on, gel.'

In the wings, Elsie said, 'What did Rosemary mean when she said "overture"?'

'Tonight, a trio will be playing music before curtain-up. And "beginners" means the people who begin the act.'

'Oh,' said Elsie, smiling. 'I thought it meant people like me.'

'No you didn't, you monkey. Ralph will have explained that to you, I'm sure.' And he had.

The curtains were down. She hardly recognised Annie who was standing in a dark grey Victorian dress with her hands on her waist, breathing deeply. On her head she wore a lacy cap. Felix was sitting at a table in the centre like a young man in a Victorian painting, his face so ruddy-brown with make-up that it looked like a brick.

Elsie stepped on to the set. Above her was a fake ceiling with what looked like a plaster carving on it. The plum-coloured walls were covered in framed photographs and paintings. Velvet drapes were hanging by the bay window, and scattered along the mantelpiece was an array of little ornaments. The shelves and furniture were dark, heavy, painted wood. It was like walking into the past.

'Splendidly Eva,' Felix remarked.

Annie held out her arms and Elsie ran into them. 'Excited?' asked Annie.

Elsie nodded.

Geoffrey peered round the prompt corner. 'Can you take your places, please?'

Nervously, Elsie sat beside Annie on the stool with her sampler, and prepared to sew. She glanced up at the two lighted gas-jets above the fireplace. An oil-lamp was glowing on a sideboard. She heard a music box playing and the sound of the curtain rising. She suddenly remembered she was the first person to speak. It was too late to ask Annie when she should start. She was nodding and smiling in time to the music box. Elsie remembered, she must wait till the tune ended.

'*Mama*,' she began.

Mrs Strachan glanced across at her and looked at her warmly. '*Yes, dear?*'

'*Lucy caught a mouse this morning.*'

'*Poor thing!*'

'*But she didn't drown it. Pa said to give any mice she caught to him.*'

Her mother gave her a worried look, thrust her hand into a sock and showed her an enormous hole.

The dress rehearsal had begun.

Elsie was dazzled by the lights. Stumbling round the set, she fought to remember where she was supposed to be and did her best to throw her voice beyond the footlights. The elastic careered backwards. She had lost Eva completely. She took a prompt four times, and each time she picked it up she went into a panic. After the dress rehearsal Mr Neville gave them all notes. Most of Elsie's were about not looking down when she spoke. 'The audience don't want to see the top of your head.'

Elsie walked silently into the wings where Miss

Benson was waiting for her. As soon as Elsie opened the dressing-room door, she burst into tears.

'Now, now, now, what's this?' panted Miss Benson.

'I've forgotten everything,' sobbed Elsie. 'I was so bad.' She collapsed into a chair and buried her head in her arms.

'Course you were,' said Miss Benson.

Elsie raised her head. 'You don't have to agree with me so quick.'

'Everyone's bad on a "dress". I told you before you went on.'

'Yeah, but not this bad!' she wailed.

'Nerves,' said Miss Benson, handing her a handkerchief.

Elsie blew her nose and then realised she had left greasepaint all over it. 'Oh, no. I've ruined it.'

'No need to be so melodramatic. It's still intact.'

'But I'm not! I'm falling to bits.'

Miss Benson was so quiet that Elsie was convinced she had left her to cry alone but she heard a gurgling sound, raised her head and peered through the mist. Miss Benson had calmly poured them both a cup of tea from a vacuum flask. Laid out on a napkin beside it were sandwiches. Then, to Elsie's amazement, she watched her take out a pack of playing cards.

'After tea we'll have a game. Meanwhile, get out of that dress and put this on.' It was her huge, hand-knitted cardigan. Navy blue. 'Then you can have a nap. I'll wake you up when it's time to re-do your make-up.'

Elsie shook her head in desperation. 'Miss Benson, I can't go on the stage tonight. Not in front of all those people.'

'And your parents and aunt.'

'Yes, yes, yes. You'll have to tell Mr Neville.'

'You don't have an understudy. Elsie, which would you prefer? To be on stage for the opening night of *Pink String and Sealing Wax* or have four more weeks of your holiday with Marjorie Bush and friends?'

'Two more weeks. We're going to Kent.'

'Don't be pedantic, gel. Well? Which would you rather?'

Elsie felt terror coming at her from all directions. 'Opening night,' she said. Her voice croaking.

'There you are then.'

'But only just.'

Elsie had told her mother she would be too nervous to

see her family for good-luck wishes before the performance, but Ralph came racing up and gave her a thumbs-up.

Miss Benson made sure that before the half, Elsie was made up and dressed so that she had time to calm down. To Elsie's surprise, all sorts of people in the company were poking their heads round the door and wishing her good luck, and Rosemary would appear periodically with little bunches of flowers and chocolates. Elsie was overwhelmed.

Down at the stage door, bouquets were arriving from local fans for the actresses and cigars and drinks for the actors. And then Rosemary gave overture and beginners, and it felt as though the contents of Elsie's stomach were about to come crashing through her bottom. She had been to the lavatory at least six times in the last hour, and now it was too late. Miss Benson removed Elsie's spectacles, put them gently on the dressing-room table, and took her hand. Elsie moved down the steps with her, as though her legs had disappeared and someone had crammed a shoe down the back of her throat. In front of them were three men, cigarettes in their mouths, in shiny old evening suits. One of them was carrying a violin. It was the

Billy Dixon Trio. She passed dressing-room two, the kitchen and dressing-room one, and then they were through the door into the wings. They stood by the prop table. Elsie stared up at Miss Benson.

'I can't–' she began, but Miss Benson put a finger to her lips.

'You must be Eva now, Elsie.'

Yes, thought Elsie, I must, and she squeezed Miss Benson's hand and turned towards the door which led into the parlour.

Annie was waiting for her on the small armchair. Elsie went over to her, picked up her sampler and sat beside her. They looked at one another intently. You are my mother, thought Elsie, and although you are always misunderstanding everything, and your choice of literature is very dull, I love you very much.

The music began and the chatter ended. As soon as Elsie heard the trio play, she began to sew. Eventually the music stopped. There was a round of applause, then silence, followed by the tap of a baton, and the music which introduced Act I. As the curtain rose and she heard the sound of a Victorian music box, she suddenly remembered a certain mouse that Lucy, the maid, had caught that morning.

*

'*Now here's the hell of a thing! Adelina Patti herself, in a carriage outside, and she's in a divil of a rage.*'

Elsie stared, amazed at Mr Neville who was playing Dr O'Shea. Suddenly, Sheila Darbisher, as Emily, gave a joyful cry, pushed her fiancé aside and fled from the room. Elsie glanced at Isla, and together they ran to the bay window to peer out.

Elsie had seen what went on behind her back at rehearsals, but she knew she mustn't turn round till she heard the curtain hit the stage. There was a silence followed by a huge wave of laughter and applause. And then the curtain fell.

'Now,' said Geoffrey from the prompt corner, and Elsie dashed downstage and stood between Isla and Annie, holding hands. The curtain sprang upward and Elsie gazed out at the packed theatre. The applause went on and on and on, and there were cheers of, 'Bravo!' Elsie couldn't help laughing from sheer exhilaration. She saw Arnold Swann bow, and she bowed with him and the others again and again, until he released his hands and stepped forward.

'Ladies and gentlemen, thank you so much for

194

being such an appreciative audience. We are delighted you have enjoyed the first of our plays, which will transfer to the Redmond Theatre next week. We look forward to seeing you again next week, same time, some of the same company, and some new faces from the Redmond Theatre, in *And No Birds Sing*, which we are sure you will enjoy. Goodnight and God bless.'

Elsie stared up at the gods, trying to spot her family, as the audience stood up to the Billy Dixon Trio playing 'God Save the King'.

As soon as the curtain fell, Elsie was amazed to see everyone vanish. Alarmed, she looked up into the flies, expecting to see scenery speeding down towards her, but there was nothing. So she made her way to the wings where Miss Benson was waiting for her. 'What's happening? Where's everyone going?'

'To their dressing-rooms.'

'But why are they running?'

'They have buses and trains to catch.'

Elsie suddenly felt depressed. She wanted to talk about the evening to someone.

'You'd better hurry too,' said Miss Benson. 'For the same reason.'

Later, in the dressing-room, when she was back in her ordinary clothes, spreading coconut butter over her face, there was a knock at the door.

'Who is it?' Miss Benson asked.

'Ralph.'

'Enter.'

'Not ready yet,' Ralph observed.

'Are they downstairs? Did they like it?'

'They loved it, but they told me to tell you they've gone to get the bus, and you're to come home on my bike with me.'

'They could have waited,' said Elsie, tearfully. 'Don't they want to see me?'

'Course they do. They'll be waiting for you at home. But if they miss the last bus we'll all be home very late. They really did like it. Honestly.'

'What did Dad say?'

'Nothing much. You know Dad. Hurry up. There's a visitor waiting for you at the stage door. Your headmistress and another woman.'

Immediately Miss Benson waved him off.

'Is she angry?' Elsie yelled after him. But already she could hear his footsteps receding.

'Close your eyes, Elsie,' commanded Miss Benson,

a cleaning rag in her hands. 'We need to get this make-up off and make you presentable.'

Elsie, her heart pounding yet again, made her way down the steps, Miss Benson walking on ahead. She had given Elsie's hair a few more strokes, and one of Miss Benson's many spare ribbons was now tied in a bow at the side. Luckily, Elsie was wearing her flared new-look skirt. To Elsie's surprise, the tall, thin woman standing next to the headmistress was Miss Dunstable, the elocution teacher. They looked very serious. Miss Benson shook hands with them as if they were royalty. Out of the corner of her eye, Elsie spotted Wilfred giving her a wink, and she suddenly wanted to giggle.

'Such an honour, Miss Castleford,' said Miss Benson, solemnly. 'I hope you've enjoyed this evening's performance.'

If Elsie could have slipped between the folds of Miss Benson's capacious navy blue skirt, she would have done so. Instead, she clasped her gloved hands in front of herself and stood still.

Miss Dunstable was beaming! 'You are a dark horse,' she said, coming over to her. 'I had no idea.'

'Was I Eva?' she burst out.

'Oh, yes,' she laughed. 'You were Eva.'

'Good,' said Elsie, relieved.

Miss Benson and the headmistress appeared to be getting on really well, looking like two stately galleons bowing to one another.

'I believe you have two weeks of performing,' said Miss Dunstable.

'Yeah!' Elsie blushed. 'Yes, Miss Dunstable,' she said politely.

Miss Dunstable drew closer. 'I need you. I shall do my best to pull a few strings. But it's a secret between us. Not a word to anyone.'

'Cross me heart and 'ope to die.'

And then they were gone. Ralph sprang up from the cubby-hole, where he had been eavesdropping, and almost gave Miss Benson a heart attack. It wasn't until Elsie was alone with her brother in the deserted street outside that she felt able to talk freely. 'Was I really all right?'

Ralph gave her a hug. 'You were splendid.'

'But they laughed at me. Do you think Mr Neville will be cross?'

'No. They weren't laughing at you, but at what you were saying. So don't play for laughs. Stay serious.'

198

He got on to his bicycle and helped her to sit sideways on the crossbar.

'But why were they laughing at serious things? Why?'

'I suppose it's because adults don't feel quite so protective of guinea-pigs as Eva.'

She noticed her brother staring at her and suspected he was already reading her mind. 'You will,' he said at last.

'Will what?' she said, testing him out.

'Be able to do it again tomorrow night.'

And she laughed, because he was right.

Thirteen

Her mother was in her nightgown in the kitchen with supper and a cuppa. Everyone else had gone to bed. Elsie's first question was, 'What did Dad say?' She wanted to hear how her father had leaped around saying how well he thought she had done, and how proud he was of her, and to ask her to *please* come with him and Harry to the allotment this Sunday. But her mother said, 'Nothin' much. You know your dad.'

'So he didn't like me,'

'Course he did. If he hadn't, that's when he would've said somethin'.'

Her mother put her arm round her. 'I thought you were wonderful,' she whispered. 'I was that proud.'

Elsie forced herself to smile. A compliment from her mother wasn't the same. Her mother was proud of them all. If they breathed in and out, she thought they were clever. It was Dad she wanted the praise from.

'Can I sleep with the boys tonight?'

'Oh, Elsie. You're gettin' a bit old for that, you know.'

'I need the sleep.'

She noticed Ralph and her mother give each other a quick glance.

'We might as well mention it now,' said Ralph.

Elsie eyed them suspiciously.

'Next week, when you're travelling backwards and forwards to Redmond, well, we thought it might be a bit hard on you,' said Mrs Hollis.

'You don't want someone else to play Eva, do you?'

'No, you silly!' said Ralph. 'But Mrs Egerton-Smythe says you can stay at her place.'

'On me own? In a room on me own?' Elsie had never slept in a bed on her own, let alone a room.

'You'd share with Jessica,' said Ralph. 'And you could take that filthy old rabbit with you for company.'

'It's up to you, love,' said Elsie's mother.

'You'd have breakfast with the actors staying there too, lucky thing.'

Elsie wasn't too sure. 'Does she snore?'

'Elsie, how do I know?' Ralph said, and she noticed him blushing.

Her mother laughed. 'Now, Ralphie,' she said,

rescuing him, 'tell me the news about the sentry. Did you ask Mr Swann?'

She was a bit nervous of knocking at Annie Duncan's dressing-room door, which was the second from the 'star' dressing-room in status. So it was really odd to discover that, in the mornings, Annie was rehearsing the part of a charwoman.

'Will you be able to see the play before you go away to Kent?' Annie asked. Elsie said that wild horses wouldn't keep her away, though she knew she wouldn't have a chance unless Ralph was given a part in it.

Meanwhile she continued to put off writing to Geraldine, and the more she put it off, the guiltier she felt. She didn't even know if Geraldine knew she was in the play. If she did, she might think it had gone to her head, and that's why Elsie hadn't written to her. Elsie wanted to ask her mother's advice, but every time she nearly plucked up the courage, it seemed trivial compared to the worn-out look her mother had written all over her face as she grew bigger and bigger. The heat wave continued, and her mother said that she didn't know if it was the baby which was making her hot and breathless, or the weather, or both. And, Elsie, not really interested in the approaching baby for reasons she didn't understand, found herself confiding about Geraldine to Annie instead.

'Keep it short and sweet,' she advised.

'Having a nice time. Sorry you aren't. Love, Elsie?' Elsie suggested.

'Bit too blunt.'

'How about, Dear Geraldine, I'm looking forward to seeing you next term too. Have lots to tell you. Will tell you then. Love, Elsie.'

Annie smiled. 'That's one way round it, I suppose.'

'The awful thing is, I'm not looking forward to seeing her. She's so sad she pulls me down unless I work hard at cheering her up.'

But Elsie did send a letter off with a 'PS, I'm in a play.' It was fortunate she did because she was mentioned in the *Winford Observer* review of the rep's latest play. 'Local girl, Elsie Hollis, carried off her part well.'

At home, Auntie Win continued trying to persuade Joan to join up and told her sister how unfortunate it was that she was married with a family. If she had been 'free' she could have joined up too, and have done something useful with her life. Elsie noticed her mother going quiet and doing something hurriedly to occupy her hands.

She heard from Ralph that her dad, who was teaching him to march, was being really tough with him. Sadly, her father made no reference to Elsie's performance, although he said he would come again with her mum to the Saturday matinée. Eventually she asked him outright what he thought of her, and he puffed at his pipe, gave a smile, and said, 'Not bad.' And Elsie was in heaven. But, come Sunday morning, there was still no invitation to the allotment.

Part Three *The Wedding*

One

The Redmond Theatre was much grander than the Palace Theatre. At the top of wide stone steps it had high pillars which flanked huge ornate doors. On the ceiling of the foyer, Elsie could see painted carvings of people floating in the sky, wearing long togas, their arms outstretched. Outside the theatre, above the foyer, were high, arched windows which overlooked a green.

'I'd better find your dressing-room so you can have your nap,' said Miss Benson, peering at a placard which advertised the play.

'Nap!' exclaimed Elsie. She was far too terrified to go to sleep.

'Nap,' stated Miss Benson pushing aside the heavy doors, with Elsie following like a puppy being brought to heel.

'I can't sit any longer,' Elsie complained for the hundredth time, wriggling on the wobbly chair in the tiny dressing-room. 'Can't I go and see the others?'

Miss Benson sighed. 'Go on then. But don't be long. They don't want to be bothered with too many interruptions.' She hauled out a huge ball of navy blue wool that she had recently dyed from a garment she had undone the previous week, and proceeded to cast on.

Nervously, Elsie made her way down the corridor. She knocked on Arnold Swann's dressing-room door. 'Come in!' yelled a voice.

Gingerly, Elsie opened the door.

To her embarrassment, Arnold Swann was sitting in his underwear, slapping on greasepaint. 'Oh, hello, Elsie. Nice of you to pop in.'

Elsie swallowed. 'I came to wish you good luck, sir.'

He whirled round and grinned. He seemed totally unaware of his state of undress. 'How kind. Excited? Nervous?'

Elsie nodded.

'Terrified?'

Elsie laughed.

'Makes the heart pump more efficiently, eh? We'll give 'em a good one tonight, eh, old girl?'

'Yes, Mr Swann.'

He returned to the mirror. Elsie stood there, tongue-tied. He stopped and glanced back at her. 'Was there something else?'

'Yes. Only I don't know how to ask it without appearing to be rude.'

'Be rude then.'

'It's about my brother, Ralph. Ralph Hollis.'

'Yes?'

'About his marchin' up and down.'

'Ah.'

'He said you'd think about it.'

'Well, I have.'

'Have you decided anything?'

'Yes, I have.'

There was a silence.

'Are you going to spill the beans? To me?'

'I have to admit, once everyone had stopped laughing at him, that the scene did work better. Had that extra edge of tension. So—'

'You're giving him a part?'

'Yes.'

'Oh, Mr Swann!' Elsie yelled, and leaped up and down excitedly.

'Now, if you don't mind, Elsie, I'd like to think about playing your father and erase the production of *No Medals* completely from my mind.'

'Yes of course, Mr Swann. Thank you, Mr Swann.'

Elsie raced up the stairs into her dressing-room.

'Is there a fire?' commented Miss Benson.

'My brother's got a part in *No Medals*! That means we can go and see the play. That means I'll be able to see Annie Duncan play the charwoman before I go down 'oppin'.'

'It appears you're hopping already.'

'I'm so happy,' said Elsie, breathlessly.

'So I see,' she said, still clicking away at her needles.

'Oh, Miss Benson, I do like you.' And she flung her arms round a surprised Miss Benson's neck.

'Careful. You'll make me drop a stitch!' But Elsie could see from her smile that she was pleased.

The audience gave them a standing ovation.

Afterwards, upstairs in the bar, the atmosphere was bubbly. Miss Benson ushered Elsie through the sumptuous mirrored marble room to one of the balconies 'That's better,' she huffed. 'Now, you stay there while I get you a drink.'

Isla was on the same balcony leaning on the balustrade, looking out at the green. Elsie joined her. Alongside them, huge Greek urns were spilling over with plants. Elsie felt as though she was in a palace in the South of France. Half an hour later they were rushing for the train. As usual, they had a carriage with no corridor, which meant no access to a lavatory unless they made a dash at one of the stations. Miss Benson sat with her knitting by the window, Elsie and Annie Duncan beside her. Opposite were Felix and Isla. Throughout the journey they all chatted and laughed except, Elsie noticed, Miss Benson, who kept giving Isla odd looks. Elsie was asked when her mother's baby was due.

'I dunno. Next month, I think. Soon.'

'Is it wise for her to go away to Kent so near the time? A hopper's hut isn't the best place to have a baby,' said Annie.

'I suppose not, but Mum loves it. She says it might be the last chance to have a proper holiday for ages. All that fresh air.'

Suddenly, Miss Benson put down her knitting, stared intently at Isla and said, 'And how about you, young lady? When is yours due?'

Isla's face froze and she blushed. Felix and Annie gaped at her. There was an awful silence.

'It's beginning to show, dear. I think, as there seems to be no husband on the horizon, it would be a courtesy to your fellow artistes to wear a wedding ring or at least a curtain ring.'

Isla gazed at Miss Benson, speechless.

'Isla?' asked Felix, gently. 'Is this true?'

Isla nodded. And then shook her head.

'Which is it, dear?' Miss Benson probed.

'Yes, I am going to have a baby. No, I'm not unmarried.' And with that she drew out a wedding ring on a chain from her blouse.

'You're married?' gasped Annie.

'You dark horse!' laughed Felix.

'But why didn't you tell anyone?' asked Annie.

'Because my father would kill me. I thought I could keep it secret till Richard was demobbed. I wasn't expecting to get pregnant.'

'Remember, there is a child present,' said Miss Benson.

'But how could you?' began Felix. 'Darling, you're going to have to explain.'

Isla twisted the ring in her fingers. 'You remember

when I went off to Salisbury to see a dying aunt earlier this year?'

'Only it wasn't Salisbury, it was the Isle of Wight,' said Felix.

'Where you saw your fiancé while he was on compassionate leave,' put in Annie.

'And you got snowed in and couldn't get back,' added Elsie. 'Ralph told me all about it. The other ASM had to play your part. Only she got drunk–'

'I think that's enough,' interrupted Miss Benson.

'That's when we married,' Isla finished.

Felix beamed suddenly. 'And you had an unexpected honeymoon because of being snowed in?'

'Yes.'

'Oh, Isla,' laughed Annie.

'Congratulations, darling!' said Felix, and he gave her a hug.

'It's such a relief to talk about it.' Isla smiled and glanced at Miss Benson. 'Is it really starting to show?'

Miss Benson nodded.

'I wondered how you were putting on so much weight,' said Felix. 'I thought you had been getting extra food rations under the counter.'

'Babies!' scoffed Elsie. 'What's so special about

having a baby? Noisy, smelly things.'

Isla just smiled.

'What are you going to do?' asked Annie.

'I don't know. I know I don't want to live with my parents. They don't even know I'm married yet. And I can't live with my father-in-law. He's still dazed from my mother-in-law's death and, in any case, he'd be out all day on the farm. I'd be all by myself. I was hoping I could work here for as long as possible.'

'I'm sure you can,' said Felix, eagerly. 'Maybe it'll be born in the theatre. I've never worked in a company where a baby's been born. How exciting!'

'It won't be born in the theatre,' said Isla, firmly. 'Oh, I hope I don't lose my job. I need the money.'

'I can make baby clothes,' said Annie, suddenly.

'You can knit it bootees, Miss Benson,' suggested Elsie.

'Perhaps I could.'

'But not navy blue ones,' added Elsie.

When they reached Winford Station, everyone went their separate ways. Miss Benson and Elsie walked to Mrs Egerton-Smythe's house. Through the stained glass windows in the front door, they could see the hall light was still on. Miss Benson rang the doorbell and within seconds Mrs Egerton-Smythe peered out.

'Good evening, Miss Benson,' she exclaimed. 'Hello, Elsie.'

Jessica leaped into the hallway in her nightdress. 'Oh, do tell her now!'

'Miss Benson, please take no notice of my daughter's antics. The reason we are up so late is that we have made an announcement.'

Elsie's heart fell. The thought of another baby filled her with unbearable boredom.

'It'll be in the local papers on Friday, and we needed to make arrangements. Do keep still, Jessica. I can't think, and Miss Benson needs to eat. I hope you don't mind the kitchen. The dining-room is already laid for breakfast.'

'Not at all, Mrs Egerton-Smythe. I'm delighted you can put me up this week.'

Mrs Egerton-Smythe ladled stew into bowls and cut bread from a fresh loaf. Meanwhile, Jessica was dancing maniacally round the kitchen.

'Jessica, do let them eat.'

'How can I? Oh, please ask her now, before I go to bed.'

'Go on, then. Get it over with, Jessica.'

'I'm going to be the maid of honour, by the way.'

'Oh,' said Elsie, puzzled.

'Only, Mummy wanted to know, and you'll have to make up your mind pretty soon because it's happening on Saturday, and you won't have to worry about clothes because Mummy's got friends who have offered to help out.'

'What she's attempting to ask, rather ineptly,' interrupted her mother, 'is, will you be my bridesmaid this Saturday?'

Two

Elsie woke up in a camp-bed in Jessica's bedroom with Bugs by her side. She had slept for a whole night without Harry. The sudden realisation that she could, quite comfortably, left her feeling both relieved and a little sad. She glanced across at Jessica's bed. It was empty but for a book lying face down on the pillow. Downstairs she could hear voices and laughter. She lay back and absorbed the room. On the faded wallpaper Jessica had stuck sketches and coloured pictures of paintings by famous artists cut out of magazines.

Miss Benson had let Elsie have a lie-in, because she had gone to bed so late. Elsie threw back the covers and kneeled down by the large bookcase next to her. On the bottom shelf were children's magazines written by Arthur Mee all stacked neatly together. Elsie flicked through the pages. They smacked of education. She put them back and picked out a *Girl's Crystal* annual.

Just then a familiar title caught her eye. *Anne of*

Green Gables. It took her back to her last day at school. Such a lot had happened since then. In three weeks, she had become one of a team in a theatre company. Some days she had laughed so much she was amazed she hadn't been physically sick or died. The book reminded her also of sewing classes and tidying up desks and waiting for the bell to ring. It was a way of keeping them still. She wondered if L M Montgomery would have wished it to be read like that, in bits, with so many different readers.

The door opened and Jessica poked her head round. 'Awake at last!' She glanced at the grubby rabbit on Elsie's pillow.

'His name is Bugs,' said Elsie.

'Don't let Miss Benson see it. She'd probably shoot it.'

Elsie lifted up the book. 'Do you mind?'

'Not at all. I love that book.'

Elsie, noticing Jessica's red plaits, could understand why.

'And not just because of my hair,' she laughed, and strode into the room and drew the curtains. Immediately, the room was filled with sunlight. Jessica jumped on to her bed and crossed her legs. She was

216

wearing a short-sleeved blouse and shorts.

'It bored me at school, but now I've started again it seems completely different,' said Elsie, 'reading it without interruptions.'

'Oh. I've just interrupted you.'

'Yes, but you're not asking me questions about it.'

'I've been quite lucky,' said Jessica. 'I managed to read some books by myself before the teachers ruined them at school. Do you like it at your school?'

'Sort of. I like some of the teachers. And I like the buildings and the garden. It's like paradise. And I like the smells. Polish, that sort of thing. And the way the corridors echo. It's just, well, I stick out a bit.'

'How?'

'My uniform.'

'Don't you all wear the same?'

'Yes, but my gymslip must have the biggest hem in history, so it doesn't hang quite right. And I could pitch camp in my blazer.'

'But everyone has to make do. Surely they're used to that?'

'The main thing is,' said Elsie, slowly, 'I don't seem to have made friends. Well, I have but–' she hesitated.

'Go on.'

'One of them is friends with everyone, so I feel I'm just one of her collection. And the other one is nearly always miserable. I can make her laugh, but sometimes I don't feel like doing it.'

'And I suppose the others won't go near you because you're with her.'

'Do you think that's why? I never thought of that.'

'Well, if you're always with someone who's a damp squib, they're not exactly going to want to spend time with you. Can't you get shot of her?'

'No. I feel sorry for her. She's got this awful dad, see. And her parents are always rowing. That's how we got to be friends in the first place. She was nice when my parents were quarrelling all the time. I can't just dump her because things are better at my home, can I?'

'I see your point.'

'So you think maybe it's not me?'

'Of course not. I mean, you get on with people in the company, don't you?'

'Yeah. But they aren't the same age as me.'

'Does it matter? We're all people, aren't we? When

you leave school you'll make friends with people of all ages. Why wait till then?'

'I never thought of it like that.' For a moment Elsie felt a tremendous weight lift from her chest.

'But when I go back nothing will have changed.'

Jessica looked thoughtful. 'Perhaps you could suggest to Geraldine that she has a moan at the first break but not at lunch-time.'

Elsie shook her head. 'When her dad thumps her, she sits next to me in this sort of cloud of gloom. She don't moan then. She just looks sort of lost.'

'Does he hit her hard?'

'Yeah.'

'But don't the teachers see the bruises?'

'She says he hurts her where you can't see. He locks her up sometimes too.'

'That's dreadful.'

'So you see, I feel I've no right to be happy when she's like that.'

'Because if you do, it looks as though you don't care?'

Elsie nodded.

'Have you got a housemistress you can tell? I mean, maybe she needs to talk to a grown-up.'

'I thought that too. But she said she'd be too embarrassed. That the housemistress might say she must have done something to deserve it. That all parents have to punish their children when they misbehave. And she'd just be told off for telling tales.'

'What if *you* went to the housemistress.'

'Me?'

'Ask her if you can speak to her in confidence?'

'I dunno. She's very posh.' And then she remembered. 'There is one teacher. The elocution teacher, Miss Dunstable. I don't have lessons with her, but she saw me in the play and she was really friendly.'

'There you are then!'

'Yes, yes, yes,' said Elsie, bouncing on the bed. And she laughed out of relief. 'I'll talk to Miss Dunstable if things don't get better. I can't lose anything, can I?'

'Exactly. Now, hurry up, Mother is ringing a friend of hers. She'll be coming round with the dresses. We'll be trying them on in the garden-room.' Elsie smiled. This was what it must feel like to have a sister.

The dresses were pure nineteen-twenties. Straight shifts in pale pink and pale green. Jessica and Elsie put them

220

on, took one look at each other and promptly collapsed with laughter. Elsie's green dress reached her shins, and made her look as if she was trapped inside a long, green tube.

'You look like a caterpillar!' choked Jessica.

Jessica's dress was too tight and too short, and the wrong kind of pink for her red hair.

Mrs Egerton-Smythe looked apologetically at a short, dumpy woman who was sitting on the settee. She was an old friend of the family. It was she who had brought the dresses.

'Gertrude, I think we may have to rethink,' she said.

'Mrs Egerton-Smythe,' began Elsie, shyly, 'you know that new-look skirt I have?'

Mrs Egerton-Smythe nodded.

'With the pale blue and cream stripes?' said Jessica.

'Yes. Well, Annie Duncan made it for me.'

'So she did!' said Mrs Egerton-Smythe, looking interested.

'I know she's rehearsing in the morning, but if you have some spare material, she has patterns.'

'Oh, Mother,' said Jessica. 'All we'd need is an ordinary blouse and a hat.'

'Which Annie Duncan could make,' interrupted Elsie.

'Gloves.'

'Which Annie Duncan might have in her collection,' added Elsie.

'White socks and sandals.'

'Well, I must say,' said the dumpy woman in an aggrieved voice, 'I thought you'd be only too pleased at my offer of help,'

'I am, Gertrude. And they're lovely,' said Mrs Egerton-Smythe, falteringly.

'But we're not,' said Jessica. 'I need to be much smaller, and Elsie needs to grow.'

'You could put a large hem in it. I wouldn't mind.'

Elsie and Jessica caught each other's eye.

'Curtains!' exclaimed Mrs Egerton-Smythe.

'What about them, Mother?'

'Upstairs. No one ever sees them. Chintz. Torn to shreds, most of them, but I bet there's enough material in there to make two new skirts.'

'Curtains!' exclaimed the neighbour. 'They can't wear curtains.'

'No one would know.'

'Charles will know.'

222

'Oh, he won't mind so much now. He has important things to think about since Timothy's arrival.'

'Another baby?' whispered Elsie gloomily to Jessica.

'Afraid so. And I'm his aunt. But he's not a bad baby, actually.'

There was a loud knock at the front door.

'That'll be him now,' said Jessica. 'Charles, I mean. Not the baby.'

The neighbour shot to her feet. 'I'll leave you in peace,' she said hurriedly. 'I expect you'll have lots to talk about. You can give me back the dresses tomorrow. I'll call for then then.'

'Thank you so much, Gertrude. I'm so sorry. I really appreciate your offer of help.'

As soon as they had left the room, Jessica began tugging at the strange shift. 'Come on,' she said. 'Let's get out of these filthy dresses.'

'How?' said Elsie.

'He's coming. Quick!' Jessica squealed. 'Hide!'

While Elsie hopped, kangaroo style, after her, Jessica dived behind the settee. There was a loud tear.

'Oh, heck!' Elsie heard. At which point, Elsie fell over and landed sprawled across the floor. Before she could manoeuvre herself back on to her feet, Mrs Egerton-Smythe and a man entered the room. Elsie was aware of a pair of shoes first, stopping abruptly in front of her.

'Is this a bridesmaid?' a voice barked.

'Where's Jessica?' asked Mrs Egerton-Smythe.

'Behind here,' said a sheepish voice. Red-faced she stood up in the pink shift, flapping now in unexpected places. 'Oh, Mother. I'm terribly sorry, but I've had an awful accident.'

'The sooner she goes to a finishing school, the better,' Charles commented.

'She's only fifteen,' protested Mrs Egerton-Smythe.

'One wouldn't think it from the state of her.'

'Don't worry, they won't be wearing these.'

'I should think not. Look, Mother, I think this whole thing is the most frightful fiasco!'

'Charles, we have a visitor,' she said, indicating Elsie. 'Let's go into the library to talk.'

'And that means you have to take turns to listen, Charles,' said Jessica.

'Don't be cheeky.'

Jessica immediately closed her mouth, puffed out her cheeks and went boss-eyed.

'How childish,' he said, leaving the room with his mother.

After a great struggle, the two girls peeled the dresses off and ran out on to the veranda in their vests and knickers, and down the lawn to the jetty.

Later, the curtains were brought down from the loft, washed, dried and ironed between tears and scorch marks. Annie Duncan agreed to make the skirts and Miss Benson agreed to do invisible hemming. Some embroidered white blouses and gloves were found in the Egerton-Smythe's attic, and one of the actresses in the cast volunteered to make little hats for them.

Before Elsie knew it, she was walking beside Miss Benson towards Winford railway station, with Jessica's copy of *Anne of Green Gables* under her arm. Sitting in the train gave Elsie time to think. She had made up her mind. She was going to be on that allotment with her father, even if it meant disguising herself as a boy. They would be off to Kent on Thursday so she would only have a few days to achieve her goal after the last performance.

'Penny for them,' said Miss Benson.

'I was thinkin' of me home.'

'Why don't you write them a letter. We could give

it to Wilfred, to pop in your brother's pigeonhole, and he could take it back to your mother. That is who you're missing, I take it?'

'And Harry. And it's strange not having Joan snoring. I don't remember waking once last night. I got more energy now and I can think straight.'

'Good. I'll give you some paper from my writing-pad then.'

'Thanks, Miss Benson.'

Once they arrived at the Redmond Theatre it was surprising how easily Elsie fell into the routine of preparing for the performance, visiting the dressing-rooms to say hello, wandering on-stage to chat to Geoffrey and Rosemary in the wings. It was a routine she liked. It made her feel safe and she hardly missed home now. Sometimes, if she was on her own or daydreaming on the train, she wondered what her mother was doing and if Marjorie Bush had found a new victim. But she knew that was just wishful thinking.

On Saturday morning the whole house was buzzing. There were flowers everywhere. Mrs Egerton-Smythe's friends bustled excitedly around arranging flowers in

226

every nook and cranny for the wedding reception, while the few of them who still had maids were baking and stacking up loaned crockery.

Breakfast was whisked through. Elsie had her hair washed and brushed by Miss Benson who, Elsie noticed, was trembling with excitement. She almost seemed proud of Elsie and when the review in the previous day's *Redmond Gazette* called her a welcome, comical young talent it received no 'congratulations' or 'well done', but an 'of course', which had Elsie in raptures.

'Do I look the part?' A young man was in the hall, twirling around in a uniform, cap, high leather boots and polished gauntlets. He was one of the actors staying at Mrs Egerton-Smythe's. He had been roped in to be the chauffeur because he could drive.

They all applauded.

Jessica's mother suddenly appeared in a pale blue linen suit and a hat with a wide brim, which she wore to one side.

'Oh, Mother!' Jessica gasped. 'I haven't seen that on you for years!'

'Well, don't tell everyone, will you?' She was holding a bunch of flowers.

'You look beautiful, Mummy!'

'So do you both, my darlings. Now, into the Alvis.'

The Alvis was a large, dark green car with an array of different sized headlamps and horns at the front. Soaring above them was an eagle in flight. The massive wheels had red spokes in them. The chauffeur gave a whistle of admiration. 'She's a beauty!'

Jessica and Elsie sat at the back on each side of Mrs Egerton-Smythe.

'Mummy, I've just realised. You won't be Mrs Egerton-Smythe any more. What's Basil's real name?'

'Rose. Couldn't be simpler. Mrs Rose.'

The young actor turned round and gave them a grin. 'From now on, as the chauffeur, I shall be tremendously deferential, so don't think I'm being standoffish, will you?'

It was when they turned the corner and were approaching the High Street, that Elsie became conscious of it being busier than usual.

'There must be some sort of fair today. Perhaps we should have set out earlier,' said Mrs Egerton-Smythe, with the first hint of nerves Elsie had seen. 'There's hundreds of them!' she gasped, leaning forwards for a closer look.

'I wonder what's going on,' said the chauffeur.

It was only when they turned into the High Street that they had the answer.

'Oh, Mother,' Jessica whispered. 'They're waiting for *you*.'

And it was true. Crowds of people were gathered on the pavements, all waving frantically. Small children were sitting on their parents' shoulders, waving flags. Some of the crowd were holding banners saying 'Congratulations, Mrs Duke'.

'I think they've made up their minds what you're going to be called, Mother,' said Jessica, smiling. 'Come on, we must wave back or they'll think we're stuffy.'

'Of course.' And she laughed.

Elsie waved frantically. People were pointing at them and cheering. Elsie spotted Joan on the pavement with her boss and the other assistants.

'It's like being the king,' laughed Mrs Egerton-Smythe.

Every passing car hooted at them. The whole High Street appeared to be in an uproar.

'I say,' said the chauffeur, 'I feel as though I'm in Hollywood.'

'Mother. Look up at the windows.'

The people who hadn't managed to get a place on the pavement were leaning out of the windows. Below them others were running along, following them.

'You won't be lonely going up the aisle now, Mother,' said Jessica.

Her brother, Charles, had refused to give his mother away.

'I wouldn't have been anyway. I have my maid of honour and my bridesmaid,' she said, putting her arms round them and giving them a squeeze.

'I'm dying to wave back,' said their chauffeur. 'It's such hard work being deferential.'

'It certainly is. So since it is *my* wedding day, I'm telling you to stop right now. Only don't crash into anyone, will you? Basil has spent ages working on this car. If it's like this for us, what is it going to be like for Basil?'

They soon found out.

The crowds outside the church were phenomenal. The place was awash with coloured frocks and ribbons and flowers. The car stopped for a moment. Ahead of them they spotted Basil, resplendent in morning dress, waistcoat, and silk cravat, getting out of another car with one of the actors from the rep. The crowds

230

surged forward. Police constables, grinning away, were attempting to hold them back. Elsie noticed that Jessica and her mother were now holding hands very tightly.

'You really don't mind, Jessica?' she heard Mrs Egerton-Smythe say softly.

'No, Mother. I really don't.'

'You see, I love him very, very much.'

'I know.'

There was a loud blowing into a handkerchief.

'I'm so sorry,' said their chauffeur, turning round.

They burst out laughing. He was crying!

'Typical thespian,' retorted Mrs Egerton-Smythe. 'Now, would you mind opening the door for us?'

'Oh, gosh. Yes. That's me, isn't it?' And he almost fell out of the door in his eagerness to get out. He then drew himself to his full height. The crowd began to point at him.

'He's really enjoying this, isn't he?' Jessica remarked.

So am I, thought Elsie. So is everyone.

They were just standing in the porch waiting for the doors to open, with Jessica behind her mother and Elsie behind Jessica, when a well-dressed man suddenly appeared at her side. It was Charles.

'Oh no!' Elsie heard Jessica whisper. 'He wouldn't try to stop her now? Surely not?'

But to their utter astonishment, he presented his arm to his mother and they heard him ask quietly, 'May I have the honour?'

They watched Mrs Egerton-Smythe gaze at him, stunned. For a moment no one moved. Then she smiled and took his arm. 'Everything's perfect now, Charles. Thank you.'

Three

Elsie couldn't speak. As she trotted alongside Miss Benson she knew that by the time they arrived back at Mrs Egerton-Smythe's, the house would be in darkness.

It had been one of the most exciting days of her life. Now it was all over. For weeks she had been looking forward to going hop-picking, but now Kent was the last place on earth she wanted to visit. As she walked dejectedly alongside Miss Benson, the tears ran silently down her cheeks. She kept her head bowed, so that Miss Benson wouldn't notice the rush of mucus heading speedily towards her entire face. She had had a taste of friendship and now it was smashed. She realised she was just another little girl who had joined the company for four weeks. The cast would now be too busy with rehearsals for the next production to remember her. She hadn't even had time to say a proper goodbye to everyone. She and Miss Benson would return to bread and something, and then it would be

233

bedtime, and Miss Benson would go home the next day.

They hadn't even been able to stay to the reception. Tomorrow afternoon she would be back at home, helping, with no one to talk to on Monday, and even though her family were attending the opening night of *No Medals*, she would have to rush off home with them. No more popping into Annie Duncan's dressing-room ever again.

The thought of this return to her former isolation and daily confrontations with Marjorie Bush overwhelmed her. Through her misted spectacles she noticed a large white handkerchief heading in her direction. Miss Benson must have had it at the ready. 'Sorry,' blubbed Elsie, taking the handkerchief and wiping her lenses with it.

'Quite normal, you know. It's your first experience of being in a play.'

'My last.'

'Nonsense. They won't let you escape. They'll use you again.'

'Do you really think so?' Elsie didn't dare allow herself to hope.

'Of course.' She stopped under a lamppost and

began rootling around in her bag. 'I was going to give you this tomorrow, but perhaps now would be a better time.' She drew out a soft parcel. 'For you.'

As soon as Elsie held it, she had a strange premonition. She tore open the package and drew out an enormous hand-knitted navy blue cardigan.

'I made it a bit large for you so that you can grow into it.'

Elsie held it against herself. It reached her knees. She would be a woman by the time it fitted her. Before she could stop herself, she collapsed into a fit of the giggles. 'Thank you so much!' she laughed, helplessly. 'It's very kind of you.'

Miss Benson began walking again, Elsie stumbling and hiccuping beside her.

'Well, I'm glad it's cheered you up,' she snorted.

Elsie nodded. She still couldn't speak, but it was for a different reason now.

As soon as they turned the corner they could see lights blazing from the windows, and from the back of the house they could hear music. 'Oh, Miss Benson!' cried Elsie. 'They're still up!'

They discovered that because so many of the actors couldn't attend the reception, they were celebrating now.

Later, down at the jetty, with the moonlight spilling on the water, Elsie sat in a pair of Jessica's pyjamas, next to her and Ralph. She soaked in the night air which was slowly dissolving into a damp dawn.

'I didn't know life could be so good. It's going to be difficult leaving it behind.'

'Yes,' agreed Jessica.

'I'm going to miss you when you go back to school,' said Ralph.

'Oh, Ralph. That is nice.'

'Mush,' Elsie remarked.

'You've no romance in your soul, Elsie,' said Ralph.

'No I haven't, thank goodness.'

'I don't believe you,' said Jessica. 'You loved being in the theatre.'

'That's different,' she yawned. 'That's exciting.'

'Anyone for breakfast?' said a voice behind them. It was Annie.

'Rather,' chorused Jessica and Ralph, and they walked arm in arm up the lawn. Elsie hovered. She had a feeling it would be the last time she would sleep in this house. Annie put an arm round her. 'Promise you'll pop in to see us when you go back to school?'

The thought of travelling to and from school

suddenly made Elsie feel sick. 'Are you sure you won't mind?'

'I shall mind if you don't. And you are coming to see me on Monday in *No Medals*?'

'Yes. Now that Ralph's got a part in it.'

'Oh, you're not coming to see my performance?' she teased.

'I am. But my parents will be coming to see Ralph.'

'And Auntie Win?'

'No. She's gone back now.

Annie gave a mysterious smile. 'I think your mother is going to enjoy *No Medals* very much. I have a feeling it might be just what she needs after your aunt's visit.'

'Why?' asked Elsie.

'If I tell you, it won't be a surprise.'

'Oh, do.'

Annie tweaked her nose. 'Wait and see. Come on. I'm starving. There's bread and dripping, and toast and marmalade on offer.'

They walked arm in arm up the lawn towards the veranda.

'How long is it till Ralph comes on?' Elsie heard Harry ask wearily.

'Act II, Scene 2,' answered Elsie. 'Only one scene to go.'

It was in Act I, Scene 1 that Elsie remembered the conversation she and Annie Duncan had had.

It was as though Elsie was watching a posh version of her mother and Auntie Win. Elsie glanced aside at her mother whose head was nodding in recognition.

'*Oh, the conceit of some of you women just because you're dressed in khaki. Perhaps you'll allow me the fact that I at least look after the health and comfort of two Wrens, one naval officer and one airman.*

'*Do you clear out two grates and re-lay two fires by seven am? No you don't. Do you do the washing and mending and ironing for all those people and yourself each week? No. Do you cook every meal for five people, clear away every meal and wash up every meal, day after day, night after night and often in the middle of the night?*'

The character was speaking for all the women who had done their bit for the war effort, unseen. Unlike the ones in uniform, there would be no medals for them.

'*You sit at a desk in clothes provided without coupons, ordering other people out to work, signing*

238

forms and granting occasional interviews – and being regaled with constant cups of tea made and brought to you by an orderly who would be doing a far better job if she helped me to scrub out the scullery. There!'

At this point there was a wave of thunderous applause from many of the female members of the audience, including Elsie's mother. The rest of the family stared at her in astonishment.

When the applause had started to die down, the actress announced, '*I feel better.*'

'So do I,' Elsie heard her mother whisper, a huge smile on her face. 'Oh, so do I.'

In the next scene, a young man in a naval uniform made his way quickly down a gangway out to the quayside. Then a young woman in a Wren's uniform walked up to him. They were husband and wife. They glanced at each other and began to speak, but then a sentry appeared and the young woman immediately stopped talking.

At this point there were great nudges as the entire Hollis family, eyes riveted to the stage, watched the young sentry. Elsie prayed that the audience wouldn't laugh. From out of the corner of her eye she saw her father lean forward and her mother gave Elsie's hand

239

a squeeze. The couple's dialogue was, for Elsie, lovesick drivel.

'*You really must love me, after all.*'

'*I believe I do.*'

They kissed. Suddenly the captain appeared.

Ralph, as the sentry, coughed to warn them. But they didn't hear him. Still holding hands there was more lovey-dovey stuff between them. How could Ralph look so serious and not be sick, thought Elsie. They kissed again. Ralph gave another cough and stood to attention as the captain came down the gangway. At last, the young woman noticed. The rest of the scene was filled with farewells. What made the mushy scene between them even worse for Elsie was that the young woman was trying to tell him she was expecting a baby. Would there be no escaping from them?

But her brother was right. The scene did work better with him there.

Elsie noticed a smile appearing on her father's face. Ralph had done him proud. To add icing to the cake, someone behind them remarked, 'I wonder where they got that young soldier from?' Elsie thought her father was going to take off, he looked so pleased.

She sat back in the dark. Her dad was proud of

Harry and proud of Ralph. Tomorrow, when he got back from work, he would be proud of her too. This time tomorrow, she thought firmly, I will be digging with him on the allotment till dusk.

Four

Elsie entered the clothing exchange shop with tuppence in her pocket from selling some of her precious annuals at the second-hand book and junk shop. She was on her way to carrying out her plan. She unpacked the carefully folded navy blue cardigan and two skirts from her school satchel, and placed them on the counter. A plump woman dressed in a green overall with a Women's Voluntary Service badge on it and a greeny-grey hat gazed at them in appreciation.

'These are beautiful! I say, Mildred, come and have a look at these!'

An older woman joined her. 'Very fashionable,' she said, disapprovingly. 'All that material for just two skirts.'

'One of them was made from old curtains,' put in Elsie.

'And very classy curtains. These are yours, I take it?'

'Oh, yes.'

'You know we don't give money for these, dear. We only exchange clothes here.'

'Second-hand with no coupons,' added Elsie, brightly. 'And I want to exchange them. My mother does, that is. But she's not feeling very well at the moment and she don't like to leave my *twin* brother alone much, him being so poorly.'

'But if she wants to exchange them,' said the older woman, 'she needs to be here to try the other clothes on.'

'But they're not for her. They're for me. Not me, I mean.'

'Make up your mind, dear.'

'Me mother sent me to try boys' clothes on, seeing as I'm the same size as me brother.'

'Did she say what she needed?'

'Shirts, shorts, boots, socks, braces, jumper.'

Once Elsie had left the WVS clothing exchange shop, she headed for the ladies' powder room in the department store. Her heart pounding, she made her way into the ladies' lavatory and changed into the boys' clothes. She took out Joan's scissors. Bending over the lavatory, she grabbed great handfuls of hair and cut chunk after chunk off into the bowl. She flushed her hair away and stuck a cap over her head.

She stood in front of the mirror and put her spectacles on to get the full effect. She had just pushed them back up to the ridge of her nose when a smartly dressed woman entered. 'What are you doing in here, young man?' she said sternly. 'This is the ladies.'

'I'm sorry,' Elsie stammered. 'I've only just put on me spectacles. It was too late once I came in.'

'Out,' said the woman firmly.

'Yes, ma'am. Sorry, ma'am.' And Elsie threw the satchel over her shoulder and made a hasty exit.

'She thought I was a boy!' she whispered excitedly. Now there was only one thing left to do. She ran to the barber's and pushed open the door and closed it gingerly. Suddenly she realised she hadn't a clue who she was supposed to approach. Two barbers were busy cutting men's hair. She was the only child. She sat down and waited. Eventually a tall man, who looked like a regimental sergeant major, approached her. She stood up politely.

'Right, sonny. Let's have a look at you then.' Elsie stared at him perplexed. He indicated her cap. She took it off.

'Blimmin' 'eck. Looks like it's been chewed up. You look like a girl.'

'That's what me dad says,' Elsie said hurriedly.

'Ow did 'e let it get that long, then?'

'I been ill. I couldn't leave the 'ouse.'

'Oh. Not this infantile paralysis thing?' he asked, taking a step backwards.

'Oh, no. Nothin' contagious.' She held out her hand, the two pennies hot and clammy in the open palm. 'He sent me off to get a tuppenny.'

'A tuppenny it is then, sonny.' He indicated one of the barber's chairs. Elsie climbed up into it and stared at herself in the mirror. He was right. It did look as if someone had chewed it up. 'Me mum tried to cut it, see,' she added, feeling a twinge of disloyalty at the lie.

'Women,' sighed the man, and he waved a silvery pair of clippers in front of her eyes. 'I don't suppose she has one of these, then?'

Elsie gulped. 'No,' she said, her voice shrinking into a croak.

'Might I suggest, sonny, you remove your spectacles?'

Elsie removed them. She was going to join her hands but thought it might look too feminine, so she

245

thrust them in her pockets and crossed her legs.

She knew about tuppennies. Her Canning Row cousins all had them before they went hop-picking. What she hadn't realised was that she saw them in late August, at the start of the hop-picking season. They all had their tuppenies in June, to last them through the summer, so that by the time she saw their pudding-basin haircuts they already had a two-month growth on them. When the barber had finished with her, the items she was most conscious of were her ears. She had never seen so much of them in her lifetime. But for a fringe at the front, the rest of her head was just stubble.

She swallowed. 'Thanks, mister,' she said, hoarsely. She put her glasses back on and slid down off the chair.

'Oh, Elsie! How could you?' wailed her mother. 'Those lovely skirts. We could have got shoes for school at the exchange there. What a waste! Oh Lord, what's yer gran going to say?'

She threw out this last remark to her husband, who was staring down at Elsie with a look of stunned disbelief.

'Why, Elsie?' asked her mother. 'Why did you do this?'

'I told you. For Dad.' Her father shook his head slowly. 'So I'd look like a boy. So you'd take me to the allotment tonight.' So you would be able to speak to me, she added in her head.

'You're not goin' anywhere tonight, my girl,' sniffed her mother. 'You're going to help me with the washing and the packing, ready for Thursday.'

'If she wears a dress, they'll think she has nits,' whispered Joan, appalled.

'Too bad,' said her mother. 'She's takin' them clothes back tomorrer and we'll get those other clothes back.'

'But couldn't I wear them in Kent?' Elsie blurted out. 'The boys won't play with me if Harry's not there.'

Now that Harry was working, he would only be visiting at weekends with the men.

'Play! You won't be playin' this year, my girl. We need to earn every penny we can get. We've got a baby comin', you know, as well as new shoes for next term.' She sunk her head in her hands. 'Next term. That's two weeks away. You'll have to walk into Winford Grammar School for Girls in that haircut!'

Her father still said nothing. Elsie gazed up at him, desperate to hear him say anything. That he understood. That even if her mum said she couldn't go to the allotment tonight, there was tomorrow night, but then she'd have no boys' clothes, so she'd look like a very strange girl. Suddenly she couldn't see her father any more. Her eyes had filled up so much that he had become a blur.

She was sent to bed without any supper.

In the morning, her mother said that she and her dad had talked things over. Dad had said that, since she had earned money at the theatre and was going to be working hard to earn money by picking hops, she might as well keep the clothes, but when she asked her mother if he had mentioned the allotment, her mother had said, 'No.' Elsie had completely forgotten she was to be paid. Mr Neville must have handed her pay-packet direct to her father. But why was Harry allowed to hand his first pay-packet over to her mum and not her? She knew the reason. That's why he had wanted her to keep the boys' clothes. It only confirmed what she had already suspected, that her father would really have preferred her to have been born a boy.

Part Four *Hoppin'*

One

Dear Elsie,

Mum had a little girl. Dad really loves her. You can see it in his eyes. He even takes her out in the pram. He don't care what people think.

He hates me more than ever now. Some days he hardly speaks to me. Sometimes he tells Mum to ask me a question when I'm there in the room.

I wish I'd never run away from him the day he come home from the war. I've tried to explain to him that he didn't look like his photograph. I left out that his voice was nothing like I imagined. And that he scared me.

But it doesn't make any difference. It's like I'm a thorn in his shirt or something, and I never know when he's going to get into one of his moods. One minute he's happy and having a joke, and the next minute he's standing behind me when I'm filling a kettle with water, watching me. And I'm thinking, please, God, please let me fill the kettle the right way. And I'm concentrating like mad, and I'm sweating, and then he explodes and starts yelling and raging, and calling me terrible names, swear words, which I won't write down, and says I'm stupid and I don't even know how to fill a kettle properly.

It's a relief when he thumps me because then I don't dread it any more. It's over and done with till the next time. But I never know what to say when he says he's sorry. The words get stuck in my throat. I just stare at him, and that gets him cross again.

Elsie looked out of the train window. It was early in the morning, before the usual trains ran. They had set off from London Bridge railway station in the dark at three o'clock, on one of the special trains for hoppers. The carriage was packed with women, two or three children or babies squeezed on to their laps, when they weren't clustered at the windows. The smallest children were now wedged on to the luggage racks. Once the ticket inspector had been and gone, they were able to crawl out of their hiding-places under the seats. Everyone in the carriage was done up in their Sunday-best. Because Elsie's mother was so heavily pregnant, there was no room for Elsie to sit on her lap. Instead, she sat on Joan's lap by one of the windows. Joan was so embarrassed by Elsie's appearance, she pretended not to know her.

It was strange not to be travelling with Harry. Staring at herself in the glass, her ears, which were now squashed down by her Sunday hat, looked odder than ever. She stuck her fingers underneath it and scratched her scalp. With her stubbly haircut, the hat irritated her more than ever.

'Don't do that!' whispered Joan.

Elsie removed her fingers and gazed out at the bombed landscape. She couldn't imagine not seeing bombsites any more. She could hardly remember a day when she hadn't seen a pile of rubble somewhere. Mum said the government would be building lots of new houses, but it was hard to believe. Elsie glanced down at Geraldine's letter. It had arrived the morning after she had had her haircut. Since then she had read it many times. She carried on reading:

'Mum's scared of him too. The other day she begged me to apologise to him because he broke my china rabbit. Like it was my fault. Like I drove him to break it. I knew if I didn't say sorry he'd just take it out on her, so I did. The only one he's nice to is the baby. I'm sorry your mum's having one as well. Still, we'll be in the same boat, won't we?

I kept the rabbit. He hasn't got any ears now, but I still like him.

I'll post this when I go shopping for Mum. I hope she don't notice I've taken out money for a stamp.

I wish these holidays would hurry up and finish. Can't wait to go back to school. We can talk lots more then, eh?

Your best friend,

Geraldine

PS What kind of play are you in? You didn't say. Is Marjorie Bush still getting to you? Life's horrible, isn't it?'

Elsie folded the letter and put it back in its envelope.

How could she tell Geraldine that life wasn't horrible? True, she had been feeling sorry for herself about Dad, but reading the letter she realised that there were worse men than her father. And Elsie had never seen her father thump anyone. He threatened a wallop, but his voice was enough to scare you. He upset Mum sometimes. But he never hit her. And since Auntie Win had been forced to leave Mum's bed and he had taken her place, everything had got better. Some nights she could hear them talking and laughing. And it was a good sound. A comforting sound. When they quarrelled she wanted to crawl under the covers of the bed and die.

'Mum?'

'Yes, love?'

'Did you bring your glasses with you?'

'Yeah.'

Elsie held out the envelope.

'Geraldine miserable again?'

Elsie nodded.

'Me glasses are in the hoppin' box. You'll 'ave to read it to me.'

Elsie glanced swiftly at the people in the carriage.

253

'Private things in it, eh?' her mother commented.

'Yeah.'

'Read it to me later. When we get a bit of peace.'

Elsie nodded and put the letter in the pocket of her cardigan. Hopping was one of the few occasions her mother could have a good natter with lots of other women. Elsie knew she would never get her alone.

'Her mum had a girl.'

'Well, that's nice. Is Geraldine a bit jealous? 'Cos that's only natural.'

'Will I be jealous when your baby is born?'

'You are already, aren't you?' she teased.

'No! I'm just not interested.'

Her mother gave her a squeeze. 'You'll always be my little girl.'

'But what if you have another girl?'

'Then you'll be my number one girl.'

'Dad wouldn't like it. If it was another girl.'

'Why do you say that? Elsie, he don't want you to be a boy.'

'Then why didn't he let me hand over my pay-packet to you like he let Harry?'

'Because Harry's job is important. It's a proper job.'

'And mine wasn't?'

'Not really, love. Your dad knows it's just for the holiday. He'll give you your turn later.' But Elsie didn't believe it.

She turned and looked hastily out of the window. A lump of bitterness was creeping into her throat and she didn't like the feel of it. Now there were fewer buildings and fewer bombsites. In their place were fields. The chatter in the carriage was almost deafening, but by the time the train pulled into the county of Kent, she was leaning out of the window with the other children, in spite of the warnings from their mothers that they would have their heads chopped off by a passing train.

'I'm not taking my gloves off this year,' she heard Joan insist. 'I have my job to think of.'

'You'll pick less hops if you don't,' said Mrs Hollis.

Elsie leaned out of the window again. The rush of air on her face was intoxicating. Her hat now hung back from her head on a piece of string. After the initial cries and pointing fingers from other children at London Bridge, she was now oblivious to their comments, and was glad of the new haircut. But she did feel sad about parting with the skirts. Not because she wanted to be in fashion, but because Annie Duncan had made them for her.

She wondered what she and Felix and Isla and Mr Neville were doing now. Annie said they would begin rehearsing *Arsenic and Old Lace* while playing *No Medals*.

'We're here!' yelled Elsie, jumping up and down. 'We're here!'

She whirled round as the women surged against the door to peer out. Elsie squeezed past them, back to her mother.

'Well, you've cheered up. The way you was goin' on I didn't think you wanted to come. Not quite like your "artistic" friends.'

Elsie reddened. Her mother's words were close to the truth.

'Come on, let's get our stuff.'

Elsie was always amazed at how many people fell out of each carriage. It was like rabbits coming out of a magician's hat. Bags, boxes, bundles, pots and pans, old suitcases, tied and piled on to wooden barrows on wheels continued to be dragged from the guard's van to the hoppers.

Mrs Hollis stood for a moment and leaned back,

her hand resting on the small of her back. The heat was overwhelming. 'Just stretching me legs!' she said, noticing Elsie staring at her. 'There's no hurry.'

They beamed at one another.

'I hope Dad remembers to get the *Winford Observer*.'

'Why?'

' 'Cos I expect there'll be a nice picture of you at the wedding, looking all pretty in your *hair* and nice clothes.'

Elsie gave a gasp. 'Geraldine!'

'What about her? You didn't leave her letter on the train?'

'No. What if she sees me in the paper?'

'She'll be pleased for you.'

'No she won't.'

'Not jealous, surely?'

'Hurt, Mum. She'll be so hurt I didn't tell her.'

'But you didn't know till the last minute.'

'Oh, come on,' said Joan impatiently.

'When we get back, I'll write to her mum and ask to visit the baby so we can all go together to see her.'

'Thanks, Mum. I don't like going on me own in case she's out and–' She bit her lip.

'And you're left alone with her dad? He gives you the creeps, don't he?'

Elsie nodded.

'Well, that's that, then. All settled. Now can we forget about Geraldine?'

'*Yes, please,*' begged Joan. 'There's our box,' she yelled. And a long trunk attached to wheels was lowered on to the platform.

Usually they hauled their luggage the two miles to the farm, but Elsie could see that her mother was in no state to pull a heavy box anywhere. Slowly they moved off the platform. A cart with a big shire horse was coming in their direction. The ruddy-faced driver yelled out, 'Anyone going to Golding's Farm?'

'Yes,' they cried eagerly.

Elsie's mother was hauled up.

'Oh no!' wailed Joan. 'I'll have arms as long as a chimpanzee's if I have to carry everything.'

Luckily for them, the driver took pity on her and room was made for their luggage in the cart too.

Gran was sitting outside her hut. The Hollis family had two side-by-side.

'I see she's all organised,' said Elsie's mother, quietly. 'Elsie, about the play, I wouldn't mention it to

Gran. She might think you're getting too big for your boots.'

Elsie nodded. But inside she felt disappointed. It meant she couldn't tell anyone. Not even her cousins.

'Elsie, walk behind us so people won't think you're with us,' whispered Joan. But it was too late. Her gran lifted her round, football-shaped face, grinned for a moment, and then her jaw dropped.

'No she hasn't got nits,' said her mother firmly. 'I'll explain later.'

'She looks like a boy in a dress! She'll have to wear her hat all the time or everyone'll think we're contagious.'

Elsie stood in front of her. 'Hello, Gran,' she said.

But her gran frowned at her and waved her away. 'Go and leave us in peace. We got things to talk about.'

Elsie nodded.

'You'd best change into your wellies,' her mother said. 'And don't go into the hut with 'em on.'

Gran took a great pride in her hut. All the women did. It was like a grand competition. A woman who didn't make her hut look pretty and homely did not have the respect of the others.

Elsie did her usual tour of the huts, waving to every

259

familiar face she saw. All the women she had got to know over the summers, she called 'Auntie'.

'That ain't Elsie, is it?' said one huge gap-toothed woman who was building up her fire.

'Yeah.'

'What have you done to your hair?'

'I wanted to be a boy, Auntie.'

Elsie saw a tall, beautiful woman in a summery frock come out of the hut behind her. 'Hello, Auntie Madge,' said Elsie.

The woman stared at her and then smiled. It was the first smile she had received. 'Elsie Hollis?'

Elsie nodded.

'Is that the Grammar School haircut?'

'No,' laughed Elsie.

'What is your mum thinking of?'

'Murdering me.'

They threw back their heads and laughed.

Elsie walked away from the huts to the next field, and gazed out into the distance, to where the alleys of growing vines would soon be cut down by the pole-pullers from their high stilts, ready for them to pluck the hops.

When Elsie made her way back to the Hollis hut

she could see the farmer had already delivered the faggots and bales of straw. The faggots were long twigs and branches and brushwood tied together in bundles. Her mother and Gran had dug out some of the turf and were laying the smaller pieces of wood over bits of paper. A pot of water was already standing beside it. Gran's bed was like a shelf which came out of the wall. Everyone else slept underneath her. She could see her gran laying bundles of the faggots across the floor.

Outside the next hut were her Aunt Lilly and two of Elsie's Hollis great-aunts, Gladys and Edie, sitting on apple boxes. Like her gran, they were both short but even stouter than last year. Elsie wondered if that was what happened to people when they grew old. Once they stopped growing upwards they grew out-wards instead.

'Don't walk in there with them boots on,' said Gran, joining them. She tutted a few times. 'You silly girl, no one in their right mind would want to be a boy, ducky.'

Elsie gave a shy smile.

'Come on, brainbox. Come here and give your old gran a kiss.'

Elsie shambled over towards her and got what

Harry called the 'octopus treatment'. But Elsie liked it. Her gran was warm and cushiony, and smelled of soap.

'Can I look inside now?' Elsie asked.

'After yer boots are off.'

Elsie peered in. From the outside the hut was a dull, grey, corrugated iron. Inside, it was a palace. Gran's dresser was by one wall with all her best china on it. She would never have dared leave it in London in case someone nicked it. And there were bits of lace draped everywhere to make up for there being no windows, even lace round the gap above the door. There were framed pictures on the papered walls and carpet had been spread on the linoleum which had been laid on the hard floor, though Elsie could only just see it underneath the faggots. On the dresser was a canary in a cage and a stuffed bird in a domed glass case, an oil-lamp, books and a large clock. Just by the door as you entered, a large tea chest was covered in a fancy tablecloth.

'It's beautiful!' Elsie exclaimed.

'Beauty does as beauty is,' her gran remarked.

Elsie hadn't a clue what she meant, only that it was supposed to be significant, so she put on a serious face.

262

'Will Joan be sleeping with us?'

She noticed her mother frowning her into silence.

'She has improved, hasn't she?' asked Elsie's gran. 'She'll have to sleep outside if she hasn't.'

'I don't snore,' protested Joan who, Elsie noticed, was still wearing her hat and gloves, and looking ill at ease. She was only related to the Hollis family because Elsie's mother, her aunt, had married one. She jumped as a passing wasp dive-bombed in their direction. 'Don't you worry, Joanie,' said Gran. 'We've got our wasp trap all sorted out.'

Elsie saw her cousin glance up at the hut and shudder. Hanging outside were several jamjars, half filled with water, half filled with jam, with some dead wasps already floating inside them.

It was later, when Elsie and her mother were pulling one of the straw bales apart, and filling a mattress cover for the large bed, that they heard a loud yell behind them. Her mother swung round. 'Dolly!'

A woman her mother's age, carrying a baby, was lumbering towards them. Two girls, Elsie's cousins, Kit and Joyce, were pushing an old pram piled high with bundles, and her cousin, Sidney, was dragging a sack along the ground behind them. A four year old,

263

her cousin Danny, was hanging on to her Aunt Dolly's free hand.

'We made it!' Dolly exclaimed.

'Sit down,' said Gran, getting up from her box. Elsie watched her gaze down at Aunt Dolly's baby. 'How old is he?'

'She. One week. I nearly didn't make it. I was that determined though. I ain't missing goin' dahn hoppin' for anything.'

'Sit down,' ordered Gran. 'Take the weight off your feet!'

'After I've unpacked.'

'I'll help,' said Elsie's mother.

'No you won't, Ellen,' said Gran. 'You're not built like us.'

'Gran! I'm not made of bone china.'

' 'Ere,' said Dolly, thrusting the tiny infant at her. 'You hold Charlotte. Get a taste of what you're in for.'

Elsie watched as her mother gazed awkwardly at the infant and began to jig it clumsily from side to side. Suddenly it stopped crying. She beamed. 'See, I haven't forgotten everythin'. Isn't she tiny though?' She gazed fondly down at it.

Mush, thought Elsie. It was then that she noticed

her cousins staring at her. Sidney was eight years old, Kit was ten and Joyce was twelve, Elsie's age. They all had the Hollis stockiness and black hair.

'You stayin' to the end this year?' asked Joyce.

Elsie shook her head.

'You still at that posh school, then?'

'The Grammar School? Yeah.'

'We're not goin' back till it's over. Beginning of October.'

'You missed goin' in the bins last year,' said Kit.

'And the party,' added Joyce.

'Yeah, I know,' said Elsie.

'She talks funny,' said Sydney.

'Don't be rude,' said Joyce.

'Well, she does.'

'I know. We all know. But you don't 'ave to tell 'er to 'er face.' Joyce smiled at Elsie. 'I got to help a bit this year, 'cos of the baby. Mum says I can keep some pocket money for meself.'

'Me too,' said Elsie.

Behind them came the sound of crying. They swung round.

'Babies!' muttered Elsie, noticing how many children seemed to be rocking the squawling bundles

265

in their arms while their mothers decorated the huts.

'I heard Auntie Edie call 'em "hoppin' babies".
She says nine months from now there'll be another lot
of 'em.'

'It's worse than the measles,' Elsie stated.

'Let's go before we have to look after Charlotte
again.'

'I like looking after Charlotte,' said Kit.

'You stay, then.'

'Nah. You goin' dahn the river?'

'Yeah! Let's,' said Sydney, excitedly.

'Joyce!' It was Auntie Dolly. 'Take Danny with you.'

'Aw, Mum, do I have to?'

'Yeah. I don't want 'im under my feet. And don't
lose 'im like you did last year. You know what a
wanderer he is.'

Elsie walked alongside her cousins towards the fields
which led to the woods and the river. It was the same
hop farm they had visited ever since she could remember.
Hopping was like having a family reunion every summer.
She wondered where her older cousins were. They would
be sharing the next-door hut with Aunt Lilly. And then,
through a clearing, she heard voices.

'It's them!' she cried. And she began running.

They were playing football in a field with four other boys. She climbed up on to the gate and waved madly. 'Mike!' she yelled. 'Doug! Albert!' She perched on the gate, shouting and yelling until she caught their attention. They stared at her.

'It's me, Elsie!'

They said something to the other boys and ambled towards her. All three were already burnt brown from the sun. Albert was the eldest. He would be fifteen now. Black-haired too. He had shot up and his shoulders had broadened. His fourteen year old brother, Mike, was like a beanpole, gawky. Little Doug was now twelve, the same age as Elsie.

'You gone all posh, Else,' said Albert.

'I'll lose it quick enough,' she said eagerly.

'Some haircut you got there!' commented Mike.

'I got boys' clothes too,' she added.

'Why?' said Doug. 'You ain't a boy.'

'I'm as good as. Can I play?'

'Bet you ain't played since last summer.'

'Have so.'

'Where's Harry?' asked Albert.

'Workin' at the paper-mill. He got an apprentice-ship. Haven't you got a job?'

'I had a job. I earn more fruit-pickin'. I'll get another one when I get back in October.'

'Are you stayin' or visitin'?' asked Mike, squinting his eyes against the sun.

'How d'yer mean?'

'He means, when are you goin' back to that school?'

Like the other children, they all missed the first month of the autumn term.

Elsie bit her lip. 'Isn't my decision,' she said, slowly.

They stared at her quizzically. Not in an unfriendly way, but as if she was an oddity. It reminded her of school.

'So,' she said, clambering down into the field. 'I'm ready.'

'When's Harry coming?' interrupted Doug.

'Sunday. With me dad and your dad.'

He nodded. 'See yer then.' And suddenly her cousins left her and sprinted to where the other boys were waiting for them. She raised her arm and was about to yell after them when she realised it was hopeless. The most she could hope for was to be politely accepted by them. She needed Harry to gain entrance to the game. Dejectedly, she clambered back up and over the gate.

Joyce and her younger cousins were out of sight now. Elsie decided to make for the river. As soon as she was through the woods she heard screaming and yelling, and through the trees she could see children jumping into the water. She began running. She was determined to make the best of things.

That night, sprawled on a sheet over the well-stuffed mattress, Elsie lay in the dark and stuffy hop hut, the door ajar to let some air in. She stared up at the corrugated ceiling, wide awake. She had told her mum about Aunt Lilly's boys, and her mother had said that once school had started she could come back at weekends if she liked, with Harry. But it did nothing to lift her gloom. Hop-picking was the climax of the year, but Elsie felt an overwhelming sadness, as though she had swallowed a sack of mud and it was lying dormant in her belly.

Outside she could hear the crackling of the fire and the murmur of her aunts and Gran, and their laughter. Inside the hut, she could hear the heavy breathing of Kit and Joyce, Aunt Dolly and the snuffling of the baby from the other side of the bed. Surrounded by aunts and cousins, she was overwhelmed with such a sense of loneliness that it physically hurt. Kit and Joyce were nice girls. Even Aunt Lilly's two girls, who were sixteen and seventeen, were very friendly, but they talked about things which didn't interest her. Worse. Sometimes they bored her. She had smiled and nodded occasionally but had begun to feel like a Mandarin doll after a while, and it had been exhausting.

And then there was her gran. Her only gran, who everyone looked up to with respect. She was one of the best pickers on the farm. She had her own bin. She could pick sixty bushels a day, sometimes more. Her fingers were broad and fat, but they moved faster than anybody else's fingers. But you didn't go to Gran unless she invited you. If she put her arms out wide you could get a cuddle, but not otherwise. And she didn't hold with self-pity.

Earlier, after supper, Elsie had overheard her chatting with her Aunt Lilly behind the huts, when they were hanging out some washing. They were talking about Elsie's mother.

'You're making too much fuss over her, Mum,' Aunt Lilly had said. 'She's only goin' to have a baby.'

'But she's been ill. She nearly lost it.'

'So what? That's nature, ain't it?'

'Look at her, Lilly. Thin as a rake. She's worn out. We gotta make sure her bin gets filled. Know what I mean? Mr Golding don't want to carry anyone. He'll sack a bad picker. I'd do the same for you. She ain't like us,' her gran had said. 'She's got class.'

'And I haven't?'

'Yeah. Course you 'ave, Lil. It's just you're more vulgar.'

'Mum!'

And at that, they had fallen about laughing.

'Vulgar is as vulgar does,' Gran said, which had left Elsie feeling totally mystified.

She wondered if her mother also felt set apart, not being a 'foreigner', which is what the home-dwellers, the local Kent people, called the influx of Londoners. And she asked her when there was a quiet moment. Her mother shook her head.

'It's such a relief to be with women. Some things you can't say with men around. They don't understand. It's lovely to be able to say anythin' off the top of your head. Even rude things.'

'But you don't say rude things, Mum.'

'Maybe not. But I have a good laugh listenin' to 'em.' And she gave Elsie such a mischievous smile that she made Elsie giggle.

And that's what she wanted to be able to do, thought Elsie in the dark. To say anything that came into her head, without being given an uninterested, disappointed or peculiar look.

Two

'Go away!'

Elsie woke with a start. She was sandwiched between Joan and her mother. She sat up and looked through blurred eyes round the mound of sleeping figures on the floor of the hut. Someone was banging on one of the doors in the next-door hut. It was the stickie. 'Come on. All to work,' she heard him yell, in the local Kentish accent.

It was the first day of hop-picking. She scrabbled around in the gloom and headed for the Hollis box, where she and her mother and Joan kept their clothes. As she fumbled through the pile, shivering, she caught sight of her grandmother's muscular arm reaching for a huge pink corset. Elsie pulled on a well-patched dress and jumper. They were damp and clammy. Lying on top of the pile were the aprons her mother had made. Elsie hurriedly threw one over her head, pulled on her socks and, spectacles in her hand, she clambered

273

over the moving bodies of her cousins.

Outside it was freezing and the mist hung heavily over the huts. The dew was so heavy it was as though there had been a downpour. She slipped on her wellies and headed for the toilets, a tin bucket in her hand. The water for all the huts was from a tap at the end of a field. If you moved fast, you could avoid standing in a queue. When Harry went hopping with them, he and Elsie would carry a long pole with several tin buckets hanging from it, fill them with water and stagger back with them.

By the time Elsie arrived back at the huts, her wellies encased in mud, her mother, Gran and Aunt Lilly had two fires going with a kettle on top.

'You beat me to it,' said Elsie.

Her mother smiled. 'I filled it up last night. But we always need water. I can use it for washing.'

'Where's Joan?'

'In the toilet.'

'I never heard her snorin' last night.'

'Gran did. She got Joyce to give her quite a few kicks. I think her snorin's got somethin' to do with her and Kitty being buried for so long in that house.'

'How d'yer mean?'

'I dunno. It's just a silly fancy of mine.' Mrs Hollis smiled. 'I'm glad her sister has found someone special. P'r'aps she'll talk to him about it.'

'When are we seeing her?'

'Tomorrow.'

'I'm longin' to see the baby.'

Elsie gave a groan.

'Go on with you,' Mum said, giving her a nudge. 'Now, have you had a wash?'

'Sort of.'

Her mother made sandwiches and poured tea into two lemonade bottles to take with them to the hop garden. They had to be there by seven o'clock. Time was money, as everyone knew. Slack pickers were not welcomed by the farmers. Soon, Elsie, her mother and Joan were walking towards the hop gardens in the mist with crowds of women and children, older boys and a few men alongside them pushing large black prams with children heaped into them. And then they were there. And the smell of hops, wet from the dew, was overpowering, bitter and lovely. The thick bands of hops were trained to grow upwards, up wires. They were four times Elsie's height and in rows of long alleys. A man was calling out bin numbers and family names.

The bins looked nothing like dustbins. They were long, baggy, deep hessian stretchers, which the pickers had to fill with hops.

As the families peeled off to their respective bins, Elsie looked to see if any of the pole-pullers and bin men were ones she knew from previous years. To her amazement, there were two land army girls and the German POW they had spotted last year.

'Mum,' she said, tugging at her mother's cardigan sleeve. 'Look.'

'Yeah?' said her mother, puzzled.

'They're still 'ere. But the war is over.'

'Demobbing takes time, love. For some, longer than others.'

Elsie suddenly remembered Isla's husband. Isla was still waiting for him to return home.

'Joan won't be pleased about the POW,' Elsie muttered.

'Bin seventeen. Mrs John Hollis and Miss Joan Walker.'

'That's us!' squealed Elsie.

As they walked over to their bin, Elsie peered round to see who their pole-puller might be.

'Oh no!' she whispered.

Smiling broadly near the Hollis bins was a tall, tanned, blond young man with blue eyes. It was Herman. Elsie watched Joan glance hurriedly away and move to the side of the bins furthest away from him. All the people in their field were Londoners. The hop-pickers in the field next to them, were 'home dwellers', the local people. Herman climbed up to the crow's-nest and cut the top of the binds.

'Pull down the binds,' he yelled, in his strange German-Kentish accent.

While Joan hastily put on a pair of gloves, Elsie and her mother pulled the binds down, and within seconds Elsie was absolutely soaked.

'You'll dry,' said her mother. 'When the sun comes up.'

But Elsie was shaking violently with the cold.

As soon as Herman was cutting binds for the next bin, which was Gran's, Aunt Dolly's and Aunt Lilly's, Joan was by their side again, pulling down the binds with them.

They laid the cold, sodden binds across their bin and started the finicky job of removing the leaves from around each hop. Some hops were pear-shaped, depending on what kind of beer would eventually be

277

made from them, but their hops, hidden under the leaves, were bulbous, like feather-like Brussels sprouts.

Her mother rubbed one vigorously between the palms of her hand and then sniffed it. 'There, smell that.'

She and Joan dipped their noses into her mother's hands. It was a strong, pungent smell.

Elsie began picking the leaves off the hops. That was the system Gran had taught her. Get the leaves off first, then you can pull off the hops in a sweep. Already the prickliness was grabbing at the sleeve of her jersey and scouring her hands. Soon insects were crawling out of the bind and over her fingers. But at least it kept her mind off being wet and freezing.

'You're too fussy!' yelled Gran from the next alley. She was talking to Joan.

'They'd never let me serve customers if me hands were stained.'

They wouldn't like their customers to know they were served by someone who went 'dahn 'oppin' either, thought Elsie. Already, Elsie could feel the familiar stickiness and see the yellowy-black stain appearing on her hands.

'You could wear gloves in the shop, couldn't you?

278

You'd pick a lot more without 'em, earn more money and be able to buy a nice pair.'

It made sense but Elsie knew that Joan couldn't bear to look rough.

'She wants to buy a new-look dress or skirt with her money,' said Mrs Hollis.

'New look!' scoffed Gran. 'All that material wasted. Lot of nonsense.'

After half an hour of picking, Aunt Dolly arrived in her wellies, her hair covered by a headscarf, an apron over her dress. The baby was snugly wrapped up with the sandwiches in an orange-box she was carrying. An umbrella was hooked over her arm. She laid the box down on the muddy ground near Gran, opened out the umbrella and put it over the box to shelter it from any falling hops. Soon after that Minnie, one of Aunt Lilly's girls, came and joined them. Elsie knew it was Gran making sure her mum didn't over-work. But her mum looked fine. She was just a bit slower these days. Minnie was short and dark-haired, with a wide, laughing sort of face. She sat next to Joan. 'You've got to have the right kind of corset, you know,' she began.

Elsie gazed at her, stupefied.

'For the new look,' she explained. 'And the padding.'

'Oh yeah, I know about the corset,' said Joan. 'I'm saving up for one. But I don't know anything about the padding.'

The idea of the new look, Elsie discovered, was to make a woman's waist look very small. You had to lace yourself up into a corset, slip shoulder pads under your brassiere straps and more pads on your hips to make the frock spread out more. Then the dress or skirt and jacket went on top.

'I don't think I'll bother,' Elsie's mum commented. And she and Elsie caught each other's eye and smiled. 'I'll have to make do with the old look.'

Elsie sat with her back to her gran. The hoppers on the other side of them were three sisters. A baby sat in a fruit box and a toddler was tied to their hop bin by a piece of string. Five children, who all looked younger than Elsie, were flinging the hops into an upturned umbrella. Elsie, still wet from the binds, picked off the leaves as fast as she could until someone blew a whistle. Everyone stopped immediately. If they didn't, the others would shout at them. It was time for a slice and tea. A slice was just a piece of bread, but it broke the morning up and it was breakfast.

'Come, you kids, out the way!'

It was the tallyman with his basket. He had come to tally up how much people had picked. Some people Elsie knew could toss their hops in a loose way to make the basket look fuller, but he would push them down. Sometimes he would push them down too much which angered the hoppers because only when a basket was full would it be one bushel, and they were only paid by the bushel.

Elsie bit into her bread and drank the cold tea. She glanced across at Kit and Joyce. They were chatting away to Mike and Doug. She felt left out.

After the break, the sun broke through, and people began to peel off their jerseys and cardigans, and then suddenly someone began singing. Within minutes the hop garden was filled with voices all singing out of time, echoing and reverberating along the alleys. Elsie joined in as she picked, and gradually her spirits lifted, even though her bare arms were stinging from the juices that were homing in on every nick and scratch on her skin.

When the whistle blew for lunch, the hop garden was bubbling with chat and laughter. A lot of the groups had come from the same street, so they were picking in sight of neighbours. Elsie looked down at her seeping beetroot sandwich, now stained with the yellowy stickiness from her fingers.

And it was hot. Scorchingly hot. As the afternoon seared on and the pole-pullers cut more of the binds and they separated the leaves off the hops and filled the bins, mothers rolled up the empty binds and made little nests with them, covered them over and then laid their small children on them to sleep in the shade or under an umbrella. Occasionally, Elsie's aunts disappeared into the bushes while they watched their little ones. The toilets were too far away to waste picking time by visiting, and at least the bushes and woods smelled fresher than the awful lime-filled pits with planks over them.

Gradually Elsie's cousins went off to play.

'Off you go, Elsie,' said her mother, but Elsie stayed, partly out of shyness, partly because she knew her mother needed all the help she could get. She noticed how she kept nodding off during the afternoon. Round about three o'clock Elsie's patience began to wear out. The work was so repetitive and dull, but the women chatted away or broke into song. It was a holiday for them. A holiday away from the men. And then the last whistle of the day was blown, and everyone waited while their hops were emptied into the baskets and measured. The tallyman wrote in his book how many bushels had been picked, and how much the pickers had earned.

Now the women carried their boxes with infants in them or hauled prams over the bumpy ground and headed back to the huts. While her mother went off to queue at a nearby barn to buy groceries, Elsie began laying a fire with the faggots left by each hut. Unless it rained, everyone cooked their meals outside. And then the air was filled with the smell of every variety of stew. Elsie was starving. As she dipped bread into her stew, she caught sight of her mother reeling with tiredness. She couldn't ever seem to sit comfortably now.

Elsie's hands and arms were still smarting. Joan had worn stockings on her arms but the stockings had snagged and slowed her down. Not that it mattered, because if Herman came across any fallen hops he would chuck them in their bin and, Elsie noticed, always with a sideways glance at Joan. Poor Herman. He hadn't a hope.

After supper, the women washed clothes and hung them on the lines behind the huts and began bathing their small children in zinc tubs, and washing their own hair and putting in curlers ready for the menfolk coming the next day. Some of the men appeared that night, including Aunt Lilly's husband, Uncle Bill. She and Uncle Bill went off to the pub, but Elsie's mother and Joan remained behind.

'I'd hold 'em up. And it's not the same without your dad. Wake me up for the singin', I'm goin' to bed.'

Joan went for a walk, her curlers now encased in a headscarf.

Elsie went off with her cousins towards one of the fruit orchards, but she hung back when she got there. They were going scrumping. Elsie's mother said it was wrong to steal other people's fruit, but her aunts turned a blind eye. Elsie wanted to join in but she didn't want to disobey her mother.

'Come on,' Doug said, when Joyce tried to egg her on to join them. 'She'll be gone next week. It ain't worth her bein' one of the gang.'

And Elsie watched them running away from her, giggling conspiratorially. On the way home, she went into one of the fields where they stacked haystacks, and felt around underneath them. Some of the chickens wandered round there, and if you looked carefully you could sometimes find an egg. She found two, and carried them very carefully back to the hut. Her mother didn't mind her taking eggs from the field. When she returned she found Gran sitting outside by the fire reading a book, squinting through a magnifying glass.

'What you readin'?' Elsie asked.

'A Peter Cheyney. Good it is too.' She glanced up at her. 'Your Aunt Win would like this one.'

'Only if there are plenty of men murdered in it.'

'Oh, there's plenty of those.'

'What you got there?'

'Eggs.'

'Good girl. You make sure your mum gets one of 'em, or she'll give both to you and Joan.'

'Is she sleepin'?'

'Like a baby.' She looked thoughtful for a moment. 'Daft expression that. Sleepin' like a baby? Made up by someone who'd never been near one I suppose.' At which point the sound of several babies from the huts opposite filled the air.

'See what I mean?'

Elsie grinned.

'So how is Auntie Win? Still tellin' everyone how to run their lives?'

'Yeah.'

'I bet she loves it in the ATS. Especially now she's an officer, I hear.'

'Yeah, she does. She thinks Joan should join.'

'Joan needs a family of her own.'

'She's got one.'

'Nah. Her own children.'

'No one'll have her.'

'There's a Jack for every Jill. She needs someone who's a bit older though. More mature.'

'She isn't gonna meet them in a dress shop.'

'Fancy working in a dress shop when you can't even make a dress.'

'She's looking for a sewing-machine. And she can knit.'

'So why ain't you with the others, then?'

Elsie didn't answer.

'Ah. Up to that lark, eh? And you didn't want to blot your copybook on account of goin' to that school?'

Elsie shrugged.

'You're changin', my girl. Don't let 'em teachers knock the spark out of you.'

'No, Gran.'

Elsie tiptoed into the hut and climbed over her mother. Aunt Dolly, the baby and Danny were asleep on the other side. She rejoined Gran with *Anne of Green Gables*.

'Now there's a girl with spark,' said Gran, noticing.

'You know this book?' said Elsie, amazed.

'Course I do. I ain't just a pretty face, you know. Course, I never actually read it, but I've seen a film about her.' She paused. 'Or was it *Rebecca of Sunnybrook Farm*?'

Gran brought her lamp outside so they had more light. Elsie sat next to her and read. She felt shattered. She must have fallen asleep instantly she climbed into bed. She didn't even hear her cousins joining her.

The singing woke Elsie up. Kit and Joyce were awake too. The hut walls didn't go straight up to the roof, so you could hear every word that someone in the next hut was saying. And if you stood on a table, you could even see the people too. Someone had started singing in one of the huts, and gradually each hut had joined in. Elsie began to sing softly, and then she

287

realised her mother was awake too because she could hear her light voice soaring above the others, clear and crystal. Even Joan was singing. There they were, all lying in the dark, singing and listening to everyone else singing, like being in a vast dormitory of music.

'Mum,' she heard her cousin, Kit, say. 'It's like Christmas, ain't it?'

Three

'Not 'ere?' said Elsie's mother. She was exhausted.

They were standing outside one of the many long army huts in a field. The squatters were homeless people who had been bombed out. Several families lived in each hut with curtains pulled across to give them a little privacy. Elsie could see that Joan was quite shocked.

'But where is she?' Joan blurted out. 'I've knitted baby clothes for her.'

'They had a bit of luck. Got better accommodation. Moved there two weeks back.'

'Where?' asked Mrs Hollis.

'Near Midden Wood Farm. Know it?'

She shook her head.

He gave Mrs Hollis a cup of tea in an enamel mug.

'You drink that up. I'll see if I can find someone to give you directions.'

'But why didn't she tell us?' Joan said.

289

'No need, love,' said Elsie's mother. 'She knew we'd come 'ere, our first Saturday of the season. And she knew someone would tell us where to find her.' She took a gulp of the tea. 'I just hope it's not too far to walk. This baby is slowing me down. Still, at least it's off me lungs.'

'Off yer lungs?' Elsie exclaimed. 'What would it be doing on yer lungs, Mum?'

Her mother squeezed her hand. 'It's not serious, love. It's just when the baby's big it seems to press on your lungs and make it difficult to take a breath. Once it drops there's more space to breathe.'

'You make it sound like a scone.'

'What are you talking about?' said Joan, crossly.

'Dropped scones,' said Elsie. 'Come to think of it, what is a dropped scone?'

'Oh shut yer mouth,' snapped Joan.

'Joanie,' said her mother softly, 'what is it?'

'I miss Kitty,' she said, and she burst into tears. 'And I wanted to see her. And she never writes to me.'

'You never write to her,' pointed out Elsie.

'All right, Elsie,' said her mother, frowning.

'And I know you're family and everything.'

'But Kitty's the only one left of your family?'

Joan nodded. 'I 'aven't hurt your feelings, have I?'

'Course not.'

'I just got all excited, and now she's not here.'

'We'll find her.'

A young woman holding a baby appeared with the young man who had given her mum the tea. 'This is Lorna,' he said. 'She's a friend of Kitty's.'

She was holding a piece of paper. 'I've drawn it all out for you,' she said. 'You're her Aunt Ellen, ain't you?'

Elsie's mother nodded. 'How is she?'

'She's fine. Lucky thing.' She glanced back at the long hut. 'I'm glad we're not right up by the stove now with this heat, but come winter I'd give up the privacy to be the other end of our hut.' And she smiled.

'Is it your first?' asked Elsie's mother.

'Second. The other one's sleepin'. I hope. Yours looks due any moment.'

'Yeah.' Elsie's mother sighed. 'Looks like I'm starting all over again, eh, Elsie?' Elsie cast her eyes up to the heavens. 'The subject of babies don't do a lot for her.'

The young woman laughed. 'You wait,' she said, smiling. 'One day it will.'

'Oh no it won't. Not ever,' said Elsie firmly.

Kitty and husband, Frank, lived in a field near a hop farm a mile away. Instead of rows of long dismal army huts, at the end of the field was a row of red and green railway carriages. Outside the carriages were similar fires to the ones they had outside their hopping huts, with poles neatly hanging across them and black kettles dangling from them. In the centre of the field was a huge bomb crater, big enough for a double-decker bus to fall into, now used for large bonfires.

Children were playing in the field and Elsie noticed there were efforts to put pretty curtains up at the windows of the carriages. And then she saw her tall, fair-haired cousin sitting outside the door of one, breast-feeding a tiny red-haired baby.

'Kitty!' Joan cried, and she ran wildly towards her sister.

'Me hands aren't free,' laughed her sister, but Joan had flung her arms round Kitty and the baby.

'Let me look at you,' said Kitty, beaming.

Joan stood back and stared at the baby in her sister's arms.

'I can't take it in,' said Joan. 'You being a mum. It don't seem real.'

'Neither can I. I don't feel grown-up at all.'

'May I?' Elsie's mother said.

'Course you can.'

'I'll wind him for you.' And, to Elsie's disgust, her mother took the tiny infant in her arms. She watched the small head fall into the crook of her mother's neck, as her mother gently tapped his back.

'So what's he called then?'

'Alan. After Dad.'

'That's nice, love,' said Mrs Hollis, smiling. 'My sister would have liked that.'

'Can I see inside?' Elsie asked, taking her mother's hand. She could see a two-hour chat about nappies and matinée jackets looming over the horizon.

'Go ahead.'

They all followed Elsie through the door. There was a small hole at one end of the roof.

'Frank's goin' to put some kind of chimney up through there. We got hold of an old stove!' she said, excitedly. 'It burns wood. And there's plenty round 'ere. We've even got a proper address. 1, The Carriages, Tiddenden Field.'

'You're lucky havin' someone who's good at woodwork for a husband,' commented Mrs Hollis. 'Is he still goin' to be a teacher?'

'Oh yeah. He starts trainin' in two weeks. He reckons he'll get a job straight after he's finished. They're cryin' out for woodwork teachers.'

Elsie suddenly couldn't bear it any longer. She wanted to see Harry again, and she was afraid they wouldn't be back in time for when the men turned up. And she was bored.

It was late afternoon when they arrived back at the huts. Elsie was running towards the field where the boys played football when she met her father carrying a bucket of water from the communal tap. They stopped in their tracks and stared at each other.

'Hello, Dad. Is Harry with Doug, Mike and Albert?'

'Yeah. Settled in?'

'Yeah. It's lovely.'

'How's Mum?'

'Slow.'

'At pickin'?'

'At walkin'. It's that baby.'

'Oh. That baby, eh?'

'Yeah.'

They stared at each other awkwardly. Elsie suddenly felt tongue-tied.

'I'll get some tea on for her then,' said her dad at last.

Elsie nodded. 'See yer then,' she said awkwardly, and she turned away quickly so he wouldn't see how disappointed she was at him not giving her a hug.

'Harry!' she yelled. 'Harry.'

To her delight, he whirled round and came racing towards her.

'Guess what. They want me in the junior football team at work. So they got to be nice to me now or else.'

'I knew you'd beat 'em. Can I join in? Please.'

Harry turned to Albert. Albert nodded.

Exhilarated, Elsie raced into the middle of the field and kept her eyes firmly fixed to the ball. At first she leaped around and ran up and down the field, thrilled at last to be one of the lads. But after a while she noticed that occasionally the ball was passed to her out of politeness, and she had the uneasy feeling that she was only allowed in under sufferance. She stayed because she wanted to win them round. At the end of the game they raced off to the river. Suddenly

Harry stopped and looked back at her.

'You comin'?'

Elsie hesitated. 'I'd like to, but Mum wants me to go to the village shop to get some extra bread and potatoes,' she lied.

'Oh,' said Harry.

'Come on!' yelled her cousins from up the lane.

Elsie could see Harry wanted to go with them but didn't want to hurt her feelings. 'I'll see you later,' she said brightly.

Harry grinned. 'Yeah.' And he turned tail and ran.

Elsie watched him go and then headed back to the huts. She was in the way there too. Her dad and mum seemed to have lots to talk about. And all the women and older girls around the huts were getting themselves dolled up for going out to the pub that evening.

That night there was a big singsong in the cook-house. One of the men had brought a piano down in the back of the lorry. Another had brought his accordion.

In the morning it was Sunday-best wear. The Salvation Army sang in one field, a Catholic priest stood in another field with a white cloth over a table for an altar, and a clergyman led an Anglican service

296

in another. After the services, there was the mile walk to the baker's, where they queued to get their roast dinners put in the oven for a fee. Then it was off to the nearest pub, dinner picked up at two p.m., and the mile trek to the huts again, with it cooling on the way. Before long the day was over, and the women and children were waving goodbye to the trucks and lorries carrying their menfolk away. And then it was a supper of potatoes in the embers of the fires and an early night, ready for the next morning and the start of another week of hopping. Elsie's first and last.

One afternoon Elsie went to play down by the river with the other children, and she enjoyed herself. But as soon as they knew she was only there for the week, she could see by the look in their eyes that she was set apart. So she returned to helping her mother who now, at Gran's insistence, took the occasional nap with the little ones while her older cousins and aunts and Herman covered for her.

In spite of Joan's lack of interest, Herman always said good morning to her and good afternoon, and managed to find stray hops to fling in their bin. In a funny sort of way, he reminded Elsie of Harry. It was his optimism. His happiness acted like a protection against rebuff. Once she heard her mother ask him what he did before the war, before he joined the German army. She imagined he must be a teacher from his cultured ways.

'Just a schoolboy. I joined up at seventeen. Eight years ago now.'

And Elsie noticed Joan look up briefly before returning to picking, head bowed again.

'Schoolboy. Soldier. Labourer. My life so far.' And he laughed.

On Saturday afternoon Elsie walked to Whitbread Farm, where she had heard a group of actors and actresses would be performing *Twelfth Night*.

There were no chairs. Everyone sat on the grass, as they did at the church services and the magic lantern shows.

'I don't understand a bleedin' word of this,' she heard a woman mutter next to her.

Elsie didn't understand it much either. But every now and then a strange phrase would make her scalp tingle as though something magical had brushed her unseen, or the actors' antics would make her laugh. So it was worth sitting there on the lumpy ground and getting through the dull bits.

As soon as the performance was over, there was a mass exodus for the pub. Elsie stayed sitting on the grass and watched the actors pack up. It was dusk when she left them. She knew she must make her way back to the huts quickly, before it got too dark. Without a torch she wouldn't be able to see a thing. It was a relief when she spotted the oast house nearest to their huts.

The evening was cool now, but as she drew nearer the oast house door, she could feel the warmth of the fires underneath the nets where the hops were dried. Being nosey, she peered in and was just about to leave when she noticed a boot lying on the far end of the floor. She decided to go in for a closer look.

A man was lying there. The fumes of the oast were heady. She grabbed hold of him under the arms and pulled, but however hard she tried she couldn't budge him. She slapped his face, but he wouldn't wake up. And then she began to gasp. Her eyes stinging, she staggered and took in deep breaths. She remembered hearing about how they burnt brimstone and that the gas was poisonous. She knew she must get help quickly. She lurched out of the oast house and along the dark path towards the huts, stopping every now and then to yell out for help. But there seemed to be no one around. They were probably all out at the pub.

Gasping, she stopped again and put her hands on her hips. She threw back her shoulders and, remembering what Annie Duncan said about how not to speak high if she wanted volume, she took a deep breath, lowered her voice and shouted out as loud as she could, 'Help!'

'What is it?' said a male voice from the trees behind her.

Elsie gave a scream. Hidden under one of the trees was a small bivouac, with Herman's head peering out of it.

'Quick!' she cried. 'The oast house. The man. I can't wake him.'

Herman was such a fast runner that he held her hand tightly to help her run faster.

'Wait here!' he ordered when they reached the oast house. 'Don't come in.'

Elsie stood impatiently in the light that spilled out, looking around urgently for anyone else who might be able to help them. Inside she could hear Herman making grunting noises.

'What's taking him so long?' she muttered to

herself. She wanted to go in and help, but she knew she would be in the way. At last, she heard him getting closer to the door. And then he was at the doorway, swaying and gasping for breath. Gradually, painstakingly, Herman dragged the unconscious man out through the doors and on to the ground. He had hardly laid him down when he keeled over on top of him.

At first Elsie stood there, stupefied. Using all her strength, she hauled Herman off the other man and shook his shoulders, yelling out his name. But there was no response. 'Now what am I going to do?' She stood up and began yelling and yelling and yelling. And then she heard the sound of voices, and to her utter relief she saw a cluster of torchlights swaying precariously from side to side coming down the lane, accompanied by the raucous singing of 'Nellie Deane'.

Four

Elsie woke to the sound of her mother laughing hysterically.

'Give over,' Elsie heard her dad say.

'I can't help it. It's the funniest thing.' Her mother's body shook.

Elsie was sandwiched between her mum and Joan. With the extra people in the hut they were jammed solidly together. If one person turned, everyone had to turn.

'It's only temporary,' he muttered.

'Only temporary,' she snorted. 'I've heard that before.'

'It's just to get them out of a fix.'

'It's the funniest thing,' she repeated.

'You go on laughing like that,' Gran barked from her special bed above them, 'you'll 'ave that baby 'ere.'

'Oh dear,' Mrs Hollis whimpered, wiping her eyes.

'What's the funniest thing?' Elsie enquired.

'Don't ask,' said her mother.

'Is this joke going to be shared?' yelled Aunt Dolly from a corner somewhere.

'No,' said Elsie's dad, firmly.

'It's something private we discussed in the woods last night.'

'I see,' said Gran.

'I don't,' said Aunt Dolly.

'Private is as private does,' said Gran. 'Now come on, Elsie. Fill us in on Herman.'

Elsie spilled out the entire story to an eager audience. An ambulance had taken both men away. One of the ambulancemen had said that Herman had saved the other man's life. He was a hero. There was such a commotion that Elsie had got away with not being told off for wandering off on her own that night. Everyone now bombarded her with questions, except, Elsie noticed, for Joan.

It was much later, when the church service had finished, that she and Joan overheard someone say that an ambulance would be bringing Herman back that morning. To Elsie's surprise, Joan suddenly grabbed Elsie's hand and dragged her away. 'Come with me,' she said.

'Where to?'

'To that place you said. Where Herman sleeps.'

'The tent?'

'Yes.'

'Why?'

'I don't want to be seen on me own anywhere near there, see? Promise me you'll come. Please? Don't leave me.'

Elsie thought her cousin was going mad, but from the strange look on her face she decided to comply. On the way there Joan kept stopping to pick flowers until she had made up a beautiful posy of wild red, blue, yellow and white flowers. Then she thrust them into Elsie's hands. 'Give 'em to him.'

'Why don't you?'

'Because I don't want him to know they're from me,' she said fiercely. 'You won't tell him, will you?'

'No.'

'You promise?'

'I promise.'

They headed for the woods. Already they could see a small crowd had gathered near his tent.

'Nosey parkers,' commented Joan.

What are you, then? thought Elsie. And then Joan

stopped and she suddenly looked distraught. 'You don't suppose,' she began hoarsely. 'You don't suppose he's dead?'

'There he is!' yelled a boy.

A beat-up old Morris car was bumping over the tracks towards them, driven by a WVS woman in her green uniform. To Elsie's amazement, when Herman stepped out, instead of the crowd breaking into applause, or shaking his hand, they just stared at him and gave him a nod, and then gradually began to disperse. The car drove away, leaving Herman standing there blinking, half dazed in the sunlight in a pair of old trousers, the braces over a button-up vest.

'Oh blow this!' said Joan, with a great surge of anger in her voice. She snatched the posy from Elsie, pushed her way through the hoppers and thrust the flowers into Herman's hands. Then she abruptly turned on her heels and, red-faced, chin held high, she marched back past Elsie. Open-mouthed, Elsie stared after her furious figure stamping forcefully along the lane. When she turned round, Herman was burying his face in the flowers. And then he looked over Elsie's shoulder and beyond, beaming.

'Beautiful!' she heard him murmur.

But Elsie didn't know whether he meant the flowers or Joan.

It was later that afternoon when the bombshell dropped. Elsie knew that she and Joan were to travel back that evening with her father and Harry. They were all sitting on the grass outside the public area of the village pub. Elsie was sipping lemonade, making it last, and keeping a look out for stray glasses. You got a shilling when you took them back.

'But you're always saying what a classy job it is,' she heard her mother saying. 'You don't want to risk losing it, do you?'

'I don't know, but I do know I don't want to go back tonight. I want to be near Kitty for a while longer. I want to be here till the end of the season. I've never done that. I want to be like the others. I want to be at the party and get thrown in the bins on the last day. I want to stay.'

There was a silence. Elsie sensed there was another reason too.

'But you have to have at least two or three to a bin,' her mother said eventually. 'You'd never get a bin to yourself. You're not a fast enough picker.'

'There'll still be two of us, with you.'

'That's what I wanted to tell you, Joan. I'm goin' back tonight with Uncle John.'

Elsie almost choked on her drink. She whirled round. 'Is it because of that baby?' she said, alarmed. 'You're not gonna have it yet, are you?'

'No.'

'Then why?' Joan asked.

'I want to be there to see Elsie back to school. Get 'er uniform sorted out. Get 'er settled in.'

'And then you'll come back next weekend?'

'Possibly, but it might not be till the weekend after that.'

'Oh? Why?'

'Your uncle's accepted a bit of part-time work to help someone out of a jam.'

Suddenly Elsie's father scrambled to his feet. 'Another one?' he said hurriedly. 'All round? Harry?' he yelled across the green.

Harry waved back from the gang of boy cousins.

'Another lemonade, you lot?'

'Yeah,' they yelled back. 'Ta.'

Her dad collected up the empty glasses and disappeared.

Elsie felt relieved. She had had no idea she had been worried about getting all her school kit together on her own until she realised that her mum would be helping out.

'Then you could come down weekends till the season's over, with Elsie,' said her mother, smiling.

'I'm stayin',' said Joan, quietly.

'I don't want to see your heart broken, love.'

'I don't have a choice, Auntie Ellen.'

'You're certain?'

'Ever so.' And she smiled, looking, Elsie thought, all soft.

Elsie's mother nodded. 'We'll sort it out. Get Minnie to help you on your bin.'

'Thanks, Auntie Ellen.'

Elsie gazed at them, mystified.

'So what's this job Dad's doin'?' Elsie interrupted, before there was a danger of mushiness creeping into the conversation. Her mother began laughing.

'Well?' said Elsie.

'Oh dear. It's the funniest thing.'

Elsie and Joan looked at each other and raised their eyes. They knew they would get no sensible answer from her now.

It was a long journey home, a truck ride with all the men and boys back to London, where they were dropped near London Bridge railway station, and then a series of train journeys to Winford. Elsie's father had allowed her to travel back in her boys' clothes. It wasn't till they all stumbled, exhausted, on to Winford station platform in the middle of the night that her father suddenly placed his hands on Elsie's shoulders and looked at her directly, so directly that Elsie thought he was about to break her some bad news.

'Now, you know I like a straight, no-nonsense answer, don't you, when I ask a question?'

'Yes, Dad,' said Elsie, wondering what she had done wrong.

'You liked being in that *Pink String and Sealing Wax*, then?

'Yes, Dad.'

'That's all I need to know.'

Mystified, Elsie and her family all trooped out of the station towards the High Street, her father dragging their hopping box on wheels along the pavement.

'Dad, there won't be any buses this late,' she said,

wondering why they hadn't gone the other way, over the bridge.

'Got a call to make.'

'Mum,' said Elsie, 'where are we going? What's going on?'

'You'll see soon enough.'

To Elsie's utter astonishment, they stopped outside the door to Mr and Mrs Neville's flat and rang the bell.

'Dad, he'll kill you,' Elsie whispered.

The door opened. Mr Neville towered above them, the usual cigarette in hand, looking tired but distinguished. 'Ah, John.'

Elsie's father gently took hold of Elsie's hand and stood her in front of him. Elsie was deeply hurt and humiliated. Was he trying to make sure that Mr Neville would never use her again?

Mr Neville peered down at her. 'Elsie? Is that Elsie?'

'Yes, sir.'

He stood up to his full height again and beamed. 'Perfect. Couldn't be better. A perfect Teddy.'

Utterly perplexed, Elsie watched Mr Neville and her father shake hands, as if making a deal.

'Thank you,' said Mr Neville. 'That's a great weight off my mind. I'll contact Miss Castleford in the morning to see if she'll give permission.' As he was about to step back inside he noticed Harry. 'Is this another Hollis?'

'Oh, no,' said Harry, backing away. 'Not me.'

'Pity.' And he gave a laugh. I'll see you tomorrow, Mr Hollis.'

Elsie's father gave a nod and the door was closed. Then, without further explanation, he turned on his heels and headed back up the High Street again, Elsie running to keep up with him.

'Dad, what's going on?'

'You're going to be in the next play. It's called *The Farmer's Wife*. They need someone to play a ten year old boy. You're him. Unless your headmistress says otherwise. You might have to miss a bit of school,' he said, glancing across her head to her mother. 'Because of rehearsals. But it's all education, ain't it?'

Elsie looked at her mother who was still smiling.

'It's true, is it then? I'm goin' to be in a play again?' she squealed.

Her mother nodded. 'I'm so proud of you.'

'But when?'

'Rehearsals start this week. You're only in Act III, so they won't need you till Thursday.'

It wasn't until they reached the bridge that she remembered Mr Neville's last remark. 'Dad, what did Mr Neville mean when he said he'd see you tomorrow?'

Five

'All alone in the world?'

Elsie leaned over the rail. She was watching *Arsenic and Old Lace* from the gods with her mother and Harry. Ralph was playing yet another elderly man, an American called Mr Gibbs. He was sitting with Annie Duncan and Eloise Neville, who were now in the roles of two dotty sisters who regularly murdered old men and buried them in the cellar. Having just discovered that Mr Gibbs had 'no family', the ominous 'What, all alone in the world?' was their cue to add him to their list of victims. Unaware of his plight, he was about to drink a glass of elderberry wine laced with arsenic.

'Oh no!' Elsie heard her mother whisper.

Suddenly the nephew of the elderly sisters, noticing what was going on, leaped to his feet and proceeded to wave his arms wildly. *'Get out of here! Do you want to be poisoned?'* he yelled. *'Do you want to be killed? Do you want to be murdered?'*

Ralph, looking terrified, fled the stage.

'Weren't he good?' Elsie whispered. 'I wish Dad could've seen him.'

'He probably has done,' her mother whispered. 'From backstage.'

Her father was going to appear in all the Winford performances of *Arsenic and Old Lace*. But he refused to tell them what he would be doing. 'I want it to be a surprise.'

'His debut,' said her mother, and she hid her mouth in her hand.

'Is he the dead body in the window seat?' said Elsie, in the first interval.

'No. Least, I don't think so.'

When the curtain rose for Act II, they peered down again, looking intently for him. When every new person walked on stage they leaned a little further forward. After a while, Elsie was so carried away by the play that she forgot he was going to be in it. It wasn't until the end of Act III that she suddenly remembered him again.

Through the loud applause, Elsie yelled out, 'Where's Dad?'

'Dunno, love. It's a mystery.'

314

'Perhaps he chickened out,' said Harry, in a mock American accent.

The curtain was now rising again and the cast stood there, taking their bows. Suddenly they parted in the middle, and from out of the cellar door came twelve elderly men, the victims of the two old ladies. As they joined hands in a line at the front of the stage, there was uproar. The laughter and applause from the packed auditorium was deafening.

'There he is!' yelled Elsie, pointing frantically. 'Sixth from the left.'

His hair was white, his face covered in wrinkles, and he had a drooping, grey moustache.

'Dad's smiling,' said Harry, amazed.

'They all are,' said Mrs Hollis.

Not surprising, as the audience was so appreciative. Elsie felt so happy she could have howled. In two weeks she would be back on that stage, opening in *The Farmer's Wife*, playing a boy! And Mr Neville hadn't even heard her read the part. Dad would have his wish at last. He would see her being a boy.

When everyone started to leave the theatre, her mother gently touched her arm. 'Let's stay for a bit. I want to avoid the crowds, love.'

'We'd better move soon, Mum,' she said anxiously. 'If you want to reach the foyer before they lock up.'

'Harry, you go on ahead and make sure they don't.'

'Do I have to?' he said, looking embarrassed.

'I'll go,' said Elsie.

Her mother looked hesitant. And then she nodded. Elsie had hardly reached the aisles when her mother called out, 'Do you really want to see Annie Duncan tonight?'

Elsie swung round, alarmed. 'Mum, you promised!'

'Yeah, yeah, yeah. But not for long, eh?'

Once through the doors, Elsie leaped down the steps. She spotted the commissionaire in the foyer. 'Excuse me, sir,' she began.

'Elsie Hollis! Your brother was good tonight. Bigger role, eh?'

'Yes. No younger though.'

He laughed. 'You look worried about something,' he said, noting Elsie's jigging up and down.

'It's me mum. She's a bit slow comin' down on account of the baby inside her.'

The commissionaire looked alarmed.

'Oh no, she's not having it for ages. It's just she's a bit, well, enormous. And it's taking her for ever. And she's worried the doors will be locked.'

'Don't you worry, little Elsie.'

'Where were you? Mum needs a hand.' Harry had come up to her.

Immediately the commissionaire swept up the stairs and escorted Elsie's mother down like royalty.

'I shouldn't really be 'ere,' she said apologetically. 'But with two of the family in the play tonight, I didn't want to miss it.'

Elsie was bursting to get to Annie's dressing-room. But her mother moved at a snail's pace.

As soon as they reached the stage door, she rushed inside.

'Elsie?' gasped Wilfred.

'Miss Duncan hasn't left yet, has she?'

'That's some haircut you've got there. No, she hasn't left yet.'

'Mum? Come and meet her.'

'No, thanks,' said her mother, shyly. 'Anyway, I don't think I could make it up them steps. You go on.'

Elsie leaped up to the swing doors, raced along to dressing-room one, and knocked on the door.

Eloise Neville opened it.

'Good evening,' said Elsie, politely. 'Could I see Miss Duncan, please.'

Annie was already thrusting her head round the doorway. 'Hello, poppet,' she said, and then she gawped at Elsie's haircut.

'Please, don't say anything, because I've heard it all before. And I can't explain now because my mother said I have to be quick. She's a bit tired because of that wretched baby.'

'That poor maligned infant,' commented Eloise Neville. 'Cursed before it's even born.'

'Where is she?'

'At the stage door.'

'Waiting for your father, eh?'

'Yes.'

'That was a turn-up for the books.'

'You can say that again,' laughed Elsie.

'How was the hopping?'

Elsie presented her black-stained hands.

'Ouch!'

'They don't hurt any more. I've being trying to get it off with a pumice stone, but it's not had any effect yet.'

'Think you could do a Kentish accent for me?'

'Yeah. Course I could.'

'Might come in useful for *The Farmer's Wife*.'

'Are you goin' to be in it too?' asked Elsie, excitedly.

'Yes. And I heard your headmistress has given permission.'

'Yeah. Good, eh?'

'Come on,' she said, taking Elsie's hand. Annie swept her down the corridor, through the swing doors and down the steps. Elsie's mother looked up at them and blushed. Elsie suddenly realised that her mother was in awe of Annie, as if Annie Duncan was a film star or something.

Annie held out a hand. 'I'm Annie,' she said. 'I'm so pleased to meet you. I've heard lots of lovely things about you.'

They shook hands.

'I'm afraid it'll take quite a bit of time for your husband to get all that make-up off, so why don't you put your feet up in our dressing-room?'

'Will it really take some time?' said Elsie's mother, anxiously.

'There's twelve of them queuing up with two ASMs and a tub of removing cream. It depends where he is in the queue.'

319

'Oh, I see.'

'You look done in.'

'May I have a word. In private?'

'You're not gonna ask her questions about me, are you?' said Elsie, worried.

'No, Elsie. Nothin' about you at all. Women's talk.'

'You two wait down here,' said Annie.

Wilfred leaned out of the cubby-hole. 'Fancy a cuppa you two?'

Harry and Elsie glanced at one another and grinned. 'Yeah!'

Elsie and Harry hovered outside dressing-room eight. They knocked again but there was so much chatter and laughter coming from inside that the knock was pathetic in comparison.

'Did you see that bloke in the third row! I thought he'd fall over, when we come on.'

Harry and Elsie gazed at one another. 'Dad!' they chorused.

He sounded as though he was actually enjoying himself.

'It's no good, Elsie,' said Harry. 'We'll just have to open the door. They'll never hear us through this racket.'

320

Elsie turned the handle, but there was someone leaning against the door. She gave it a push.

' 'Ere, what's goin' on?' A man with a red-brick face smeared in removing cream peered out at them.

'What do you nippers want?'

'Me dad,' said Elsie. 'Mr Hollis.'

'What's 'is first name?'

'John.'

There was a yelling of, 'John. John Hollis.'

Eventually their father, still grey-haired and moustached, appeared. He was grinning. 'Well? What did yer think? Do all right, did I?'

'You were smashin', Dad,' said Harry, eagerly. 'You got the biggest laugh of the night.'

'No! Really?' he said, with an attempt at nonchalance.

'Yeah!'

'Where's your mum? At the stage door? Bit much for her to come all the way up 'ere, I suppose? You could touch the moon from this dressing-room.'

'That's what we've come to tell you,' said Elsie. 'She's having a baby.'

'Elsie, I've known that for months.'

'Now, Dad. In dressing-room one.'

In an instant there was silence and several men's faces appeared haloed round her father's head.

'Don't you worry, mate,' said a voice from behind his stunned face. 'We'll stand by you.'

By the time the district nurse arrived, the corridor outside dressing-room one was packed with every member of the cast. Unperturbed, she swept calmly through them, like Moses parting the Red Sea. The door was closed firmly.

It was like a railway station. There were people crammed in dressing-room two and the kitchen, in addition to those walking up and down the corridor, Elsie's father included. The other eleven 'dead' men took turns to put their arms round his shoulders or pat his back, or regale him with their birth-stories.

Elsie had been dying to see Annie Duncan and now, not only was she ousted from her dressing-room, but that blimmin' baby was in there instead of her. Suddenly the most extraordinary sound broke the chatter. The sound of a newborn's first cry.

For a moment no one moved, and then the men made way for Elsie, her father, Harry and Ralph along the corridor.

They hovered outside the door. At last it opened, and the district nurse appeared with a tiny, towelled bundle in her arms. 'Mr Hollis?' she said, peering out at the crowd.

'That's me,' said Elsie's father, a catch in his voice.

'I believe this belongs to you.' And she placed the baby in his arms.

Everyone surged round him and peered over his shoulder, grinning. 'What you gonna call him?' said one of the men, suddenly.

'I'll name 'im after the chap who wrote this *Arsenic and Old Lace* play, so we'll always remember this day. Joseph, aint it?'

'That's right,' exclaimed a voice behind them. It was Ralph.

'I'm afraid it'll have to be Josephine,' said the district nurse. 'It's a girl.'

Elsie watched her father's face, riveted. But he was beaming at the baby. In fact, he couldn't take his eyes off her.

'Josephine,' he murmured. 'Josie. Josie Hollis.'

The district nurse had just closed the door to tend to Elsie's mum when they heard her say, 'How lovely to have been born into such a big family.'

323

'Do you have a large one too then, Nurse Wilson?' Mrs Hollis asked.

'No family at all, I'm afraid.'

'What,' they heard Annie exclaim in a dazed voice, 'All alone in the world?'

At which point the entire cast of *Arsenic and Old Lace* collapsed into helpless laughter. 'For pity's sake,' yelled a male voice from the end of the corridor. 'Don't touch the elderberry wine!'

Six

She hadn't grown at all. At least if she had, it didn't notice. Her school uniform was as voluminous as ever. Sitting by the window, her gymslip flapped round her shins in spite of the mammoth hem, which made the box-pleats look misshapen. She had chosen a window seat because she wanted to think. It meant she could look away from the other girls without appearing to avoid their horrified glances. She was trying to sort out in her mind what not to tell Geraldine, so that she wouldn't upset her by letting her know how much of the holiday she had actually enjoyed. She would have to say that she only did *Pink String and Sealing Wax* to be away from Marjorie Bush, that the theatre was desperate for anyone local, that the wedding was really boring and she must only talk about the uncomfortable side of hop-picking.

The thought of Marjorie Bush made her feel sick. Still, she didn't have to worry about her till she went home. She glanced down at her hands, now encased in woollen gloves even though the sun was streaming in through the bus windows. Why were the first days of being back at school in the autumn term so often the best part of the summer?

'She's so brown, she looks like a gypsy,' she heard someone remark from a seat across the other side of the gangway. But red was the colour Elsie thought she must look. Red-faced from the heat of her school blazer, red-faced with embarrassment at her appearance.

'And I must not tell her about Monday night,' she murmured to herself. How Mr Neville had offered her father a cigar. How there was nowhere to put Josie, so that people took turns to hold her. How there was the most extraordinary party afterwards, that it was years since a baby had been born in a theatre. In fact, no one could remember a baby being born in the Palace Theatre ever.

It wasn't until Elsie spotted the tall, sprawling, imposing building through the bus window and the wide steps leading up to the high arched entrance, that she suddenly realised what she was doing.

Did she want to spend the whole of the term telling Geraldine white lies, either watching what she said to avoid being insensitive to Geraldine's already damaged feelings, or trying desperately to cheer her up? Swinging from being subdued to being a clown? She still suspected that if she suggested Geraldine talk to a housemistress or Miss Dunstable, she would argue, 'What good would that do?' And, to be honest, Elsie didn't know either. But maybe a grown-up could listen to her in a different way. Elsie decided to give her one last chance. If Geraldine still wouldn't talk to a teacher then she, Elsie, would do it for her. It might cost their friendship, the only friendship she had. Not true. She had made friends at the theatre, hadn't she? And with Jessica? No, she said sternly to herself. She had heard her gran once say, 'Start as you mean to go on.' It was better to be alone and not feel guilty for being happy, than have a friend who wanted you to believe that all life was awful.

Then she remembered the baby. She didn't know what to make of the baby. She didn't love her. How could she? She was a small person she didn't know. But she didn't hate her either. After all, it wasn't Josie's fault she was born. Elsie still hadn't held her, but she had taken a quick peek at her now and then, when she was asleep. Tiny, with black hair, she had an amazing grip, as Elsie discovered, when she accidentally let her little finger drift in the direction of her sister's hand.

By the time Elsie tumbled out of the bus with the other girls, she was determined to do something about Geraldine. She searched intently through the crowd for her, half wanting to see her, half dreading it. She spotted Alice having an animated conversation with a short, dumpy, curly-haired girl. From the little Elsie had overheard, the girl had stayed with Alice on the Isle of Wight and they were obviously picking up from where they had left off. They looked like bosom pals now. Alice didn't even appear to notice Elsie.

A teacher was ushering them all into the large hall. The new first years were lined up at the front, looking shy and bewildered. Elsie's form were lined up behind them.

Elsie wondered if the last one and a half months had been a dream, or whether that was what was real and this huge Gothic building with its waxed floors, its portraits on the walls, its high ceilings, its trophies in cabinets was the dream. Sitting on a wooden bench, sandwiched between the other second-formers, she peered round for Geraldine. She couldn't look for her too conspicuously because she kept finding everyone staring at her, and trying to edge away from her as if she was diseased. So Elsie kept her gaze firmly ahead.

Miss Castleford was sitting on the stage, with the other teachers in their tweed suits flanked on either side of her. Miss Dunstable was sitting at the end. She was staring at Elsie, but she appeared friendly.

Miss Castleford welcomed the new girls, gave a potted history of the school and talked of the honour of being a Winford Grammar School girl, and what was expected of them. And then, to Elsie's horror, she looked directly at her.

'While you girls were enjoying your vacation,' she intoned, 'sailing, or sampling the joys of the beach, or taking brisk walks in the country, one girl in the school chose to extend her education in the artistic field, and after being auditioned by Mr Adrian Neville at the Palace Theatre, was chosen from many other young girls to play the demanding role of Eva in Roland Pertwee's *Pink String and Sealing Wax.*'

By now Elsie's face was burning so much she was convinced she could have fried an egg on it.

'Those of you who were fortunate enough to have seen that production will, I am sure, agree with me that this girl excelled herself, and was an honour to the school.'

No chance of being invisible now, Elsie thought.

'Dedication and self-sacrifice are traits that we have always demanded from our girls.' Here, Elsie noticed that Miss Castleford's voice was wavering. 'But Elsie Hollis has taken these traits to their ultimate. Mr Adrian Neville has again offered Elsie the chance to appear as a boy in the new play at the Palace Theatre, and such is her dedication that she has had all her hair shorn off for the role.'

'Oh thank you, Mr Neville,' Elsie whispered.

'Her beautiful hair. A girl's crowning glory.'

Not that beautiful, thought Elsie.

'For the sake of Truth and Art.' She beamed down at Elsie. 'Elsie. I would like you to take off your hat and come up here on the stage.'

Elsie gawped at her. But Miss Dunstable was smiling and nodding. Elsie checked first that her woolly gloves were still firmly on, removed her velour hat and slowly stood up. A wave of gasps swept through the hall. Trembling, Elsie climbed over the knees of the other girls, walked up the aisle and ascended the steps. Miss Castleford and the staff began clapping, and as

Elsie stood staring down at three hundred girls, they were clapping too. A great cheer broke out, and Elsie couldn't help grinning and enjoying it all. She suddenly realised that if she hadn't decided to change her ways, she would have fought back that smile for Geraldine's sake. Liberated, she gave a bow which raised a huge laugh.

As she left the stage, and Miss Dunstable led her down the steps, she whispered to Elsie, 'I'm doing extracts from *Great Expectations* this term. I'd like you to play Pip. Interested?'

'Yeah,' whispered Elsie. 'I mean, yes, Miss Dunstable, but I don't do elocution.'

'We'll talk about that later.'

As Elsie walked back to her bench, she found the girls had moved up to give her a place at the end.

Form Two was in a classroom overlooking a patch of grass. Beyond it was a sunken tennis court surrounded by high bushes of pink and mauve hydrangeas. Elsie claimed a desk and waited for Geraldine to find her, since she had still failed to spot her.

Miss Digby, their new form mistress, was younger than the other mistresses but, like them, wore a suit. Although her hair was scraped untidily back into a bun and her glasses kept sliding down her nose, as did Elsie's spectacles, she exuded energy. Elsie liked her instantly.

As soon as everyone was settled in their desks, Miss Digby began to call the register. It was then that Elsie realised Geraldine wasn't there. Perhaps she had missed the first day because of illness. Elsie had a dreadful premonition. Suppose Geraldine's father had given her a thumping the day before and the bruises showed?

As soon as Miss Digby closed the register, Elsie put up her hand.

'Yes, Elsie?'

'You forgot to read out Geraldine Brown's name.'

Miss Digby reddened. 'Geraldine won't be returning to Winford Grammar.'

'But she told me in a letter she couldn't wait to get back,' Elsie stammered. 'Is she being put in another class?'

By this time, the teacher's face was scarlet. 'No, Elsie. It's family reasons.'

And then, before Elsie could stop herself, she blurted out, 'Her father hasn't killed her, has he?' She had begun to shake violently.

'No,' said the teacher. 'I believe the family are moving away. Now,' she said hurriedly, 'Anthea, will you hand out the new jotters on the shelf there. I'd like you all to write a composition, the subject being "What I Did in my Holiday".'

At first Elsie stared down at the jotter, her mind as blank as the piece of paper in front of her. Not true. She was blanking out what she shouldn't write down. I'm doing the same thing as I was doing with Geraldine, she thought. Angrily, she pulled off her gloves, revealing her heavily stained hands. But how could you write down seven weeks? Some of the events which happened were too private and special to write down. And she was still too shocked by Geraldine's absence to think coherently. Perhaps Geraldine thought Elsie had deserted her when she didn't write letters back. Finally Elsie began writing, but in a daze.

> *Started holidays in 1880. Saved the lives of the guinea-pigs and my brother, Albert. Went down hopping. Saw Gran. Sung myself to sleep. Helped save a life from an oast house. Heard my sister being born. Read books. Went down the river.*

But still haven't been invited to Dad's
allotment.

It was a jumble of words that didn't make sense, but it was all she could cope with.

The next class was algebra, but Elsie heard nothing of it. At break-time, she was called to the front of the classroom. Miss Digby waited until the other girls had left the room.

'Miss Castleford would like to have a word with you in her study,' she said quickly.

Miss Castleford's study had blue, red and green stained glass in the windows, which were arched like the doors. It was a world of dark wood and books and order. To Elsie's surprise, Miss Dunstable was seated at the front of Miss Castleford's enormous oak desk.

'Sit down, Elsie,' she said, indicating an empty chair.

Elsie had decided she would reveal her hop-stained hands, in all their glory, in the lap of her gymslip.

Miss Castleford was about to launch into whatever it was she had invited Elsie to talk about when she spotted them. 'Is that tar, Elsie?'

'No, Miss Castleford. It's from the hops.'

Miss Castleford's face went slightly taut. 'You have been hop-picking?' she asked slowly.

'Yes, Miss Castleford.'

'This is not suitable. This really is not suitable.'

'For research, was it?' Miss Dunstable interrupted. 'For your new role?'

Elsie could see that she was trying to help her out, but Elsie knew she had to make a choice: the truth and the consequences or, lies and tiredness.

'No. The family go hoppin' every year. It's the only chance we get to see each other. And it means Mum can earn a bit of money for me school coat or shoes.'

'I see,' said Miss Castleford, curtly.

'And it's good fun,' added Elsie, firmly.

Out of the corner of her eye she saw Miss Dunstable drop her head slightly.

'Yes, well, the least said on that subject, the better.' Miss Castleford cleared her throat. 'I expect you're wondering why you've been asked to see me.'

'Is it to pull me socks up because of me last report?'

'No. Though that's always a good idea.'

'Is it about Geraldine Brown? Is she ill? Has she caught infantile paralysis?'

Miss Castleford looked startled. She glanced away

335

briefly and then looked squarely into Elsie's face.

'No, Elsie. Nothing like that. I suppose, since we're on that subject . . .' She paused. 'I'm going to ask you some questions, Elsie, and I want you to think about them and answer them truthfully.'

'Yes, Miss Castleford.'

'You were Geraldine's best friend?'

'Yes, Miss Castleford.'

'Did you spend time with her in the holidays?'

'No, Miss Castleford,' said Elsie, guiltily. 'I meant to but the time sort of went too quickly. Me mum was going to write to her mother but she was too busy.'

'So you had no contact at all?'

'Only by letter.'

'Letters,' she repeated awkwardly. 'And what did she tell you in her letters?'

Elsie felt herself redden. 'Private things, really. About her family.'

Very gently, Miss Dunstable took hold of Elsie's hand. 'You see,' said Miss Dunstable, 'the police may need to know.'

'The police!' said Elsie, alarmed.

'Geraldine's father was arrested last week for,' she faltered, 'what he was doing to Geraldine.'

'Did he hurt her really badly this time?' asked Elsie. 'Is she in hospital? She wanted to be in hospital. She said she'd be away from him then.'

She noticed the teachers glancing at one another.

'You'd better tell us all you know, Elsie,' said Miss Castleford.

So Elsie did. The words tumbled out of her in a great wave, and she realised that keeping Geraldine's secret had been just as much a strain on her as it must have been on Geraldine.

'But why didn't she tell us?' asked Miss Dunstable.

'She thought you'd think she'd done something to deserve it.'

'Well, had she?' asked Miss Castleford. 'Did she do anything to provoke this behaviour from her father?'

'No,' said Elsie. 'She did everything she could to make herself invisible. But whatever she did, well, it didn't seem to work. But why are the police interested?'

'All information would be very useful to them, and especially for Geraldine's sake.' She paused. 'But, because of his arrest, it means that Geraldine must leave home for a bit. Be looked after by someone else.'

'And then she's coming back?'

'No, I'm afraid not.'

337

'Why?'

'Because I think it would be very difficult for her to return here with everyone knowing. It will be in the papers, you see.'

'But that means she'll be getting punished for him thumping her.'

There was silence for a moment.

'This thumping, as you call it. Did she go into any details about it?'

Elsie noticed a certain awkwardness in Miss Castleford's manner, and it puzzled her.

'Not really.'

'There's something else I need to ask you, Elsie.'

Miss Dunstable squeezed her hand.

'Were you ever alone with Geraldine's father?'

'Yes, Miss Castleford.'

'And did Mr Brown attempt to thump you too?'

'No. In fact he wanted me to sit on his lap. He was very friendly. Soppy, really.'

'I see. And did you?'

'No fear. I'm not a baby.'

'And where was Geraldine when this was happening?'

'In her room. He'd locked her in there.'

338

'Oh? And why was that?'

'She'd used a certain word.'

The headmistress pursed her lips.

'I see.'

'What was the word?' asked Miss Dunstable.

'I don't think we need to know that, Miss Dunstable.'

'I never found out. Nor did Geraldine.'

'Surely she knew?'

'No. She asked very politely. She said, "I'm sorry I've upset you, Dad, and I apologise for using the word which upset you." And he said, "Which was?" and she said, "I don't know, Dad. Will you tell me so I don't use that word ever again?" And he called her a liar, and other things, and she said, "Please, Dad. Please tell me what the word is." And he just kept saying, "You know, Geraldine." ' Elsie paused. 'She said he often did that. It made her a bit nervous of talking sometimes. He did it with things she did in the house too. He wasn't like it all the time. Just every now and again, when she was off guard. But even when she was on guard he still did it.' She stared at them. 'What do you think he meant? I didn't understand it then. I still don't. What does it mean?'

But when Elsie looked at them for an answer, Miss

Castleford only gazed back at her in silence. And then Miss Dunstable said, 'It means it wasn't her fault. The brute,' she added.

'Miss Dunstable,' cautioned Miss Castleford.

'Well he is, isn't he?'

'That's not for us to judge. The war has unhinged a lot of men.'

'That's no excuse.'

'Perhaps not, but please, Miss Dunstable. Not in front of the child.' She looked troubled. 'If only Geraldine hadn't kept it to herself, some of this might have been avoided. It could have been nipped in the bud.'

'Do you know where she is?' Elsie asked. 'So I can write to her?'

'Elsie, I know this may seem hard, but Geraldine needs to make a fresh start. Go somewhere new. Make new friends.'

'But, Miss Castleford—'

'Those are my instructions. Now,' she said, 'this may be difficult for you to take in at the moment, but I asked you here for quite another reason.' She folded her hands on the table. 'I asked you here because I would like to offer you a special scholarship.'

340

'Oh, yeah?' said Elsie, still too confused by what she had heard to make sense of this. 'Sorry, Miss Castleford. I mean, yes, Miss Castleford.'

'That's better. In fact I can see you could benefit from just this scholarship. Of course, we'll need to talk to your parents. We would like you to have an elocution scholarship so that you can join in the elocution classes.'

'We'd be doing choral verse-speaking, mime, improvisations and scenes from plays. That sort of thing,' added Miss Dunstable.

Elsie was speechless. She didn't really want to talk any differently, but she was sharp enough to know that more doors would be open to her if she could talk like the teachers. And she could always learn it like an accent. Eventually, a feeble, 'Thank you, Miss Castleford,' emerged from her mouth.

'I take it you're pleased, then?'

'Yes, Miss Castleford. Annie Duncan has already been helping me a bit with diction exercises and resonance. That sort of thing.'

'Ah, yes. Annie Duncan. Good, good. That's all, Elsie. I'm glad we had this little chat. Miss Dunstable will take you to the playground.'

As Elsie was about to leave, she suddenly remembered something which felt very important to her. 'Miss Castleford, Geraldine doesn't know. She thinks it's her. Someone's got to tell her.'

'Tell her what, Elsie?'

'What Miss Dunstable said. That it wasn't her fault.'

'Oh, I'm sure she knows that.'

'She won't. I know Geraldine. If you don't tell her, she'll think she's the bad'n, not him.'

'But, Elsie, why on earth should she think that?'

'Because you won't have her back.'

'That's not the reason. It's just—'

'Please!' Elsie begged.

Miss Castleford looked confused for a moment, and then her shoulders collapsed into resigned acceptance.

'I promise I'll write to her, Elsie. That's the least I can do for the girl.'

'And you'll tell her it wasn't her fault?'

'Yes. I'll tell her.'

'That's all right then,' said Elsie. 'After all, she is a Winford Grammar School girl, isn't she?'

'She is indeed.'

342

Miss Dunstable walked down the corridor with her to the playground.

'I should have spoken to someone sooner, shouldn't I? I should have helped her more. I was going to tell someone. This term.'

Miss Dunstable stopped and took her by the shoulders. 'You listened to her. That was something. It's out of your hands now. Go out and play.'

When Elsie stepped out of the corridor into the sunlight, she felt an enormous weight lifted from her shoulders, so much so that she felt ashamed of the relief that flooded her. She stood in a daze, soaking in the warmth of the sun, while everyone seemed to whirl and yell and run around her. The bell rang and she stumbled over to her form's rank of girls.

'Miss Dunstable told me you're joining the elocution class.' A girl, not much bigger than her, with thick, black, wavy hair in plaits, was standing beside her. It was Rebecca Stein. She was smiling, and her smile was infectious.

'Yes,' said Elsie.

She stared at Rebecca. It was strange to think that after a year she hardly knew anything about this girl with the slightly foreign accent. In fact, she hardly knew anything about anyone really. When she had gone to elementary school, before their street was bombed, she was at school with the kids in her street. She knew where they lived. She knew who their brothers and sisters were. And she saw them after school. But the girls at the grammar were names and quirkinesses and the subjects they were good at or bad at.

'Can I sit next to you?' Rebecca asked.

'Yeah. Course you can,' said Elsie, surprised. 'I'll ask Miss Digby.'

Miss Digby gave them permission and to their surprise Elsie and Rebecca got on as if they had known each other for ever. They had the same quick sense of humour, and they were both chatterboxes. In fact, they got on so well that in class Miss Digby threatened to separate them if they didn't both calm down.

In the dinner hall, two of the girls at their table were exchanging stories about their holidays. They had been trying to impress everyone with their exploits about grand goings-on with other equally grand people. Once they had exhausted that subject, they turned to the professions of people's fathers. They pointed at the other tables and made sneering remarks about some of the other girls' fathers. Suddenly, they rounded on Rebecca and said, 'We know what your father is, don't we?'

'Yes,' said Rebecca, simply. 'He's a musician.'

'No he's not,' snapped the girl. 'He's a bus driver.'

'By day,' said Rebecca. 'He's a musician at night.'

'Snap!' said Elsie.

'What do you mean, snap?' said the girl. 'Your father doesn't play music. He works at the paper-mill.'

'By day,' said Elsie.

'Oh, yes? And what does he do at night then, smartypants?'

Elsie beamed at Rebecca. 'He's an actor.'

Seven

There was one more thing Elsie needed to do before the day was over, and that was to challenge Marjorie Bush. Geraldine's sudden disappearance had shocked her deeply. Trying to make oneself invisible was no solution, you only risked injustice and being snuffed out for ever. Elsie was no longer going to be at the receiving end. She knew she was no match for Marjorie Bush and her gang, but today she was going to go out fighting.

As her bus drew nearer to her street, she kept the image of Miss Benson firmly in her mind. She was going to give Marjorie Bush the paper tiger treatment. By the time she spotted the half a dozen children sitting on the wall waiting for her, she didn't need to put on an act any more. She was really angry now. Not just for herself, but for Geraldine too. 'We will not be silenced,' she muttered to herself.

She leaped off the bus and on to the pavement,

346

flinging her bulging satchel and hat on to the ground. She stood, legs astride, opposite the gang. Then, with a great roar of anger, she raised her fists into the air and howled with rage. The group of children stared at her, startled, and one of them fell backwards off the wall. Elsie could hear him whimpering from the other side.

'You want me!' yelled Elsie. 'Then come and get me!'

To Elsie's amazement, two of the children slid off the wall and ran away, and another began to back off.

'Don't you go running off,' she shouted. 'Come 'ere!'

'Steady on,' said a tall, skinny boy. 'I don't want no trouble.'

'But I do,' shrieked Elsie. 'I do want trouble.' And she swung her arms round in circles. 'I've had enough. This is it. No more. I'm not takin' no more from you lot.'

Two more of the gang ran off, leaving the boy on his own. He put his hands up in defence. 'I got no trouble with you,' he protested. 'It's nothin' to do with me.'

At which point Elsie opened her mouth and gave another great roar.

The boy looked even more startled. 'It's Marjorie. We was just doin' what Marjorie told us.'

'Where is she, then?' Elsie swung round and yelled at the wall. 'Come on out, ya yellow-livered *hombre*,' she shouted, remembering a phrase from one of Harry's comics. 'I'm ready for you.' She whisked round quickly in case Marjorie was attempting to creep up from behind.

''Aven't you heard?' stammered the boy.

'Heard what?' Elsie snapped.

'About Marjorie?'

'What you on about? I've no time for this,' said Elsie, throwing her arms about like a demented boxer.

'She's got that infantile paralysis, 'asn't she?'

Elsie stared after him as he ran away, totally deflated, her moment of glory snatched away from her by the very illness Geraldine longed to have. It was all so unfair.

'When?' she suddenly yelled after him. 'And where is she?'

But he was out of hearing.

She found out where the Bush family lived by knocking on doors in the next street. Like their street, it had had its share of bombing, but nothing as devastating. How narrow their worlds were, she thought. For years she had lived so close but there was their street and their world, and the next street was like another planet. It seemed peculiar when her family traipsed all the way to Kent each year to see their relations, yet they seldom popped round the corner.

The house the Bush's lived in was like Elsie's house. Two rooms upstairs and two rooms downstairs, only it was divided up for two families. The Bush's had the downstairs part with the scullery and yard. Elsie knocked at the door. A grubby-faced girl peered out of the front window. Inside, she could hear someone yelling, 'Mum! Mum!' Elsie waited patiently but no one came. She knocked again.

'All right, I'm comin', I'm comin'!' yelled a woman.

The door was flung open, and there stood an even bigger version of Marjorie, only middle-aged and fat, with a black eye. The child at the window was peering round her apron. The woman had a baby in her arms.

'Yeah?' she sighed, looking exhausted. 'Who are you? What d'ya want?'

'I heard about Marjorie. I came to see her.'

'She's not 'ere. I told her not to swim in that river.

She got no consideration. Who are you anyway?' And she suddenly gave a gasp. 'You're that blimmin' Hollis girl? Come round to crow, 'ave you?'

'No,' said Elsie, perplexed.

'Well, she won't want to see you, will she?'

'I just wondered how she was, that's all.'

'She's in some hospital. They won't let you in though. You're not a relative, see.'

'Mum!' came a voice from the kitchen.

Through the hallway Elsie could see three small heads peering out at her. 'What's that toff want?' said a belligerent-looking boy of about eight. 'Wants to know about Marjorie, silly cow,' Mrs Bush murmured under her breath. 'Not you, dear,' she added. 'Marjorie.' She opened the door a little wider. 'You'd best come in. I've got the address of the place writ down on a piece of paper.'

'Is it far away?' asked Elsie, following her down the passage.

'Dunno. I can't go and see 'er with all these nippers, can I?'

'Who has seen her then?'

The woman swung round. 'What's that supposed to mean?'

'Nothing,' said Elsie, quickly. 'I thought perhaps I could ask them.'

'She got nurses and doctors, 'asn't she? Having a bleedin' holiday if you ask me.'

Elsie didn't know whether to feel sorry for her or shocked by her callousness.

The kitchen consisted of a table, four chairs, a range and a bed under the window. A heap of clothes lay draped on the back of one chair in front of the range. Elsie stood awkwardly while the children stared up at her. The woman dumped the baby in the oldest girl's arms. The girl could only have been six years old. 'It's 'ere somewhere.'

Elsie hovered in the doorway while Mrs Bush went into the next room. With the door ajar, Elsie saw one big double bed and a mattress on the floor, and orange-boxes round the sides of the floor filled up with clothing.

Eventually Mrs Bush lumbered out with a scrap of paper.

' 'Ere you are.'

Elsie opened her satchel and scrabbled around for a pencil.

'What yer doin'?'

'I'm just goin' to write it down in my jotter.'

'Why? Keep it.'

'But you'll want it,' stammered Elsie.

'No I won't. There's no one to look after the kids. Me old man won't. I'll 'ave to wait till she gets back.'

Astounded, Elsie folded the piece of paper and tucked it neatly into the inside pocket of her blazer. She was about to step out through the door when she plucked up courage and asked, 'Why does she hate me so much? Is it because I'm small?'

Mrs Bush looked at her as if she was mad. 'You tryin' to be funny?'

'No. She's never told me why, you see.'

'Thought it's obvious.'

'No.'

'It's that,' Mrs Bush said, grabbing the lapel of her blazer. 'That blimmin' uniform.'

'You mean she failed the eleven-plus?'

'Failed it? She came top in her year. Top!' Mrs Bush emphasised angrily. 'We never wanted her to go in for it, but that fancy-mouthed teacher put her up to it behind our backs, didn't she? And she passes with flying colours, don't she? And she gets offered a place, don't she?'

'But you couldn't afford the uniform?' said Elsie, slowly.

'Even if we could, we wouldn't let 'er go. Lot of nonsense. She's the eldest. I can't 'ave her doin' all this book-readin' stuff. I need her to help me with the kids. She'll be fifteen in a couple of years, and then she'll be workin'. Bringin' in a wage-packet. If it hadn't been for this government she'd be working next year.'

And that's when Elsie realised what was so odd about Marjorie Bush's home, how it didn't seem quite right. There was no reading matter about the place, not a book or newspaper in sight. She had always taken it for granted in their home. But in the Bush's home it was like a desert.

'Do you want me to take Marjorie a message?' asked Elsie.

Mrs Bush grew alert and then dissipated into a slumped mound of exhaustion. 'No,' she said, and closed the door.

Walking away, Elsie was aware of a spring in her step. It hadn't been *her* Marjorie Bush had been attacking. It was what Elsie represented. Every time Marjorie Bush set eyes on Elsie, she must have been reminded of what she longed to have, what she had earned even, but could never have. The sight of her must have caused such pain that the only way of relieving it was to try to get rid of the object which caused the pain. 'It's not me,' Elsie said aloud. 'It's not me. It's nothing I said or did. It's just what I do to her. It could've been anyone. Any girl! It's not *me*!'

She noticed two women staring at her as if she had lost her marbles, but Elsie didn't care. She gave a great whoop of delight and then ran crazily down the street, her hat dangling behind her, her satchel banging heavily on her hip from the weight of the textbooks she had to cover in paper that night.

It was quiet when she let herself in through the back door and into the scullery. To her surprise, she heard movement in the kitchen. Perhaps her mother had decided to return home early. She rushed into the room. Mrs Duke was there with Queenie, cooking up a meal on the range.

Elsie stared at them. They looked so out of place in their kitchen.

'Someone looks happy,' Mrs Duke commented.

Elsie smiled and flung down her satchel on to the table. She looked at all the old well-thumbed paperbacks and magazines stacked higgledy-piggledy on the shelf near the wireless, and all the bits of wood her father had whittled away during the evenings. But now she looked at them with new eyes. 'I am happy,' she said.

'Homework tonight?'

'Not much. A bit of reading. And covering books with brown paper. Mum's got it put aside from last term. Where is she?'

'Upstairs. Sleeping. So's the baby.'

'Oh. I thought she was going to stay with you.'

'So did I, but she misses you lot too much. And it is a bit noisy with actors coming in late at night and learning their lines out loud in bed.'

Elsie giggled.

'So we've invaded your home. To help you over this week.'

'And I'll be poppin' in regular like,' said Queenie. ' 'Cause I know Joan's away.'

'So, spill the beans,' said Mrs Duke. 'You look about to explode.'

Mrs Bush was right. Elsie wasn't allowed to visit Marjorie, but as Wednesday was one of the only two visiting days in the week and she was her first visitor, Elsie was allowed to stand at a window at the end of a ward with Mrs Duke.

They watched as a nurse wearing a surgical mask took one of Elsie's precious *Girls' Crystal* annuals to a long box which hissed rhythmically like a steam engine. A large tube from the box led to what seemed to be giant bellows which sucked themselves in and then filled out again at intervals. Sticking out of the other end of the box was Marjorie's head.

She looked so small, thought Elsie. Strange to think Marjorie had once terrorised her.

The nurse leaned close to Marjorie, showed her the book and held up a mirror.

'She probably can't move her head,' explained Mrs Duke.

Elsie waved, not knowing if Marjorie could see her reflection or not.

It looked as though she was attempting to ask something.

'Why doesn't the nurse answer her?' asked Elsie after a while.

'I don't think she's finished speaking. She has to wait till the machine pushes her lungs and helps her breathe out. I think that's how it's done. She can't talk till then.'

'She won't be able to turn the pages,' said Elsie, suddenly realising.

'I expect they have volunteers who'll do that.'

Eventually the nurse gave a little nod and headed in their direction. She stepped out into the corridor and pulled down her mask.

'Did she see me?' asked Elsie.

'Yes.'

'How long will she have to stay in that box?'

'A very long time,' said the nurse, and she looked seriously at Elsie. 'But she has youth on her side, and she has the constitution and strength of a steel-worker.'

'I know.'

'And she's not in any pain,' added the nurse reassuringly. 'But she'll have to work very hard for every tiny step towards recovery. It's exhausting. But she'll succeed. I'm sure of that.'

'What about school?'

'She won't be doing anything like that yet. But later–' she began. 'When she gets better. She'll probably be sent to a special boarding-school.'

'Can you tell them that she's very clever?'

'I think they'll decide that for themselves, young lady.'

'No. You don't understand. She won a scholarship. Her elementary school teacher will have the details. Please tell someone.'

The nurse smiled. 'I certainly will. Actually, the heads of these schools are very keen that their pupils get a good education.'

'So she might be able to take her school cert.?'

'If she's as clever as you say.'

The sister began to look a little embarrassed. 'I have a message from her to you. She wanted me to ask you something.'

Elsie knew what the question was already. Marjorie wanted to ask for her forgiveness. And yes, Elsie would gladly give it. She bore no malice towards Marjorie now, and the anger she had felt had all disappeared.

Elsie indicated by a nod that she was ready.

'I don't know quite how to ask this,' said the nurse, awkwardly.

'I know what it is,' said Elsie, gently. 'Go ahead.'

'She wants to know,' said the nurse hesitantly, 'if you have nits.'

*

Mrs Duke didn't come inside. She dropped Elsie outside the door.

Her father was in the kitchen, hanging nappies over the range and a tiny little nightdress. On the table, wrapped in brown paper, were all her textbooks. 'I left you to write on the covers,' he said.

'Thanks, Dad!'

'How was Marjorie Bush, then?'

'Poorly. Her mum don't care about her at all. And her mum had a black eye.' She remembered Geraldine and her father, but couldn't bring herself to say anything about them yet. 'Has Harry gone to bed already?'

'Yeah. You should be in bed too. You got rehearsals tomorrow.'

'Yeah. Won't you be late for the theatre?'

'I'm not on till the end, remember?'

'But what about the make-up?'

'They let me be last in the queue. Your mum's feeding Josie. Want to say goodnight?'

Elsie tiptoed into her parents' bedroom, but when she opened the door she found her mother was already asleep. Josie lay on a patch of mattress where there was no pillow, beside her, her eyes closed. They looked all of a piece, Elsie thought. Like two parts of a jigsaw which fitted together. Content. She stood there for a while gazing at them. 'Goodnight,' she whispered, and she closed the door quietly behind her.

'Yer mum says you've got to look smart for this rehearsal business tomorrow,' her dad said, downstairs. 'But I reckon you ought to get used to wearing shorts and boots, don't you?'

'Yes, Dad,' said Elsie. She giggled. 'Miss Benson will have a bit of a shock, won't she?'

'I don't think anything will shock Miss Benson.'

They looked at one another, and there was an awkward silence.

'Goodnight, Dad,' and she gave him a wave.

' 'Night, Elsie.'

About ten minutes later, Elsie was about to doze off when she heard her door being slowly opened. She listened for a moment. 'Elsie?' a voice whispered. It was her father. He was obviously checking up to see if she was asleep. The door closed. She was about to sit up when she heard footsteps coming towards the bed. She kept her eyes firmly shut. Then she felt his hands diving under her pillow. She froze. He whispered, ' 'Night, love.'

She heard him move away and the door close

behind him. She waited until he had shut the front door and had walked past her window and down the street. Perplexed, she sat up and felt under the pillow. She pulled out a long, cylindrical shaped bundle tied with a piece of string and a bow. She didn't need to guess what it was. It was a comic. Not a second-hand one, either. It was brand, spanking new, and it was a girl's comic! It was then that she realised it was wrapped round something bulky. She undid the string. A heavy object fell on the bed. It had a wooden handle with leaves and flowers and winding stems carved into it. Her father must have made it for her while she was in Kent. It was attached to a triangular-shaped piece of curved metal. As she held it up to the shaft of streetlight that filtered through the threadbare curtains, she could see what it was only too clearly. It was a trowel. Her very own trowel. It was her invitation to the allotment. And not as a boy, but as a girl!

She wanted to leap out of bed and sing and dance and yell out at the top of her voice, but she knew she couldn't because it would wake everyone up, so she did the next best thing. She tucked the trowel snugly in beside her, put on her spectacles, smoothed out the comic and, by the light of the streetlamp, she began to read.

EGMONT PRESS: ETHICAL PUBLISHING

Egmont Press is about turning writers into successful authors and children into passionate readers – producing books that enrich and entertain. As a responsible children's publisher, we go even further, considering the world in which our consumers are growing up.

Safety First
Naturally, all of our books meet legal safety requirements. But we go further than this; every book with play value is tested to the highest standards – if it fails, it's back to the drawing-board.

Made Fairly
We are working to ensure that the workers involved in our supply chain – the people that make our books – are treated with fairness and respect.

Responsible Forestry
We are committed to ensuring all our papers come from environmentally and socially responsible forest sources.

For more information, please visit our website at
www.egmont.co.uk/ethicalpublishing

The Forest Stewardship Council (FSC) is an international, non-governmental organisation dedicated to promoting responsible management of the world's forests. FSC operates a system of forest certification and product labelling that allows consumers to identify wood and wood-based products from well-managed forests.

For more information about the FSC, please visit their website at www.fsc-uk.org

FSC
Mixed Sources
Product group from well-managed forests and other controlled sources

Cert no. TT-COC-2063
www.fsc.org
© 1996 Forest Stewardship Council